OF DEATH & STARLIGHT
BOOK 1

AMANDA AGGIE

Printed in the United States of America. For more information, please visit www.AmandaAggie.com.

Cover Illustration by Amanda Aggie

Interior Map Designs by Amanda Aggie

Interior Chapter Illustration by Amanda Aggie

ISBN: (paperback) 9798321763568

ISBN: (hardback) 978-1-963184-00-6

First Edition | Book Dragon Publishing, April 2024.

10 9 8 7 6 5 4 3 2 1

A FATED VOW

To the girlies out there collecting morally gray book boyfriends like Pokémon.

WARNING

This book contains triggers! You will find some adult situations and language intended for individuals 18+ years of age. If you believe magic and sorcery is the Devil's work, ***please close the book now.*** This book is intended for those who like a bit of spice with their fantasy but please be aware that this is a SLOW BURN. Though there are intimate situations in book one, if you're someone that demands nipple play in the first chapter, you're not going to find it in book one… but maybe book two.

If you have read my Dark Halos trilogy, please know that the extended epilogue in The Crimson Queen has been altered. All of the events occur as they do in the original epilogue, but it is not word for word and has been modified on purpose due to rights and limitations.

TRIGGER WARNING:

Gore, steamy scenes intended for those 18+ years of age, monsters, animalistic behavior, blood, murder, death, violence, biting, magic rituals, immoral practices, arranged marriage, and other disturbing images that might not be suitable for all audiences.

Now… Be a good little reader and turn the page/scroll on. ;)

Forest of Lost Souls
Bell Hold
King's cove
Dragmorr Sea

Grim's Keep

The Mainland

Dragmorr Sea

Vanderlyth

Larendorr

Evercryst

The Elven Islands

Grim's Keep
Boundary Wall
The Forest of Lost Souls
Dragmorr Sea

Prologue

ONCE UPON A TIME, the Devil became a father.

However, it wasn't the dream of having a family that made him one.

It was war.

The Devil wanted a nephilim child he could use as a weapon, and his wife dreamed of becoming a mother. So together, they chose the perfect soul, and a prince was born, but the child grew to become a monster.

And his name was Asmodeus Morningstar.

1

Asmodeus

I had two goals for today, to move back into the keep I grew up in and maybe get a cat. *That's it.* Yet, as I stare at the shithole I plan to call home, neither of those things seem remotely possible.

Breathing in the musky forest air, I let the salty tang of the nearby ocean soothe the rage burning through my veins. This place used to be magnificent. It used to reach into the sky, adorned with gold and black banners hanging from stone walls. But while I was trapped in the Realm of Monsters, the keep was abandoned, and time wreaked havoc on its beauty.

Those same two-toned banners are now a muted, drab brown, the fringed hems in tatters, consumed by the elements. Even the embroidered snake twining around a rose in the center is hardly visible, nothing more than an angular head, mouth open to reveal poison-tipped fangs.

It's the *Morningstar* crest, the royal family of the Seven Realms. My true last name still seems foreign to me, like some fragmented memory of a previous life.

It'll take more than a few layers of paint to restore Grim's Keep back to its former glory, but much like these crumpled remains, I've seen far too much death and sacrificed enough for one lifetime. Moving back here is a new beginning—a future I can mold and shape and escape into, assuming the bones are still good.

Something cracks beneath my boot, and I pause, lifting just enough to see the pieces of colored glass. It's from the windows, though I'm not sure how pieces of them made it this far away from the base of the keep. It's like an explosion sent them flying. Glancing at the grass and vines that nearly smother the pathway, I find more fragments peeking out from the plant life. It appears Mother Nature has claimed the estate as her own.

Every inch of this place is in ruins, and my heart aches at the sight. It's like a giant chewed it up, spat it out, and then crushed it underfoot in a fit of rage, destroying most of the left wing. Grim's Keep used to pulse with life and magic. I don't even want to know what condition the library is in. If any of the ancient tomes are salvageable, I'll be surprised.

I was the only one who cared enough to look after this estate, and it's not like I had any warning to ensure someone could pick up the torch in my absence—or rather, my *banishment*. My departure was too sudden.

The lords of my father's court revolted, demanding my death, and that his hand be the one to deliver the blow. Fortunately—or maybe *unfortunately* for me—my mother had other plans. She lured me to the Realm of Monsters before I could be caught or executed and didn't hesitate to shove me inside. It's a prison, a place built to contain the immortal creatures deemed too dangerous to live among the rest, a place not even the Devil dare go. She trapped me there, and with tears in her eyes, my mother begged me to survive.

From that point on, everything became about living one more day, one more hour, drawing one more breath. The luxuries of a roof over my head, drinking tea on Sundays, or reading late into the night were nothing more than a memory.

Now, my parents are both dead, the war is over, and my little brother and his wife sit on the throne of the Seven Realms. They freed me in exchange for my help during the war, and when it was over, my life was my own again. They even reinstated my title as Prince of the Seven Realms and welcomed me to live in the castle, though I insisted on a place to call my own and requested Grim's Keep, the place I grew up.

Perhaps I should've laid eyes on it first…

It's been years since the war ended, since I've gained my freedom, and I've yet to put down roots. It's not that I don't enjoy my brother and his wife's company; I adore their children, too. It's mostly due to how deep the tensions still run among their subjects. I can't wander through town without hearing the whispers of the locals. They still believe I'm a monster, claiming that if I wasn't one before I was shoved across the boundary, then I must be one now. I'll forever be known as the demon prince who lost the ability to control his magic and incinerated everyone in Hell Hold, including the woman he loved.

Birds burst from the trees and brush around the base of the keep, taking flight—fleeing from something. Narrowing my eyes, as if that will help me see clearer, I spot the curved top of a head peeking up from the overgrown rose bushes.

"Who's there?" I shout, lacing power into my words to project my voice down the twisted path. No one answers. "Show yourself."

The head moves, followed by the rustling of leaves and the snapping of twigs, and the stranger yanks the hood of their cloak up, disappearing into thin air. *Magic.*

The question is, are they still here, or did they teleport away? They could still linger about, unseen to the naked eye. As I allow my power to surface, my eyes darken to obsidian voids, determined to find out.

Not all demons can see magic—not even my brother, even though we share the same parents. Only I inherited my mother's true sight. She was a mage with the power of a goddess, capable of crafting intricate, nearly unbreakable spells. That is, unless you know what you're looking for.

All magic has threads, shiny golden strings woven through spell work. Though some magic is stronger than others, the threads tighter together and held with more complex knots, all spells start with a single piece, and if plucked, the magic will crumble in an instant.

Unfortunately, the only time I can see those shiny threads is if I'm in my demon form. It's not something I enjoy shifting into, but there's a fox in my henhouse, and I'll be damned if it's going to sneak up and bite me.

Talons push through my fingertips, as sharp as blades, and the skin covering my hands and forearms turns inky, like I've reached into a cauldron of soot. My vision sharpens as I stroll toward the keep, quiet as a mouse. With predatory eyes, I search the courtyard, the bushes around the base of the stone walls, the woods surrounding the keep. I watch for those golden threads. For movement.

"You should know you're trespassing," I call out into the stagnant air, my voice echoing off the ruins.

I stop at the base of the keep, a few yards from what remains of the front door. The air shifts, and gold catches the light to form a transparent silhouette, only revealed by a web of threads wrapped around it. The figure tears through the courtyard, breaking through the wild foliage that's all but eaten up the cobblestone paths. They're darting at a breakneck pace for the front door of the keep, like it's a lifeline.

Interesting.

Tilting my head, I wait for them to get closer. Honestly, I'm surprised they got through the enchanted walls. They were erected ages ago to conceal the estate from the rest of the realm—unless that too has faltered with time.

With a flutter of my eyelids, I teleport. Bright webs of light and shadow spin around me until I materialize just inside the keep's front door.

The hooded figure hasn't noticed I disappeared. Gold threads wrap around their otherwise-invisible silhouette as they burst through the open doorway, oblivious to me waiting just inside.

There you are.

I hardly move an inch, my leather boots rooted in place, as if the vines pouring through the cracks in the marble and broken windows hold me here. Darting out a hand, I grip invisible fabric while simultaneously drawing my dagger from the sheath on my thigh.

A slender shape flickers in and out of view as I pin the trespasser to the soot-covered walls. They jerk wildly against my hold, but the moment the cool blade reaches their throat, they freeze. The magic still obscures their face from view, but I snarl, leaning closer, pinning them harder against the stone.

"Who are you, and why are you in my house?" My voice is dark, gutting, as if my words alone could flay flesh from bone. "Speak," I command when they don't answer.

The featureless outline of a person doesn't move. Doesn't breathe. The magic threads weave around them still, the lines messy, unpracticed. *Undisciplined.* Whoever it is, they lack the know-how to cast decent spells. My baby niece could do better than this.

"Fine. Don't talk," I growl through clenched teeth. Holding the figure to the wall, dagger in hand, I reach a dark claw up into the space between their face and mine, curling it around the thread holding their sorry excuse for a spell together. The originating strand always glows just a little brighter than the rest. The others knotting around it are more gold and yellow, while the origin strand is pure white.

Tugging gently, I test my theory. As expected, the other threads strain just enough to make the magic falter a moment. My lips pulling into a wicked smirk, I watch the person's cloaked head jerk left, then right. I can taste the fear wafting off them, mixing in the air with the sweetness of our mingling power.

Then, the thread snaps.

The magic crumbles in an instant, laying the cloaked stranger bare to my scrutinizing gaze. Still, they don't take off the hood. The dark blue fabric falls just to the tip of their nose, and I hold my breath as I find lips too full, too *feminine*, to be male. They part on a sharp gasp.

Tilting my head to the side, I furrow my brow. *It's… a woman?*

My jaw clenches as I let my head fall back, the faint outline of the triplet moons now visible in the darkening sky… through the *gaping hole* in the foyer's ceiling. *How the hell did that get there?* It goes straight through the second and third stories. *The gods must be laughing at me.*

With a huff, I sheath my dagger. I won't be needing it, even if she is a pest currently taking up residence in my home. Giving a sharp tug on the woman's hood, she jolts as the dark fabric pools over her shoulders, revealing her flawlessly beautiful face.

"Well… What have we here?" I arch an eyebrow, making no effort to step away.

Dark, bone-straight hair splays across her face. Her breaths are even despite the circumstances, dark green eyes narrowed at me like looks alone could kill. But it's the tips of pointy ears peeking through her hair that seems to make my blood go cold, just for an instant.

"You're awfully far away from home," I muse. Far is putting it nicely. She's an entire ocean away from the Elven Islands. The elves don't come to the mainland unless the lords are convening. Even then, everyone but the elf lord stays onboard their intricately carved ships. Ships that are covered in more gold and crystals than there the entire castle in Hell Hold possesses. And that's where the King and Queen of the Seven Realms live.

The elves stick to themselves, too *esteemed* to associate with other species. It's as if we're beneath them. Or so they believe. They also think they're blessed by the old gods and protected by the dragons since one of the furies was nice enough to make their lands rich with crystals.

Sure, they have magic. They have more crystals to power their magic and spells than any of the other six realms, but relying on said stones is their biggest crutch, too. Without their special rocks, they're powerless. Whereas we demons siphon it from our very souls.

My eyes drop to the red stone pendant she's clutching in her white-knuckled fist. I might not be able to view the stone itself through her delicate fingers, but I can feel it pulsing, the power it breathes into the air dancing over my flesh like ghostly fingers.

I curl a claw around the golden chain, breaking it with ease. "I'll be taking this."

"The hell you are," she snaps, gripping the pendant tighter.

Gently, I circle her wrist, prying her fingers away from the pendant one by one. She grits her teeth, fighting *so hard*. It's almost cute.

Pendant in my grasp, I dangle the chain in front of her. "You can have it back when you answer my questions."

She darts a hand up, trying to snatch it away, but my hand flicks into a swirl of shadow, and the pendant disappears. Her gold-flecked emerald eyes widen, and she lets out a shaky exhale through her nose. "What did you do with it?" With a clipped tone, her defiant eyes narrow on me.

"I'll answer your question if you answer mine."

Her nose twitches, ever so slightly, her gaze turning lethal. "Where is it, asshole?"

My heart flutters as I lift my chin, a grin forming on my lips. "My, my... For a lady, you clearly have a way with words." Reminds me of Alice. The queen has a collection of colorful insults that put 'asshole' to shame. "It's safe."

"I'm sorry, was I supposed to be polite to demons? All of you are the same, cunning, selfish tricksters. I'm not in the mood for playing games."

I let my eyes wander over her features, the button nose, the ethereal cheekbones, almond eyes... She's elegant, but I know in elvish culture that her beauty likely means nothing thanks to the dark hue of her hair. For elves, the more silver the better. Regardless of what kind of elf they are, silver hair is a symbol of nobility and the darker their hair is, the more polluted the genes are.

It's fucked up. No one can control their hair color, nor can they control their heritage. The color of their hair determines nothing beyond physical appearance. It doesn't make them brave or wise. It's just one more reason to deem the elves snobbish.

And she calls me selfish. At least I believe in basic rights.

"How did you get past the enchanted wall?" I grit.

"What?" She arches a perfect eyebrow, rolling her neck, feigning impatience.

"The stone wall that surrounds the keep. You can't miss it. It's enchanted to keep people from stumbling upon this place. So, either you toyed with it or—"

She cuts me off with a shake of her head. "There's no enchanted wall. I've been living here for weeks. If there were wards somewhere other than the rocks we're standing in, I'd know."

"You've been living in my home for weeks?" My brows disappear into my hairline.

"I didn't know it was *your home*. It looked abandoned."

It was… but she doesn't need to know that.

The woman scans my face, but her scowl softens a moment as if she's just now noticing my scars. She quickly darts her eyes away when she realizes I've caught her gawking. It's a pretty common reaction. At this point, I'm used to it.

She inches to the right, but I put my arm out, my fingers splaying over the cool stone beside her head, talons gone. I'm not sure when they went away.

"I'm not done with you, little girl. I still have questions."

"I owe you nothing, *demon,*" she says, as if the species itself is dirty. "Now move and I'll be on my way."

"Would it kill you to say *please?"* I just need a moment. If the wall is down, there's no telling what else is lurking around the keep. If she leaves, with or without her crystal, I could very well be sending her to her death. Yet, if she stays… What? I'll stay here all night?

I could take her to Hell Hold. Alice and Kai could put her in a room for the night and find her a ship back to the islands tomorrow. *But* Alice would insist I stay in Hell Hold, too. She'd try to convince me to move in with them permanently while we 'look' for somewhere else that's fitting for a prince. I've never been able to tell the woman no. Nor, have I ever been able to stick to my wits when she bats her baby blues at me. She's my best friend, as hard as that is for me to admit. I prefer to stay to myself, yet she's wormed her way into my heart.

I hate and love her for it at the same time.

Not to mention, Alice would use the children against me. That's how she kept me there for weeks already. She'll convince them to beg me to stay, and if she's hard to say no to, those little spitting images of her are much harder. They've mastered the puppy eyes.

No… Going back to Hell Hold, even if it's to take this woman there, is not an option. *I'll make it work here.*

"Sorry," the elven woman's voice hits my ears, yanking me from my thoughts, and as I return my gaze to hers, white-hot, searing pain explodes in my middle. She leans in, putting her mouth near my ear as she whispers, "Keep the crystal. I don't need it, anyway."

My lips part as I stagger back a step. It's impossible to take a deep enough breath, the air leaving me in short bursts. The woman pulls up her hood, shoots me a closed-lip smile, and glides out the front door of the keep. Before I can wrap my mind around what just happened, she's disappeared into the woods.

My spine arches as I buckle forward, bracing myself with a locked arm, using the wall for support. Gritting my teeth, I wrap my free hand around the leather-bound hilt of my dagger, then yank it free from where it's buried between my ribs. A grunt escapes me, the air hissing through my clenched jaw.

If I were mortal, the wound alone would kill me. Yet, this blade in particular is going to make me wish I was dead in a moment. It's been dipped in pix root poison, strong enough to bring an immortal, like me, to their knees. It could take days before the drug works its way out of my system, unless I can take the antidote.

Which, to my fucking luck, is in the castle's apothecary in Hell Hold. Pressing my hand to the wound, dark blood seeps through my fingers, dripping steadily onto the dusty marble floor.

I curse out loud, hearing the echo of my voice bounce off the stone ruins.

She stabbed me.

With my OWN BLADE.

Then had the gall to leave me for dead.

Yet, I'm the asshole?

2

Asmodeus

I'M TOO WEAK TO teleport. The pix root from the blade won't let me heal, and I fear using my magic will only sap my energy and make me succumb to the poison faster. If the wall around the keep has fallen and the enchantment is gone, there's no telling what might lurk in the woods.

There are plenty of creatures to fear, especially now that the Realm of Monsters has been freed. The boundary that contained it was destroyed. Now, countless beasts have crossed into the other six realms, the worst of which come alive at night. They'll be able to scent my blood from a mile away.

Needing to preserve my energy, I lean my head back against the wall, seated on the dirty, cool marble. The poison has sunk its claws in already, making me see double. My muscles ache, pulse weak, and the room spins. My mouth waters, a metallic tang on my tongue as I swallow yet another gulp of blood, too tired to spit it out.

Hands trembling against the wound, I try not to think about how clammy they've become. Nor do I acknowledge how pale my skin looks in the dim light of the moons. I have to do something… I'll lose consciousness soon without the antidote. Seeing as that woman was able to walk through the front door, the wards on the keep are broken, too. Anything could sweep in here and have its way with me…

and let's just say I made quite a few enemies during my time in the prison realm. I've made enemies in all the Seven Realms, really. There are plenty of people and creatures who'd love to see me dead.

The lump in my throat bobs as I swallow.

What do I do? Attempting to teleport with magic might not be to my advantage. My head is too foggy to form a clear image of my destination. I could end up lost in the ether, in the veil between life and death. For all I know, I could drop into the open ocean, and it the very process would take enough energy from me that I'm not sure I'd have the strength to fight effectively if I landed in the wrong place.

Teleportation is out, though I might be able to bring someone here to me...

Alice. I'll summon the queen.

Picturing her face, I let the image of her consume me. Her long dark red curls that bounce when she moves. Her intelligent blue eyes, framed by the soft freckles that cover her nose and cheeks. I can hear her laugh, wherever she is, wherever I'm about to rip her from. Then a blinding white light illuminates the back of my eyelids.

But when I open my eyes, she isn't there.

Fuck... No... It didn't work. Worse, I can feel the energy I just expended draining from my soul.

Searching the room, I pray to the long-lost gods that I overshot it. That I popped her in somewhere else—the courtyard, maybe. With a shake of my head and a deep, steadying breath, I try to slow my heartbeat. It's frantic in my chest, the panic flowing deep in my veins, which will only make the blood spill faster, weakening me more with every passing second.

Leaning forward, I attempt to see past the arched wooden doors, still left ajar. The elf woman hadn't bothered to close them when she abandoned me here. I barely make out a sliver of green between the wooden slabs. Hope plummets into my stomach.

It didn't work… Okay, Plan B: find a place to hide while I heal.

I take in the holes in the plastered walls. Heart-stopping art once hung in this foyer, but it's since been reduced to charred frames and blackened canvases. It's like this place was set aflame after I left, and a small part of me wonders if the village masters and the lords of my deceased father's court torched it. If they'd tried to burn me out, not knowing my mother had imprisoned me.

A layer of dust and grime as thick as my fingernail coats every surface, save for the scuffs of old footprints on the floor. The woman's, I assume. I didn't have time to wander about upon coming inside.

Chunks of fallen stone litter the midnight-blue marble. Dozens of them have embedded themselves down the hall, leading from the foyer through the heart of the keep. A staircase wraps to the right spiraling upward in an open, hollow tunnel, leading to the third floor. It's crunched from the debris, and half of the steps rotten, the railings broken into splinters. There's no way I'll be able to crawl up there. The best I can do is slide toward the infirmary down the hall and hope I don't pass out first.

With a guttural growl, I try to use the wall to get myself to my feet, cringing from the strain.

This is bullshit. I'm a fucking demon prince. I can command death, yet standing is an exhausting effort. Staggering a step, I wince. The muscles in my stomach flex, tearing the wound wider with every disappointing step I take.

My blood drips, leaving a trail as I fight my way down the long hall. Barely making it a few feet within the minutes that tick by. Head too heavy to keep up, I tuck my chin to my chest, grinding my teeth hard enough to crack bone as I force my way forward.

Drip.

Drip.

Drip.

Fucking elves. Fuck those pointy-eared pricks.

Letting rage burn through me, fueling my efforts to keep going, I click my tongue. I can't believe I let some random, magicless stranger stab me… And for what?

I dropped my guard, took one look, and labeled her as a non-threat.

"Never… Again…" I breathe between steps, determined to get to the infirmary. My legs are weak, the strength leaving me in droves. But I'm so close.

As long as the apothecary inside hasn't been lost, I'm willing to bet the ingredients for the antidote are in there. Then so help the woman who thought it wise to stab me.

Pausing, I rest my weight on what's left of the staircase railing, holding myself up with everything I have. The paralytic effects are coming on strong. With labored breaths, I push on. I'm already on borrowed time, resting is asking to die here.

Whether or not I want to believe it, immortals can die. We might not age, but under the right circumstances, our souls can be claimed and returned to the Soul Well. And particular monsters that were released when the prison world boundary collapsed are capable of delivering such a death.

The last thing I want is to be caught here, hunted down by the scent of my blood, like a damn wolf would a rabbit. I have to heal… I have to replace the enchantment on the wall, to clear the woods. There is no other option.

Just a few more feet…

My legs wobble and I almost tip over, catching myself on the rough stone wall. Plaster from the ceiling rains down onto me, chunks rattling along the floor. I squint my eyes shut until the dust clears, but my head only seems to swim harder, my vision blurring until the only thing I can make out are vague colors and shapes.

When my feet go numb, I know the poison is taking my extremities first. Barely staying upright, I picture Alice's face again, desperate to focus. Her red curls. Her blue eyes. Her pale freckled skin. The snarky comebacks she likes to throw at me.

Then the image shifts. Those red curls become brunette waves, eyes turning to a deep brown with flawless, porcelain skin… pointed ears. My Jade.

I used to trace the veins on the inside of her forearm at night, as she hummed. She had such a beautiful voice… such soft skin. I adored the way she wrinkled her nose when she was being stubborn, and twitched her ears when she was upset. I could stare at the way the light seemed to paint the contours of her face for hours.

She was my everything… my heart, my soul, my world. I'll love that woman, my Jade, long after the reapers claim my soul and send me to the well. So beautiful… and so *dead*.

My fingers scrape along the wall as I search for the door. I'm almost certain this is pointless. I wouldn't be able to see to know what I'm grabbing for, even if I make it inside the infirmary.

I take another step, my body numb as my ankle twists. Then I'm weightless.

Falling…

Collapsing to the floor, my cheek smacks into the dusty marble, and my vision becomes lost in a sea of muddled colors.

I swear I hear my name, but it's hard to tell over the roaring in my ears. A faint echo grows louder, like feet bounding against the marble floor, the vibrations tickle my skin as they grow closer.

Hands grip my shoulders hard, wrenching me onto my back. Red hair dangles above me, obscuring most of the woman's face, but I know who it is.

Alice. The Queen of the Seven Realms.

"What the fuck did you do?" she snaps, the urgency in her voice making me smile.

"Elf…" That's all I can get out before the darkness digs its claws into my soul, beckoning me to give into sleep.

"The elves did this to you?" She scowls down at me, hands hovering over my chest.

Magic shoots from her hands, burrowing into me with such force I gasp for air. My spine contorts into an unnatural bow, my blind eyes flaring wide open, seeing nothing but darkness.

"Stay with me, Asmo." Alice's voice is clearer now. "Don't you dare die, you hear me? I'll drag your ass back to the living by myself if I have to."

3

Asmodeus

Coming to, my eyelids flutter, the chilled air making my skin pebble. Stone grits beneath my bare torso, but there's no searing pain in my middle. The only hint of being wounded comes as a steady throb in my skull.

My head lolls to the side as I blink the world into focus.

"Bout time you woke up." Alice huffs, pacing beside the altar, hands on her hips. That voice of hers is harsher than normal, but it's a tone I know well. Her *mom tone*—the one she uses when she scolds her children. "Are you going to explain why I found you on the floor?"

"I was stabbed," I admit. Something sour coats my tongue, and I smack my lips in hopes to dilute the aftertaste of the antidote. "Poisoned." That thought alone makes me more bitter than the taste in my mouth.

I've grown soft since escaping the Realm of Monsters. Who knew living in a realm where I'm no longer hunted at every turn could prove to weaken me—to weaken my mind.

"I got that much." Small, dainty fingers skim my arm. The cool metal of Alice's rings sends a shiver through me as she crouches next to my head, her bold, blue eyes staring into my soul, like she could glimpse all of my secrets there. "How did *you,* of all people, get stabbed with your own dagger?"

"I'm not invincible, you know. I make mistakes."

She's pissed, and I'm not sure I blame her. Bringing Alice here had been my best option. She's quick on her feet and so obnoxiously vigilant, that I knew she'd figure out what was wrong with me. My brother is strong and cunning, but he's built for war, not puzzles. That, and he would've likely shrugged off my summons instead of letting me pull him here.

I needed someone who would come, not get back to me later.

Still, Alice is also a chess player. She's the one who sees windows in a doorless room, who sees things others don't, and not just in a magical sense. Something within her, something not born of sorcery or creature allows her to sense things about people. I should've known she'd suspect something, that she'd read into me being hurt more than she should, but I was out of options.

Her eyes shift briefly between mine until I'm forced to avert my gaze. Whatever information she's gathered from them, I'd rather not know. Instead, I drag my teeth over my lower lip and stare at the glowing crystal sigils embedded into the walls and ceiling. Anything to not look at her as I say, "I'm sorry to scare you."

"Scare me? You're the one person I don't have to worry about. Finding you one foot in the grave is downright *terrifying.*" Alice chuckles humorlessly. "You survived living in the Realm of Monsters for years. I died on my first day there. And if it weren't for you, I'm certain my immortal soul would've died again and again until something finally ended me for good." She shakes her head.

"What do you want me to say, Alice?" I push the words through my teeth, my body shaking as if death's claws are still hanging onto my limbs, weighing me down and smothering my heart.

"I can count on one hand how many times in the last two hundred years that I've bested you and I'm the most powerful creature in this realm. Yet, someone took *your blade* off *your body* and bury it between your ribs. And judging from the lack of body parts in the hall, they lived to tell the tale. You expect me to believe that?"

Peeking at her from the corner of my eye, I watch her drag a rickety chair over and plant herself in it. Alice's arms are crossed in defiance, and her steely gaze pins me to the altar like a nail driven through stone. A red eyebrow arches up, demanding an explanation I can't admit to myself, let alone to her.

"As I said, I make mistakes." My tone is unnervingly steady. She should be worried. Hell, I'm worried. But there's nothing I can say to ease her heart.

"You don't make mistakes. You taught me that mistakes mean death. So, I'm sorry, but we're not leaving this room until you tell me what *really* happened." Alice lifts a hand, waving two fingers in a circle. Magic explodes through the air, so sweet it turns my stomach. The doorway and the windows glow as shields form in the openings, cutting the room off from the rest of the world. "Now, what do the elves have to do with this?"

"The elves?" I scrunch my face.

"That's what you mumbled before you passed out. If they're trying something, I need to know. It's no secret that the elf lord has been plotting something. He doesn't like me having a say in the court, and he despised Kai for letting me. Some of the other lords have voiced concerns. There's been whispers of him planning a rebellion to overthrow us. I'm not sure how true they are, but after this…" She tosses a hand at me, looking at the ceiling for a long moment, like it will give her strength.

Letting out a deep sigh, I trail my fingers down my stomach, prodding where the blade tore through my flesh. All that's left is a puckered scar between my ribs. Healed. Whether by my abilities or Alice's magic, I'm not sure, but it doesn't matter.

"Why didn't you tell me about the elves?" I've been in Hell Hold for weeks. It's been months since the court of lords convened last. If the elves were pulling on their leashes, testing my brother's and Alice's rule, they've said nothing. They never so much as alluded to it.

I push up from the stone altar, taking in the dust-covered shelves and dirty amber bottles as I wait for Alice to use her words. She's never been good at it. Not when emotions run high. Not when the people she loves are in danger or hurt.

Herbs hang from the walls, carefully placed around the room to keep the crystal sigils uncovered. They're still active, despite the keep's current state. I wouldn't be surprised if Alice used them to speed up the healing process. It's what I would've done.

It's not until I meet those blue eyes—the ones I'm so used to seeing locked down and giving away nothing—now so full of emotion, of *guilt,* that I put the pieces together.

She didn't tell me about the elves because she promised she wouldn't.

My brother and I have mended our relationship to a point. He hadn't been born when I was banished and thus, he'd only heard my father's side of the story. It wasn't until the war—and Alice—brought us together that we became friends and moved past the stories and rumors. Two hundred years later, and he still doesn't trust me. Not like she does.

"He wanted to tell you," she says, barely above a whisper.

Shaking my head, I clench my jaw, making the muscle in my cheek feather. "Then why didn't he?"

Alice doesn't answer.

"Fine. Don't say it. I already know the answer, anyway." I scoff.

I'd served the mad king, but it wasn't because I wanted to. I had no choice. In the Realm of Monsters, the only choices were to be killed or serve him. I'd chosen to live, but Alice can attest to my hatred for the mad king. Not to mention that I helped her and my brother defeat him. In a way, I'm partially responsible for them becoming the King and Queen of the Seven Realms.

But none of it matters.

"I'll always be a monster to the lords, to this kingdom. I'm not sure why I bother pretending to be something different." I barely recognize my voice, the rawness to it, and it strikes a chord in me. "My brother asked you not to tell me because the lords are worried I'll join the elves, because I betrayed my father by serving the mad king, just as I betrayed the mad king to serve you. Trust me, I'm aware of how it looks, but you have to know, I'll serve you with my dying breath, Alice. I've sworn my fealty to *you, always*. I won't pretend I didn't do terrible things, but I'd fall on my sword before I ever betrayed you."

"I don't see you as a monster, Asmo. I don't think Kai does, either. You're the reason I'm alive. He'll always be in your debt for that." She stands from the chair, inching closer, but I stare off into space.

"Being indebted to me and forgiving me are two very different things. It's why I didn't want to stay in Hell Hold."

I can feel her eyes on me, analyzing with that innate power of hers, reading me like an open book. "I know. It's why I didn't argue when you said you wanted a place to call your own. It can't be easy being there. Your face turns to stone every time you go down that hallway, where Jade…" she trails off and I thank the gods for it. "I can sense your sadness every time you see Kai with the kids, like it's a future you'll never have, and I hate that for you."

"Don't." My teeth lock together. "Just don't. Please."

Alice is my person. She's like a sister to me—a best friend—but not even she knows everything that happened in that prison realm. It's not longing for a family that she's seeing in me. It's grief, a void that opens up every time I'm reminded of what I've lost.

The only solace I have lies in the fact my mate's soul is safe in Hell Hold. That no one can ever hurt her again, not even me. I won't let it happen. Jade might be gone, but her soul is at peace. And one day, when I die, Alice has promised to ensure Jade and I can get out happily ever after, by returning both of our souls to the Soul Well at the same time, so we can be reincarnated together.

I should be content with that. The mad king I was forced to serve is dead. My father, who used to rule over the rest of our world is gone. Neither of them can hurt me again, yet it's not enough. I still can't find peace in this gods forsaken world.

I don't need to be in love to feel whole. Even though Alice wishes that I'll find someone to fill the void Jade left, I don't need it. I had an epic love, one written in the fucking stars. That's enough for me.

"I'll let it go if you answer one question." Alice blocks me from getting off the altar.

"One." I glare at her, but it quickly fades when her blue eyes twinkle like she's struck gold. I'm not sure when the woman wrapped me around her finger, but it's annoying as fuck.

"Do you ever think about falling in love again?"

I'm not sure how long I stare at her, but I know it's too long. The truth is, I have thought of what life could be like if Jade hadn't died, of what it could've been like if she never existed. And I hate myself for it.

I've lost count of how many hours I've spent, staring at my ceiling at night, missing the feel of holding someone in my arms, or wanting to have someone to wake up next to. But for every one of those times, guilt follows. Guilt from the fact I ended Jade's life and took her from this world even if it wasn't my fault. Moving on from her feels a lot like forgiving myself, like cheating on the person who should have ownership of my heart for all eternity. It's not an option.

"No," I lie, leaving no room for interpretation. "Never."

Alice's face falls, her shoulders too, as she takes a step back. "Okay, then."

"Thank you for helping me." I take a deep breath, blinking long and hard. "It wasn't the elves, but *an* elf. When I got here, there was a woman hiding in the keep."

Something about that comment sends a new spark of life through Alice. Any hint of her sorrow from my lack of love vanishes in an instant. "An elf woman?" Her lips twist into a knowing smirk.

"Yes. She was invisible. I didn't know who or what she was until I pinned her to the wall and demanded answers. When I discovered who was trespassing, I was debating on whether to take her to Hell Hold. The night was falling fast and the wards are down. It wouldn't have been safe to make her leave, but the keep isn't exactly inhabitable, either. While I was thinking, she grabbed my blade and stabbed me."

Her smile turns down-right wicked as she licks her lips, resuming her seat in the chair. "And where did this woman go?'

"The fuck if I know, and I don't care. She's not in my house any more and considering she *stabbed me*, she's not my problem."

"Once upon a time, I stabbed you, and here we are." She tilts her head, soft red curls falling off her shoulders. "Was she pretty?"

"For fuck's sake…" Darting my gaze to hers, I furrow my brow. "Does it matter? I don't need a woman in my life. I'm happy on my own."

She shrugs. "It was just a question. No need to get defensive about it."

Dragging in air until my lungs can't inflate any more, I slide off the altar, boots smacking against the stone floor as I straighten. I'm not sure where my shirt disappeared to, nor do I bother finding it. As is, I only ever wear them for Alice because she thinks not doing so in the king's court is improper. "If you'll excuse me, there's a wall I need to enchant."

"Then I'll help you. I'd prefer not to save your life twice in one night." Alice waves a hand and the spell she cast dissipates.

"I'm sure the kids need you. I've got this." Not wasting a beat, I rush from the infirmary, traveling down the hall until the cool night air assaults my senses.

"The king is just as capable of getting them to bed. If you're set on living in this death trap, I'm going to help. I'll sleep better knowing you're not poisoned on the floor." She falls into step beside me, her leather vest gleaming in the light of the moons. It's made from dragon scales—impenetrable by magic or steel—and a small golden crown is pinned on top of her head. Long white sleeves spill out from beneath the vest, billowing around her wrists, and swaying as she chaperones me to the woods.

My boots crunch against the earth with every stride, yet she keeps pace. The forest is thick, the air still as we travel deeper into the darkness. A silence so pure, so resounding, blankets this place, and it makes me wonder where the animals have gone.

Reaching a stone wall in the woods, Alice places her palms against the rocky surface. "There aren't any wards left, like all the magic was stripped out of it. The woman, could she siphon?"

"It didn't seem so. She had a crystal. If she had magic of her own, why use one?" I shift, letting my demon form see what my naked eyes can't, but it only confirms what Alice has said. There's not a trace of magic here, not a single thread in sight.

"I use crystals to amplify my magic. Sometimes when I siphon, I can't hold all the power within my body. Crystals give me a place to store it for later use." She gets to work casting, weaving together the magic while I do the same.

"Maybe, but elves rarely possess magic on their own. Even the elf lord needs crystals to cast. Though, her hair was darker. It's possible she was a half-breed."

Power pulses beneath my skin, heating my veins, boiling in my middle as it burns brighter and brighter. Together, Alice and I replace the enchantment on the wall, rendering the keep invisible to the creatures in the woods. It's stronger than the magic cloaking this place ever was before, and my hope is it'll hold against whatever brought it down.

4

Asmodeus

When we're finished, Alice pulls a dagger from her hip, using the blade to slice her palm before handing it to me to do the same. Blood wells in the wound crimson pooling in my palm until it drips from the side o my hand.

Like most of the castles and large settlement structures on the mainland, Grim's Keep has been built over a buria ground. And in order for the spell to be activated for the wall, we must walk the perimeter of it, creating a circle with our blood. Only then will the spell be finished, and bound to the titan bones beneath our feet, belonging to one of the first creatures to ever bless this realm long ago. The magic in the titan's bones fuels the wards and allows me to do as I please without worrying about intruders. Otherwise without shackling the spell the dead, it would be tied to me at all times, draining my magic by the day, and should I die it'd crumble, leaving anyone here at risk.

"Who knows what you're dealing with. That elf woma could be anything mixed with anything, if you truly believe her to be a half-breed," Alice says as we make our wa through the woods. "Mage, fae, dragon… the possibilitie ae endless. Until you can be sure whatever took this wal down is gone or dead, you'll need to be wary. Keep a close eye on it. Whatever siphoned the magic from it took every drop. It's powerful."

"Yes, mother," I tease, and Alice shoots me a stern glare.

"You play, but I mean it."

"I will check the walls. Promise."

The only light within the dark forest comes from the glowing mushrooms littering the ground. Though dim, we can make out the rough shape of tree trunks. The air is sticky with an eerie stillness that has my nerves on high alert. The forest should never be this quiet, unless something predatory lurks nearby. Animals can sense it. They flee, but not even my magic, nor the darkness whispers of what could be out there.

My blood goes cold just thinking about what foul creature could be watching us, lurking in the shadows. I've seen every kind of monster there is, but only a few wield the power to drain an enchanted wall dry. I'd rather not run into any of them.

We finish the circle, and the wards snap up, weaving tight around the estate.

"Sure you don't want me to stick around? Help you clear the woods?" Alice turns, scrutinizing me from beneath her long dark lashes.

"No, it's okay. I'll be fine. I'll be up until morning rebuilding the keep, anyway."

She sucks in a breath, letting it out in a deep exhale. "Fine, but be careful. Go slow. Don't drain your power stores to fix it all in one day—"

Cocking my head, I smirk down at her. "I'm aware of the consequences of using too much magic, Alice. I won't overdo it."

She twists her lips, stepping closer to put her hand on my bare chest, just above my heart. "I don't trust you, so..."

Trailing off, she sends a tidal wave of power through her fingers and into me. It fills me up until I fear my skin will split at the seams.

It's so easy to her, like what she gave me was barely a drop in the well she carries.

"Considering you just came back from the brink of death, a boost will do you some good until you can fully recover." She pats my chest then puts a solid step of space between us. "Use it wisely."

"Thanks, but I wasn't dying. Not directly, anyway."

"Right." She smirks. "It just would've been imminent the moment you bled out on the floor and the creatures in the woods sniffed you out." A smile pulls at her lips. "Don't forget. End of the week. If you're late, I will hunt you down."

"How could I forget?" Dinner in Hell Hold. *Why would I ever want to miss a family reunion?* The sarcasm flowing in every spoken word is thick enough to be syrup, but Alice says nothing, just blinks out of existence and leaves me alone in the dark.

THE NIGHT SOMEHOW FEELS colder with Alice gone. It's not something I can explain and definitely not something I'll dare to let myself think about. I'm the Prince of Death for fuck's sake. I'm not supposed to miss people, but if I lived up to my reputation in every way, I'd be cold and heartless. My hands would be as bloody as they are now every waking moment, and that's not even remotely true.

And as much as I hate being seen that way, it's for the best, so long as those I care about know otherwise.

It's not all untrue, either. I *have* killed people, more than I can count. I'm not sure I can even say it in past tense considering blood is coating my body like a second skin, but I'm the person my brother calls when things need to be handled. That's who I've always been—even to the mad king. I'm the one that can do the things others can't stomach.

Though, to say my hands are always bloody, is a stretch. Most of the time, I opt to use magic. It's clean and precise. It's foolproof. Blades are messy, but when one has to clear monsters out of the woods around their home, they're the go to.

Lots of monsters, especially those that escaped the Realm of Monsters, have become immune to magic. No doubt, thanks to the mad king I used to serve. He bred the ability into them, then surrounded the only side of his castle that wasn't bordered by ocean with a forest full of beasts no one would dare face. It's partly why I carry blades dipped in poison. It might be the only reliable thing when facing creatures like these.

Cringing a little at the dark, oozing blood creeping toward the tip of my sword, I daringly wipe the steel clean on the fabric of my pants. It's the last thing I want on me, but it's better than having it drip to the hilt. My grip could falter and that could prove to bare deadly consequences than needing to wash my pants.

The lifeless mass of sticky fur and broken bones sits before me on the forest floor. A dread wolf. They're nasty creatures that descend from the fae, but there's nothing remotely humanoid about them. Though, unlike the fae, these things only know blood rage. They take pleasure in hunting anything that moves and there's not a shred of civility remaining within them, making them brutal to take down.

This one nearly took my arm. Its teeth drove into my bicep, split muscle from bone. Thankfully, the wound is healing, just not as fast as I'd like it to, thanks to the poison still working out of my system.

Alice would kill me herself if she knew I was hunting. She'd have wanted me to go back into the keep, shut the doors so the wards would go up, and call it a night, to worry about the rest tomorrow. And she'd be right for telling me to do so, but a small part of me needed this. I needed the release just as much as I needed the peace of mind that I didn't send that woman—as awful as she may be for stabbing me—out to her death. Without her crystal, she's practically human, and a piece of me wants to believe she stabbed me out of fear and not because she wanted to kill me.

I probably could've handled our meeting better. In my defense though, she was in *my home* and *she ran.* If that's not suspicious, then I don't know what is.

Does it mean I'll forgive her? No.

Does it mean I'll at least try to take care of some of the beasts around the keep, knowing she's likely lingering nearby? Yes. That's as far as my sympathy goes.

Blood trickles down my arm, the one without a sword, and drips onto the dried leaves, mixing with the mud. On the bright side, I won't have to hunt for the next one. Any other predators creeping around out here will come find me, thanks to the scent of it. I just became a magic-infused gourmet meal.

Soaked from head to toe with sweat and the gods know what else, I leave the body to collect in the morning, along with the other five I've already taken down tonight. There's a den of them here—*somewhere*—but not even these beasts could be responsible for the destruction of the keep, nor the wall. Dread wolves are vicious, but they can't cast or siphon magic. They're just immune to it.

That part is still a mystery to me.

I'm starting to believe fellow demons did it… The damage looked ancient, like centuries had passed since those walls of the keep caved in. No one had known about my mother pushing me through the boundary, trapping me in the Realm of Monsters. I suppose, with the witch hunt my father called on me, his royal subjects might've trashed the keep looking for me all those years ago. It would've been empty, and had my father been present, the wards would've let him and anyone he was with go right in since he shares my bloodline.

I hate to think of that, to imagine what would've happened had they found me inside, but it's the only possibility that fits.

Something burns up my arm, and my feet slam to a stop. There, in the inky circle tattooed on my palm a speck of light flickers around the dark rim. I created it, bound it to the enchantment we just placed. And though it's merely a pinpoint, it means someone crossed the wall. Unfortunately, with my magic still returning, Alice and I had only cast a detection spell. It's strong enough to zap things crossing it, but not enough to keep everything out, though it'll alert me, like now if messed with.

We'll have to create a true boundary when my magic comes back to full strength, since my gift is the only thing capable of truly trying the wards to the bones. It's what makes my death magic unique. It also takes an enormous amount of energy and effort to bind the wall fully, and I didn't want to risk something siphoning it the moment we placed the spell back. So, until I figure out what ripped the enchantment from the wall, a detection spell is the best we can do.

But this circle in my hand, that small pin-prick of light, means someone has come to say hello.

Forgetting the throbbing pain in my shoulder, I sprint toward where the tattoo suggested something crossed. If I'm lucky, whatever took the magic down will be there, and I can end this once and for all.

5

Valeria

Water surges into my lungs until I choke, desperate for air that will never come. No matter how hard my limbs thrash against the unyielding ocean, I sink into the depths—into the dark.

All I can do is watch as the light shining through the wave-ridden surface grows fainter, and with every passing second the world I know becomes farther out of reach. It doesn't stop me from clawing and kicking, but my fingers slip through the water like it's nothing.

My efforts are a waste of energy. There's no way I'll make it back to the surface, and that realization saps every ounce of fight from my being. There's nothing but salt-laden ocean, feet of it, between me and life… but it's too much. I'm too tired to keep flailing.

I almost give up, but then those invisible hands of death scrape my skin. A reaper, and it's ready to wrap those talons around my soul and drag me away. That faceless, shadowy figure looms before me, its outline waving in the undercurrent.

I've only seen one. Though, it had a face that time. Still, I know what it's here to do.

Reapers are what's left of the angels who lost their grace. Most turned into demon-like creatures long ago and were banished to our world for their sins in another, taking on the physical forms of nightmares. Now, they serve the King of the Seven Realms. Their job is to collect the souls of the dead, guide them through Limbo—through judgment—then return to the Soul Well to be reborn as someone new.

The reaper stares at me for a long moment, and though it has no eyes, I think it recognizes me, too. Spindly fingers made of night, stretch toward me. One delicately strokes over my cheek as if to wipe away a tear.

"Valeria Nightborn, we meet again," its graveled voice speaks inside my head. It's more monster than man, yet almost ethereal, like even though the reaper is nothing close to the angel it used to be, it's clung to at least a small shred of its divinity.

Those phantom hands hold me, suspend me in the water that seems to still, as if it can command the tide, too. Yet, I don't move. I don't even attempt to pry at its grip. It's the only thing keeping me from descending farther down into the unforgiving dark. Into death.

An eerie, tranquil silence fills my ears until time and space lose all meaning. The darkness seems to pull into a smirk, crooked and cruel, and something else I can't quite put my finger on. Knowing, maybe?

"It is not your time. Not yet. Though, it'd be wise of you to stop dying." That voice… It sends a chill down my spine.

I'm incapable of replying. I'm not even sure how I'm still alive—*coherent*—as if magic has kept me here. Perhaps the reapers?

The shadow raises a hand and snaps dark fingers. Light explodes in front of my face. Tendrils of it whip through the water, curling around my body until that magic is the only thing I can see. I have to shut my eyes against the blinding light and a surge of raw, unbridled fear has me thrashing against its hold.

Every cell of my being seems to stretch and pull and bend. My heart thunders, every beat louder than the last. *Then, the ocean disappears.*

I shoot up from where I've been resting on the forest floor, gasping in air until my chest burns from the onslaught. It's as if I'm… as if I'm *drowning. Again.* I blink in rapid succession, taking in the dark twisted tree trunks, the glowing mushrooms.

It was just a dream.

A memory.

I am still alive, I remind myself.

Pressing my hands against my throat, my skin tingles as if those dark, dagger-like nails are still dancing on my skin, still suspending me in the ocean. Minutes pass before I can stop panting long enough to get to my feet.

It's been two weeks since I nearly drowned in the ocean between the mainland and the Elven Islands. Two weeks since our ship was attacked by some creature of the deep. It'd wrapped its scaled tentacles around the deck and splintered the wooden hull to pieces as if it were a twig and not made from the strongest trees in existence.

Elven ships don't sink. At least they didn't before the boundary around the Realm of Monsters came down.

In the two-hundred years since that realm-sized cage broke open, we've lost more ships than we have in all recorded history. Merchants refuse to cross the waters. Goods stopped coming in and out of Vanderlyth. And for a group of islands that are composed predominantly of crystals and stone, we rely on that trade. There's only so much food we can grow in the crystal rich soil.

Pushing up from the dewy leaves, I dust off my clothes and pull the suede cloak tight around my shoulders, warding off the frigid night air. On the bright side, I'm in the southernmost part of the mainland. It doesn't get nearly as cold down here when the hell flame is gone. Had I been in the north, I'd be frozen solid by now.

"Two weeks," I swear under my breath as I sheath my microscopic dagger into my boot. I've slept with it in my palm every night since leaving home. Though, whoever's idea it was for my betrothed to give me the tiniest dagger known to elvenkind, wasn't taking into consideration the possibility of being stranded in a realm full of demons. Not that I'm in any hurry to be rescued. In fact, I'd rather not be.

I'd almost drowned. If it weren't for the reaper using his magic to chuck my body at the mainland, I might've taken death as a way out of my impending marriage. That monster attacking our ship saved me from a lifetime of misery.

Still, I can remember the way whatever spell the reaper cast gripped me. The next thing I knew, I was being catapulted out of the water. My body skipped across the open ocean like a stone, and I'd landed in a heap that was far from graceful. I've never thrown up so violently before, and I can't say whether it was due to the need to expel water from my lungs or from my brain being jostled in flight. But none of that mattered because *I was alive.*

I don't have the slightest clue why the reaper had shown me mercy. Maybe it's because I knew him. Maybe it's because of the bargain he made my mother long ago, but whatever the reason be, I'll forever be grateful for it. Even if he could've been gentler about his approach.

Everything was getting on just fine here. I'd adjusted to living in the wreckage of the old castle, to forging for food and water. The wards within the keep were active and when I used my magic to turn into light, it allowed me to slip inside undetected. Most importantly, it was safe from the things that roam the woods at night.

Hell, some are bold and wander about in broad daylight. I'd come across a couple of those wolfish creatures during my time here. They'd chased me into the keep and it was a godsend that the wards could hold those *things* out.

Now, I'm not sure where to go. Worse yet, I don't have my crystal and therefore, I'm powerless.

The *man* has it—whoever he is... *Whatever* he is.

I'm certain he's demonic, those endless obsidian eyes were proof of it. Yet, he seemed like *more*. The only time I've felt power like that was when the current King of the Seven Realms came to visit the islands. My father made me stay in my room, but I felt when he entered the castle. The king's power, even stories away, pulsed over my skin like a lover's caress. It made the little hairs on my arms and the nape of my neck raise. It's a feeling I won't soon forget.

The man in the keep's power was just as intense. He houses more magic than I care to know or ever see again, and it means he's more than *just a demon.*

There's a chance he descends from a strong bloodline. There are demons born from the gods who roamed these lands long, long ago. Though, it's more likely he's nephilim... and I really hope I'm wrong.

Creatures like nephilim have little to no limitations to their magic. It comes from their soul and the more they wield the more risk there is to destroying their morality to fuel their spells and magical whims, just like the infamous Prince of Death had.

Stories of how he went mad are told across all Seven Realms. They're used as a warning—an example—to use magic only when necessary in the elven culture. Even though elves need crystals to use their fury-given gifts, instead of our souls, like the demonfolk, power can still warp the mind. It can make weak individuals greedy and crave more.

So, we scare our children early with tales of the Prince of Death. We tell them about how he snapped, and in his fit of rage, tried to kill his father, the late king. In doing so, he murdered countless innocent people within Hell Hold's castle.

The shadows of his victims are still burned into the walls of that castle. Those poor people never knew what hit them and didn't even have bodies to bury. The magic had leveled them to nothing more than free floating souls and painted silhouettes on the dark stone hallways.

The sitting King and Queen of the Seven Realms are nephilim. That's why I could feel his magic when he visited our lands. Everyone within the royal family or of nephilim blood has the capability of going mad, of letting the power snuff out their morality. All they'd have to do is draw a tad bit too much on their magic and they could destroy their soul for good.

It's why my father wishes for them to step down, to allow someone else to hold the throne. In his eyes, no king or queen should have that much power while teetering on the edge of morality. And from what I understand, or from what I knew prior to being shipwrecked, his cause is only growing.

Allowing the monsters from the prison realm to go free after the war was the tipping point for several lords on the king's court. They've been planning to overthrow the crown ever since.

But if that man was in fact nephilim, I might've already driven the nail in my coffin by stabbing him… There is nowhere to hide from a creature like that. All they need to do is picture your face and they can step through the layers of time and space and appear before you in a blink of an eye.

The best thing I can do is get my crystal and run like hell. I'll need to find somewhere I can ward against demons and nephilim and hope and pray he forgets about me.

A trickle rolls down my spine at the thought of going back to that abandoned keep, but what choice do I have? I need my crystal. Without magic I'm a sitting duck to all the other things that go bump in the night.

If what I know about his magic is true, he couldn't have hidden it far. It's likely still in that keep. And considering the amount of poison on his blade, the scent of it alone had singed my nose, it would've been enough to render a full-blooded god immobile. At least for a bit.

I don't dare try to lie to myself. I've worked with enough poisons to know pix root won't kill an immortal. Not outright. They'll heal over time as long as something else doesn't get to them first. By now, that poison is likely deep in his veins, and I should be able to get in and get out with my crystal without him being able to stop me. It's my only shot.

Still, it doesn't stop my hands from becoming sweaty as I inch through the forest.

When I woke up today, I hadn't planned to sneak about the woods like a thief in the not-so-proverbial night. In fact, I'd intended to read a book I salvaged from the keep library, but then that man showed up.

I didn't know the keep was his home. The place had been ransacked. It looked abandoned. Yet, instead of letting me leave in peace, he wanted to interrogate me *like some criminal.* Though, I suppose that term describes me accurately now. After what I'm about to do, I'll have stolen from him, even if the loot was mine to begin with.

I don't even want to think about his face, that inexplicably beautiful face… It's infuriating, that's what it is. It's a trap. You stare just a second too long, and the next thing you know you've handed over your soul in a bargain, complete with a tiny little bow.

But he's seen my face… That alone will allow him to haunt me forever. He can pop into my life at any moment in time and with that power… It's possible I'll be at his mercy, but I've already stabbed him, is stealing my necklace back worse? In fact, he might applaud me for getting one over on him. Demons are weird that way. They respect cunning plots.

Surrounded by the kind of silence that screams, I finally reach the wall. The moment my hand comes close to it, I stagger back, careful not to touch the mossy stones. Power, like the twisting cords of electricity, travels up my arm, then dissipates. I flex my fingers. *It hadn't been enchanted before…*

Hovering my hand over the surface again, I feel for the magic, careful to not let my fingers grace the surface. A vibration thrums against my palm, confirming my worst fear. The bastard enchanted it. And if he could do that, then that means *the poison didn't work.*

I steal a quick glance up, panic whittling into my bones. The wall is easily ten-feet tall. The only way over it is to go above the magic. Trying to physically scale the wall could trigger whatever spell he's cast. But trying to scale a tree with nothing more than five feet of stubbornness and wit, doesn't sound like a good plan, either, but that would be the only way I can get over it without touching it. And staying out here with all the things want to eat me for supper, sounds worse than anything a tree could do to me.

Turning in a tight circle, I find a tree with a thick branch that looks like it could hold my weight crossing above the wall. Another tree on the other side, isn't far. I can probably jump to it, but if he's awake, and not paralyzed, do I want to?

He didn't come for me. There's a chance I could escape right now—magicless, but free. If I go for my crystal, I risk pissing him off more. I don't think I could survive out here without it, but to go after it would make me a mouse picking a fight with a cat if I get caught. I'd be entirely at his mercy and there's no way he'll make the mistake of seeing me as harmless again. Not after I stabbed him.

And those claws…

That power…

Imagining it turned on me…

He had morphed into something out of a nightmare with obsidian eyes and here I am, sneaking back into his territory like I've got a death wish. I'm already living on borrowed time as is and I doubt the reaper will spare me a third death.

Maybe it's best if I just go. There have to be more crystals somewhere—

My thoughts fracture into pieces as a growl sounds from somewhere in the forest. It's close, whatever it is.

Nope… That settles that.

6

Valeria

Turning toward the tree, I find my first foothold and climb. The rough bark bites into my palms as I move with precision, staying silent as best I can while I ascend. Foot after foot, hand after hand, the ground below grows distant. And when I make it to the limb I spotted, and pull myself to a sitting position to rest, I glimpse one of those beasts prowling near the wall. It growls low in its throat, as if it's looking for something on the other side of it.

Even from way up here, panic at the thought of that thing seeing me claws at my gut. My mouth goes dry, and my body tenses as it halts mid-stride. Its head whips as it glances for something in the dark, *listening*. Then it bounds off along the wall at the sound of a guttural wail.

Choosing not to stick around and find out what kind of creature could scare off that *thing*, I seize my opportunity. Quickly getting to my feet, I hold my arms out to balance, putting one foot in front of the other until I near the end of the branch. Gauging the jump, I hunker down and pounce, whirling my arms as I glide through the air. Slamming into the tree trunk, too low for what I had planned. I slide down the rough bark, feeling it bite into my skin without mercy, feeling the scrapes form and the bark burn my flesh.

Gnashing my teeth together and hanging on for dear life, the ground rushes up to meet me.

It's too fast. I'm falling *too fast.* If I hit the ground like this, I might break a leg if not two. Forced to act last minute, I kick off the trunk, redirecting my motion toward the wall and I drop into possibly one of the biggest piles of leaves I've ever seen.

An *oof* escapes my lips as I collide with the hard ground, sparks of pain rattling my bones. Having sank into the pile like a rock in water, I'm buried alive in the crunchy leaves. They're in my mouth, in my hair, and some have snuck under the hem of my pants and shirt. They're *everywhere.* But my pieces are intact and that's what matters.

With a groan, I push to my feet, cringing at the sting in my hands, arms, face… My entire body is on fire. I pop through the top of the leaf pile, but even standing, the leaves still come to my shoulders. Swishing my arms, I wade through it, praying that whatever is going on with the creatures in the woods is still happening and is loud enough to cover the noise I'm making.

Free of the leaves, I push my hood back and start picking foliage out of my hair, along with other places that leaves should never go. Then, with my dagger in hand, I head toward the keep.

The strip of forest between the wall and the fortress isn't thin, but I make quick work of moving through the underbrush. And when I reach the edge, I stick to the shadows, peering over a thick bush, scouting for movement or any sign of the demon man lurking. If I'm lucky, he might've gone back to wherever he came from after putting the magic on the wall. Maybe it's empty and I can at least sleep in the keep until the hell flame comes up—assuming I can even get in without my crystal.

The wind blows against my nape, sending an icy cool breeze down my spine, cutting straight through the thin fabric of my clothes and nipping at my skin. Still, I don't take my eyes off the keep. I will *not* go in there blind. Without my crystal, spying is going to be my best bet to not get caught.

Warm air blankets the crook of my neck, then my shoulder.

"See anything interesting?" *That voice. No.*

My spine straightens like I've been electrocuted from behind and I whirl, coming face to face with a smirk I'm certain will star in my future nightmares. His brows arch closer toward his hairline as those deep amber eyes take me in, traveling down my body and taking their sweet-ass time doing so.

I lift a foot, ready to bolt for the hills, but his voice stops me dead in my tracks. "Hands."

"Excuse me?" I barely get the words out, too busy cycling through scenarios of where I can hide.

"I said, show me your hands," he breathes, tipping his chin at me, his fingers flexing on the hilt of the sword sheathed at his hip. The motion draws my eyes down a scar-ridden chest, splattered with dark blood. The copper scent of it singes my nose, laced with a sour tang of the pix root poison, like that on his blade earlier.

Are all of his blades dipped in it?

The moonlight catches on his tan, sweat-slicked skin, painting him in strokes of silver, bronze, and shadow. His dark shoulder-length hair is half wet, and raked through by ruthless fingers, leaving only a couple rogue strands to frame his face.

The man could be a god… Hell, he might be. Power radiates off him, clouding my mind. My head spins with the pulse of it, and somehow, the sweetness that magic emits overpowers everything else. It's intoxicating, and I have the sudden urge to move closer, to allow it to curl around me, to reach out and spread my fingers across his broad chest, to paint with the blood splattered there.

He bares his teeth, not bothering to hide the ire in his tone. "You can eye fuck me later, princess. Hands. I won't ask again." The sternness has warning bells blaring inside my head, pleading with me not to push him.

Demons like to play games. Maybe flirting with him, *playing with him*, will allow me the chance to escape, seeing as I'm armed with nothing more than a sharp tongue and the world's tiniest dagger. Both of which are practically useless compared to the magic at his fingertips. I slowly raise my hands, revealing that itty bitty blade. "Worried I came to finish the job? You can't possibly believe I'm dumb enough to stab you twice." I give him a sultry grin, forcing my spine to remain strong even though every cell of my being is screaming to run. *Hide. Escape.*

"I think you were dumb enough to stab me the first time, then ballsy enough to risk coming back. If it weren't for the fact I just watched you fall out of a tree, this conversation would be going much differently," he says, glaring at me down the length of his nose.

He saw that?

The man steps closer, eyes locked on mine as he pats me down, sure to keep his body—his blades—out of my reach. I don't so much as breathe as his warm hands slide down my sides, between my legs, and over every curve of my body. And I'm almost certain he can feel my rampaging pulse through the layers of my clothes.

Pleased with the fact I'm relatively unarmed, he steps back, but remains expressionless as he shoves his hands into his pockets. “So, if you’re not here to play murderer, why are you here?” A smile teases his lips. “It can’t be that you lost something, can it?” Laced with a hint of amusement and challenge, his tone makes my heartbeat kick up a notch.

“I thought you’d be gone by now.” It'd be pointless to lie. I’ve never been a good liar, and he’d smell it from a mile away. Demons are perceptive that way.

“Oh?” He arches a brow as he pulls a single hand from his pocket, twirling his wrist in the space between our faces. My necklace appears out of thin air, dangling from his crooked, blood-stained finger. “So, you weren’t searching for this? Good to know.”

I school my features into a wall of expressionless stone, giving away nothing. “Actually, I’d just planned to go on a midnight stroll.”

His laugh is low and cunning, a sound that sends shivers down my spine in the least unpleasant way possible. “A stroll?” Those amber eyes become sinister as they lock with mine. “Here. Take it, but know you’re not welcome on my lands, and as you can see, I’m rather busy. So, if I were you, I’d make yourself disappear before I tire of this little game you’re playing. I get rather murderous when I’m bored.”

I reach for it, our fingertips brushing briefly as I grasp my necklace. The world seems to tilt from the charge in that touch. It sends an echoing pulse of something dangerous, something *wild* through every nerve in my body. "You’re just giving it back?" I manage, clutching the crystal like it's my last shred of sanity.

“Not out of the goodness of my heart, no. I’d rather not have to pick up your pieces come morning. The woods are riddled with dread wolves. I’ve killed over half a dozen already.”

Not daring to look away, I clutch the crystal to my chest, hissing at the sting that radiates up my arm. "Well, I'd hate to inconvenience you further by dying, so I'll be on my way." I take a single step, halting to peer at him out of the corner of my eye. "Thank you, for my crystal." Pinching my lips between my teeth I force myself to look at him. "And for not killing me."

The corner of his lips quips up. "My pleasure."

I can feel his gaze roaming over me as I leave, and against my better judgment, I steal a glance over my shoulder, finding him leaning his back against the tree he was near, arms crossed. And if I didn't know better, I'd think there was a flirtatious glint in his eye.

It's not wise to give a creature like him my back, but my hope is it'll appear as though I'm not scared of him, even if the truth can't be more opposite. I only make it a few yards away before I hear that angelic voice once more.

"What's your name?" he calls.

My lips pull into a smirk, but I don't dare look at him as I say, "I know better than to give my name to strangers."

"I'm not fae," he says, like the word is dirtier than his blood-caked nails. "Give me a little credit, will ya? I'm a demon and the only way a demon can trick you is if you make a deal and seal it in blood." His voice is much closer, as if he's standing right behind me, but I'm too frozen to look.

With menacing slowness, he barely disturbs the ground as he circles me, chin tucked toward his chest. Those amber eyes glow from beneath his dark lashes, only inches separating us while he watches me with such *intent*, I'm not quite sure what to do.

"I could've killed you, you said it yourself. Yet, I didn't. I returned your necklace, despite you coming to barge into my home unannounced… *again.*" I tense as he scoops up a dark lock of my hair from where it was resting on my shoulder, then proceeds to coil it around his pointer finger. "Doesn't that deserve some reward?"

I clear my throat. Clearly, he needs this. I knew it was too good to be true, and I don't think he ever had intended to let me leave without giving up something. But he's right. Demons can't make deals without consent and just knowing my name isn't dangerous in itself. For lesser demons, those not as powerful as the one standing before me, they'd need a name to track me down. This man? He's already seen my face and for nephilim that's enough.

"Valeria."

Tipping his head to the side, he studies me, his movements dripping with feline curiosity. "Valeria…"

My heart skips. My name has never sounded so beautiful, so *sinister*, nor has it ever been spoken with such grace.

"Do you have a last name, Valeria?"

I tense, eyes darting from his. "Just Valeria."

He'll know I'm lying, but if I tell him the truth, there's no good way this will end. My engagement was meant as a distraction. My father knew the King and Queen would need to give their blessing in order for my betrothed to be sworn in to the Court of Lords upon his death. Without their blessing, as his only heir, I would be appointed.

My father would much sooner roll in his grave before that ever happens.

We saw elven ships break away from ours, it's what left us vulnerable when the beasts attacked. I'd known my father was up to something, but using his only living child as a distraction is low, even for him. The moment those ships left us and headed away from King's Cove, I knew.

They'd had cannons and weapons of magical destruction strapped to every available surface of those ships. It didn't take a genius to know that they intended to attack Ogre's Landing, the only major port east of the mainland.

There are some ports farther north, but not even my father is mad enough to go there with anything short of a fleet. The seas in what used to be the Realm of Monsters, are far more deadly and it's not just the monsters of the deep they'd need to worry about. Pirates in the outer realm own the water. The demons might be savage brutes, but the pirates there are much more ruthless.

Regardless, if anyone found out my last name, it wouldn't end well. Who knows what my father did to that port. It couldn't have been anything good, and for all I know, he might've declared war on the demons by now.

How much would the king and queen pay to have their enemy's daughter in their clutches?

Would they use me as bait?

Would they send my head to my father in a satin-lined box?

No one can know. Not here. Not in this realm. Not ever.

Here, I will be anything other than a Nightborn.

"Well, then. Don't tell me." The man tips his head toward the dark forest, all hints of the flirtatious smirk gone, as if it never existed. "Over the wall with you then."

Incapable of doing or saying anything more, I give him a curt nod and stroll off into the dark.

7

Valeria

The morning light bursts through the tree canopy above me, and I squint against the onslaught. Birds chirp from somewhere high above me, their songs filling the silence… The silence I've become so accustomed to.

Come to think of it, this is the first time I've heard birds since washing up on the mainland.

With a groan, I unravel my cloak and push back my hood as I lift to a sitting position. Large tree roots curve up alongside me, large enough that they almost form a cave. I slept here last night. It was enough protection in the dark that most things slipped past me without knowing I was here. It was the best I could do on short notice. I didn't trust myself to sleep in the trees. Not after knowing how much it hurts to fall out of one.

Wiping the sleep from my eyes, I crawl over the leaves until it's clear for me to stand up. Though, I don't get that far, not before a rough, tired-sounding male voice hits my ears.

"Good morning to you, too."

My head lolls to the side as I meet his gaze. His bare back is pressed against the trunk of the tree, right beside the root I slept under. Dark circles hang beneath those otherwise bright amber eyes. Though, where the blood had been splattered is now wiped clean, revealing layers upon layers of scars. Some of which, in the light, make symbols.

I've seen those symbols in the keep's apothecary. They're etched into the stone with crystal slabs, but I haven't been able to derive their meaning yet though. They're Enochian, I think. The language of the angels and demons. The elves don't see a point in learning it, but I had tried during my time at the keep, just to no avail.

"Tell me, do you always sleep out in the open where anything and everything could pick your bones clean if they wanted to?" His head slumps forward, his eyes narrowing on me slightly.

"No." I don't play into his hand, keeping my face blank as I cross my arms over my chest.

"What do you call this then?" He tosses a hand at the tree roots. "A luxury castle?"

"I call it being evicted from my home an hour before nightfall."

The man flinches like I've physically struck him. "Well..." He gets to his feet, appearing far taller than I remember. I don't falter as he glides forward, eating up the distance between us. And this time, his voice is smooth, like one would speak sweet nothings to a lover. "I would've let you stay had you not stabbed me. You made your own bed." He glances at the tree. "Or perhaps mother nature did. Either way, it's of your own doing."

My brows knit together as I stare him down, refusing to be shaken by his coy, flirty, *beautiful* face. "Why are you here?"

He lifts a brow. "Was I supposed to let you get eaten?" I inhale sharply as he leans an inch closer. "Did you want to be?"

"No." My eyes narrow to mere slits. "Believe it or not, I don't wish to die."

He presses his lips together and releases them with an audible *pop*. "I don't think we're on the same page, but I'm here because whether you're gnawed into pieces on this side of the wall or my side, I'm still going to be stuck smelling your rotting body. Besides, you snore like a broken gear." The man scoffs and shakes his head, as if my breathing is despicable.

"I do not." Recoiling, I take a step back, desperate to put distance between us. He's far too close for comfort.

"You *do*, and had I not used my magic to conceal the sound, everything in earshot would've known your location. You should be thanking me."

"Thank you? You're the one who put me in this mess."

"Ahhh. There are the words I was looking for." He gives in over dramatic bow. "You're welcome."

"I wasn't—"

He holds up a finger. "Now, I'd planned to offer my services. I have no interest in sleeping in the trees every night as you wander on your way, so where would you like to go? I'll take you there."

Anything to be free of you. That's the part he doesn't say.

He extends a hand.

I stare at his palm, head canting as I take in the burned mark there. A sigil of sorts. "So, you are nephilim?"

"Something like that." When I don't take his hand, he lets it fall to his side.

"I'll be just fine. I don't require your help." I take another step back.

He scrutinizes me, those amber eyes brightening and darkening as if he's reading words written on my skin, my clothes. "Did I offend you? I thought I was being friendly, all things considered." A single finger skims over the space between his ribs where a fresh puckered scar has formed.

"You are," I say, trapping my lips between my teeth. "I just don't need your help. I'll find my way on my own. Surely, you're a busy man. You're the lord of this estate, yes?"

He lets out a short "Hah," and his lips pull into a smile that's all teeth. "Something like that." Mischievous amber rings gleam at me in the morning light. "Is this my land? Yes. Am I a lord on the king's court? Not a chance, and gods, I hope I never am."

My shoulders ease, the tension leaving my body with every passing second. "Then what are you?"

"I know better than to disclose all of my secrets to strangers."

Something about the use of the line I'd given him when he asked for my name has a smile pulling at my lips. So much so, my cheeks heat. "I see... Well, you know my name, and considering you know my sleeping habits, I'd hardly consider us strangers."

He looks into the forest for a moment, then dusts off his peck like some invisible layer of dust exists there, then slowly, his eyes return to mine. "I suppose you can call me Asmo. That's the most you're going to get. The last thing I need is you trying to summon me. It's not a pleasant experience."

"Very well, then. It was a pleasure meeting you, Asmo, but I have a home to find." Turning on my heels, I suck in a breath when he appears out of thin air in my path.

"I meant it. Tell me a place." His hand is extended in the space between us, palm up, beckoning of mine. "I could take you to the Elven Islands. It'd be for the best, anyway. Relations with the elves are strained at the moment."

"I don't have a place to tell you because I don't have a place to go."

Asmo's face falls blank, eyes toggling between mine. "You were banished? Let me guess, half-breed?"

"Not banished, but something like that."

He knows I'm lying. Despite my hair being darker, I otherwise look like a pure-blooded elf. It's hard to miss. Yet, by some gods-given grace, he doesn't pry. I wouldn't know what to tell him if he did. How do I explain that I was shipwrecked? That the reaper didn't let me die?

His features pinch as if he's trying to put the pieces together.

"It was nice meeting you." Shuffling around him, I head into the forest.

"I have a deal to offer you."

"Not in the mood," I say over my shoulder. No way in hell am I making a demon deal right now.

"You haven't even heard my proposition." He's before me in the blink of an eye. "You already know the keep. I'm rebuilding the place. I need someone who can come and go when I'm not here. As long as you make a deal, claiming you won't attempt to murder me again, you can stay, but know things are going to change around here. No more crumpled walls." Asmo pulls the dagger from the sheath on his thigh. "Do we have a deal?"

Looking him up and down, I mull the words over in my head. *There's no way that can be twisted, right?*

When I've settled on my revision, I square my shoulders. "If I die, you do, too." Simple enough. "Those are the terms."

The corner of his lips tugs up. "Deal." He slices the blade over his hand, the motions for me to do the same.

Hesitantly, I grip my dagger, hissing in a breath as it slices through my skin, the crimson beading in an instant. Lifting my hand, I press it to his and magic rushes around us like a warm, sweet-scented wind. And it's gone in seconds.

"In that case, welcome to Grim's Keep," he purrs, his fingers sliding between mine. I barely have time to process the fact his home is named after the oldest reaper when the world spins. Ribbons of air, of *magic* weave until they form white and black smoke around us. My body vibrates, my eyes widen as I frantically glue them on his, anything to keep me steady, to keep me grounded.

I'm not sure how, but the world seems to fold around us and when those wisps of darkness and light spin out, we're standing in front of the keep. Except it's not the crumbled broken pieces I remember. Now, it's… It's *magnificent*. The dark gray stones gleam, as if they were crafted yesterday, the garden and hedges trimmed and brimming with vibrant flowers of every hue.

The charred remains of the front doors that barely swung on their hinges hours ago now consist of heavy wooden slabs, carved into an array of falling feathers. Even those broken and missing windows have changed, now catching the hell flame light, scattering colorful rays along the stone, the green grass, and everywhere else the light can reach. Based on the windows I can see from the ground, they depict dragons of every color, swirling around one another, like they're flying through the clouds. Some look like a painting that carries on from window to window—a black dragon chasing a silver one across the stretch of the keep.

It's like these stone walls rose from the ashes, from the crumpled rubble, and pieced itself back together again. Then I see the long banners, cascading down the side of the twisted towers, from the place sentries would sit if they were here. The fabric is made of a voidness black; the hems decorated in gold, and in the center is a golden phoenix.

"The queen thought it was fitting." Asmo glances up at the banner. "Seeing as they keep coming back from the dead and all."

It is, except for the phoenix on that banner is exactly like the tattoo on my back. *How did he know?* My jaw falls open, but I haven't the ability to shut it. "How?" I breathe.

Asmo glides toward the front doors, turning backward without faltering a step as he waggles his fingertips at me. "Magic."

He knew about my tattoo by magic, or does he mean he rebuilt this place with it?

Gripping my shoulder, I feel the pulse of that tattoo, of the magic there. It had been placed on me the day my mother died, a physical mark of the deal she'd made with the Grim Reaper to exchange her life for mine, so that I could live, much to my father's dismay.

I stand in awe, my heart a captive to the view before me.

"Well, don't just stand there." Asmo appears in the now open doorway, beckoning me to follow him inside.

8

Valeria

I follow him inside, and all I can do is gape. Gone are the flamed remains of plaster, of bent canvases. Now, the walls are dark, glowing and receding in places as if they're made of the night sky. Those gleaming lights are somehow captured within them sparkling like the crystals from my land. Everything glows in a soft light, and when I look at Asmo, he points toward the ceiling with a single finger and I follow it. Above us, dozens of floating orbs illuminate the room, adding the sea of starry crystals on the walls.

"These…" Asmo begins, his voice like dark velvet and burning embers as he steps closer. His gaze follows my entranced stare, up and up, until his head rests back as far as it will go. "These are inspired by the bloom festival. There's a little village in the Realm of Monsters that hosts the event, every year after the blackout."

"The blackout?" I ask, admiring the way those glowing orbs reflect off his eyes, off the scar that slices down the side of his face.

He relaxes his head, glancing in my direction just long enough to remind me I'm staring. "You wouldn't know about it, but occasionally, in the north the hell flame disappears for three days straight, sometimes longer. When it returns, that village uses magic to make orbs like these rise from a fountain in the middle of town. They float above the streets, like lanterns. It's one of the most beautiful things I've ever had the pleasure of witnessing."

I drop my gaze, seeing that he even replaced the floors. Where cracked midnight blue tiles were, are now an endless piece of obsidian marble with the most subtle hints of gold and silver streaked through it.

Each room he takes me to is adored with stone and moss and shadow. The kitchen is large enough for me to get lost in alone. Somehow it seems bigger than it was when I stayed here, but that could be due to the crumbled wall taking up easily half the room. The dining room has been filled with a long wooden table, surrounded by at least a dozen or more seats. It hints at his desire for future gatherings, while the sunroom, now framed in clear windows, is the perfect place to curl up in the quiet afternoons. I could see myself laying in here, bathing in the golden light of the setting hell flame, lost in thought or book.

He leads me through the apothecary, which for the most part looks the same, just less dusty. The air still vibrates with magic in here, the crystal wards on the wall glowing faintly in the dim light. Then there's the throne room, toward the front of the keep. It's a large, mostly empty, space, besides the various round tables scattered about and the two large stone thrones on the far side.

"Those thrones are older than this keep. They were given to the lord who ruled here as a present. This place hasn't seen much company, even if the rooms look ready for it. At least not in my lifetime it hasn't." Asmo waves for me to follow him, and I let him lead me up the stairs to the second floor. "Up here, is my office." He nods to one of the large rooms off the landing.

"Glad to see you kept the piano," I say, following him like a lost puppy.

He stops, twirling to face me so fast, I nearly topple into him. "You play?"

"No, but it's fun to pretend I do."

He chuckles, shaking his head. "Well, lucky enough for the both of us, I do. I consider it an unfathomable crime to own a piano and not know how to play it." He nods at the other four doors that surround the landing. "There's not much else here beyond bedrooms. The smaller ones, that is. And I can imagine you know where the terrace is."

Asmo gestures for me to continue up the stairs to the third and final floor of the keep. The winding staircase curls around the open center, giving a clear view down the foyer, but as we reach the landing, this floor is grander than either of the two before it. The ceiling is made entirely of glass, glass that had been broken, leaving most of the floor open to the elements before. Except now, it's not the sky above me, it's some sort of liquid of blending blues, silvers, and whites.

"What is that?" I ask, staring up at that swirling liquid. It moves on its own accord, but as I peer closer, I can make out a map of our world behind it. It's not just moving colors. The blue forms almost perfect circles, shooting through the white and silver only to stop at different places on the map.

"They're souls. It's a reaper window. They take souls to the ferryman in the Soul Well, but this map shows where all souls in the Seven Realms are." Asmo's hands are in his pockets as he watches me from the opposite side of the open landing, the circular hole that extends down the middle of the curved stairwell to the foyer spanning between us now.

"Did the Grim Reaper use this?"

The blue light reflects off his face, making the striking amber of his eyes more brown from here. "No. He made it for me."

"You?" My brows knit together as I resume watching the colors shift.

"He raised me, and he disappeared all the time unannounced. It was part of the job, so he made this for me. That way, when I woke up to an empty keep, I could close my eyes, think of him, and know where he was." As if to demonstrate, Asmo closes his eyes, his long lashes fanning his tan cheeks. The colors above us stop swirling, the white and silver forming a perfect circle around a clear section of the map. In a swift motion, one of the blue dots shoots toward the center of that opening, stopping on a place called Witchelm.

When he opens his eyes, he seems to lose himself in that little blue dot. Then as if remembering I'm here, he shifts, clears his throat, and returns that molten stare to mine. "Anyway, the library is just through there," he says, pointing to an open archway. "Unfortunately, I was poisoned, so my magic is limited. I'm not sure I could fully restore the books anyway, but I'll replace them."

I scoff. "Limited? I'd hardly say this is limited magic." Gesturing to the room, I do a quick twirl.

"Well, I had help. Not even I can create things out of nothing. I can manipulate and glamour items to look like something else. I can summon them from other places or send them away, but not create. There's only one person in the Seven Realms with that ability."

"The queen," I breathe. "I was taught that she was of witch and nephilim blood, but I didn't know it made much of a difference. I thought it just meant that she had no need for spells."

He snorts. "She's as different as they come, but she does use spells from time to time. They're not always needed though. However, her witch side allows her to siphon magic from things around her. It gives her an endless supply of magic, whereas demons, nephilim, and most other magical creatures who can use magic innately, tap into their souls. We can only use so much before it has to rest and regenerate. It gives her the ability to create things anew."

Because drawing too much magic, draining the soul completely, would destroy it, along with all sense of morality. That's the part he doesn't say. It's the part my people worry about.

"She helped you restore this place?" I slowly make my way around the banister, toward his side of the landing.

"Not by choice. By the time I returned from clearing the woods, she was here, putting the keep back together so I'd have a place to sleep, to clean up afterward. And like you, she seems to not listen to a single word I say. I tell you to get lost, you come back. I tell her I don't need her help, she builds me a fucking keep. And since she's seen all of my memories, she made it exactly how I remembered it, with a few upgrades."

I tilt my head, wondering how someone like him could know the queen, to have her care so much for him that she worried he wouldn't have a place to sleep… Then it hits me. The king and queen have children. I'm not sure of their ages, but it would explain his magic.

"She must care about you a lot," I say, trying not to pry while letting my curiosity get the better of me. Except, he doesn't take the bait. He doesn't elaborate at all beyond agreeing with me.

"Your bedroom is just through there." He nods to the door on his right, then moves toward the one beside it.

"And that's yours?" Daring to move closer, I watch his hands fidget in his pockets.

His head twists, angling slightly. “If you’re thinking of sneaking in while I’m asleep, don’t.” With lazy steps, he turns toward his door, opening it ever so slightly. “If there’s anything you need, we’ll get it for you tomorrow. For now, just settle in. We’ll have company by dinner.”

I don’t get to ask if it’s the queen coming. I don’t get to do much of anything as he slips inside his room and shuts the door, putting a definitive end to our conversation.

Retreating to what’s been dubbed my room, the door clicks shut behind me, sealing me inside what can only be described as a sanctuary sculpted from the darkness itself. For a moment, I stand rooted to the spot, my heart going quiet in my chest, frozen by the sheer awe this place instills in me. It's as if I've stepped into the queen’s quarters, not merely a bedroom within a demon's forgotten keep.

I inch forward, my steps silent against the obsidian marble that gleams beneath my feet. I almost feel guilty to be wearing muddied shoes in a room so clean—so perfect.

The floors reflect the odd dot-like designs. Symbols of some sort. Regardless, they seem to move on their own accord, shifting along the wall, as if I’m the center of their universe and those thin silver strands connecting those dots gravitate around me.

It’s a masterpiece, full of light and shadows, just like the man it was modeled for.

Pushing deeper into the enchanted space, my fingers ache to graze the surface of those walls, to trace the hard lines and intricate patterns, to sense the magic there pulse against my flesh. I’m certain it would be like everything in this keep, a contrast to what I’d known hours ago. It would feel like a living, breathing entity. It’d feel alive and hum with energy.

How ironic, considering this place is named after the Grim Reaper—a collector of the dead.

I don't dare touch those walls though, for fear that disturbing it would somehow wash away the magic. That I'd corrupt it somehow. Instead, I move farther into the room, exploring the place I'm to rest my head tonight, and possibly every night after. That is, assuming Asmo puts up with me and honors his deal.

I'm still not sure why he made it with me. I'm not sure what it gives him.

It doesn't take someone born of magic to know he has enough that people would volunteer to look after his keep if he vanished from the realm. In these lands, I wouldn't be surprised if others made sacrifices in his honor or started a waiting list to bow at his feet.

So, *why me? Why forgive what I'd done and offer me sanctuary?* My hand closes around the crystal pendant around my neck, feeling it vibrate against my skin. *Why give back my crystal? Why not get revenge for me stabbing him, and let me die in the woods?*

The enormous bed sits regally in the center of the room. Blanketed in dark velvet covers, it appears soft and inviting, promising dreams and warmth. Above, there's a glass dome ceiling that opens up to the daytime sky. The hell flame light filters through those paned windows, bathing the room in a golden glow, making the air shimmer with dust. It's a stark contrast to the dark theme that dominates my chambers, though I'm sure it fits right in at night.

On the far side of the room, two solid doors are inset into the wall, and behind the bed sits two large glass panes, lacking door handles, open to the terrace just beyond it. I approach the first solid door, curiosity nipping at my heels as I peer inside to find a closet. For the most part, it's empty, but there is a set of folded pajamas, made from satin, and a note on top of them.

To the woman who's agreed to live with Asmo,

Long ago, I moved in with a man I didn't know. A man who wanted me to feel welcome and loved, but knew nothing about me. He filled my closet to the brim with frilly dresses, and things princesses could only dream of, but all I desired in that moment were boots and fighting leathers. So, this closet is enchanted. Speak what it is you desire to wear out loud and it will create it just for you. Consider it my present and my sincerest apologies that you've chosen to live with my grumpy, cynical, obnoxiously stubborn best friend.

Alice

Alice… As in *the Queen of the Seven Realms, Alice Morningstar?*

I let the door drift closed, turning my attention back to the room. *How did the queen know I'd be moving in?*

Her note in hand, I exit into the landing, rapping my knuckles on the door I saw Asmo disappear into. It takes me knocking four times before the wooden slab opens just enough for an amber eye to peer through the crack, flicking over me. Then he lets out a rattled huff and opens the door fully.

"May I help you?" His teeth clench tight.

"I… um…" All the words I had planned die on my tongue as my gaze takes in the dripping-wet dark hair, the water droplets sliding over rippled muscles, the silver scars… My eyes track all the way to where his hand clenches a towel around his waist. My mouth is suddenly dry as I force my attention back to his face, finding it harder than it should be to keep it there. "I found a note and I'm sorry to *interrupt,* but how did the queen know I'd accept your deal? That I'd agree to living here?"

Asmo snatches the note out of my upheld hand, his eyes ticking back and forth as he reads it. Then, as if it's nothing important, he hands it back. "She's the queen, and a witch who can scry the future. What I'm more concerned with is the fact that she gifted you a fucking enchanted closet and all I got was a rubber duck near the bathtub and a note reminding me to be on my best behavior. Now, if you'll excuse me, my duck friend is rather lonely, and I'd like to finish my bath."

The door snicks shut, leaving me fighting back a grin on the landing.

9

Asmodeus

The last thing I wanted to do when I woke up this morning was save Griffin. Yet here I am, heading to the gods forsaken Enchanted Forest.

Hands in my pockets, the shadowed wisps evaporate into nothing, revealing the gnarled, crooked trunks of poison apple trees. The air is thick with the scent of syrupy magic that puts my senses on edge, but I do my best to swallow down the bile rising in my throat.

Unfortunately, a rubber ducky wasn't the only gift Alice left me. Along with it was a note. In her curly scrawl, I was reminded to behave and have manners—as if I frequently forget. I was all but ordered to shower. It's like she knew I'd returned to the woods to continue ridding the beasts that got past the wall. And last, came a favor. And when the queen asks a favor, especially after resurrecting your keep, you comply. No questions asked.

"I need you to do something for me. Preferably, without making an enemy of the mage clan in Solaria. Griffin has been 'ensnared' by one of his 'conquests'... I'm sure your imagination can figure out the rest. I'll need time to break it without harming him. I thought I'd broken it once, but the spell work is more complex than what I saw at first glance. The knots and threads must be internal. The best option might be to let it wear off in a place warded against such magic.

Regardless, I need time and he needs a safe place to stay. I trust you'll look after him. On the back of this letter, you'll find a map with where to find him."

And just like that, I've now gained not one, but two roommates in a twenty-four-hour period. The first being a woman who tried to kill me out of spite, and the second being my notorious nephew.

I've always despised this forest. Traveling through it has brought nothing good, and not once in my years of serving the mad king did I come here and not have the sudden urge to lose my breakfast. The power magic users have differs from mine. All magic smells sweet, but being around a horde of mages and druids can quickly make the air unbearable to breathe.

As expected, the air reeks of them, of their magic, and only a man with a death wish would come here without being invited. And by the strength of it pilfering the breeze sweeping through the fruit trees, I'd say there have to be dozens in that mansion.

I have nothing against druids, mages, or witches for that matter, so long as they keep their hands off the blood grimoires. However, this clan used to make up the mad king's personal guard. When the boundary fell and Solaria was united under the crown that reigns over all the Seven Realms, most of them died in uprisings. Those that remain… Let's just say they never truly got over it, but have since learned to keep to themselves and not cause trouble. For that mercy, they've been allowed to live here.

Though, holding Griffin hostage might change things.

I push open the gate that's been made of decaying vines. The hinges holding it upright whine, the sharp pitch of it slicing through the eerie silence. In the shadowed heart of the clearing, surrounded by those poisoned fruit trees, the dark mansion looms before me. Pillars made of thick, twisted vines, support the carved wooden roof. Even from a distance I can make out the rune wards that decorate every inch of exposed siding, preventing anyone from entering any other way than the front door.

Who knows what else those runes protect from. It's possible that the moment I enter, my magic will be out of reach. Though, being magicless isn't something I'm unfamiliar with.

Only my nephew would put himself in such a *delicate* situation. I'm not sure I'll ever understand what possessed Griffin to wander into their hornet's nest with a hard on, but I think it's safe to assume the mages and druids living here didn't take too lightly to the Duke of Solaria standing on their doorstep. And he risked this for what? To get laid? There are plenty of other prospects. His looks alone rival that of his grandmother, who quite literally was the embodiment of lust and beauty, and to say men and women fall at his feet for simply existing is an understatement.

So why choose someone who despises the very blood in his veins?

Shaking my head, I kick a toadstool growing in between the cracks of the old, cobblestone path leading to the mansion. The shadows seem deeper here, and though the clearing is open to the hell flame, the light seems to be snuffed out before it ever reaches the roof. It's like a dome of midnight encircles it, making the place look more imposing than it is.

Overrun in weeds and vines, the wooden siding is barely visible. If the wards didn't have a slight golden hue to them, one might not know they're there. Even the windows have been blocked out by the wild thatch work of blooming jasmine.

Nearing the steps of the wrap-around porch, my boots click against the creaking wood, screaming beneath my weight. This place has aged since I visited last. Granted, that was over two hundred years ago, and my trips here were far and few at that.

Resting a hand on the wobbling rail, the vines at the base of the steps writhe, as if they could reach out and touch me as I pass. It's now that I notice the bones in the planter beds. I spot the curved edge of a humanoid rib cage, its holes filled with flame-colored tulips. The trellises lining the side of the mansion are constructed of long femur bones, held together by twine.

"Oh, Griffin…" I breathe, keeping my voice quiet. "What did you get yourself into?"

Mages and druids wouldn't have bone decor.

But what is Griffin doing with blood witches? They're what becomes of magic users who dabble in dark magic and blood grimoires. It's powerful and wild, but requires sacrifices—*extensive sacrifices*—and it's magic that even the mad king outlawed when he reigned.

No wonder this clan has been so quiet. They're likely not seen in town because they don't want to waste power to glamour themselves. They don't want the locals to see their rotting teeth, the lesioned skin, or soulless eyes. Not even glamours can conceal all the physical ailments that are caused by wielding blood magic, and if the crown discovers the spells they're weaving here, they'll be put to death for their crimes.

For all I know, Griffin might've tried to fuck one. A shiver rakes through me at the idea of him doing anything with one of these creatures… He might as well sleep with a corpse, seeing as blood witches are closer to the realm of the dead than the living. Maybe that's why they've held him here. Maybe he discovered their secret, and they took him hostage to prevent him reporting the truth.

All I can hope is that those aren't his bones being devoured by the daisies… Those twisted spells could strip the living flesh off his bones in moments, siphoning the life out of every cell to fuel the witch's power that sacrificed him. It would be his soul the magic would feed off last.

Alice had used a locator spell to find him, but it doesn't prove life. Unfortunately, his soul might linger here, but it doesn't mean it's still united with his body any more. Shaking the thought from my mind, I step up to the large wooden door, lift a hand, and rap the knocker. Silence ensues for far too long, making my pulse quicken. I'm just about to turn around, to search for another way in when the sound of footsteps echoes through the door from inside.

The knob twists, the hinges creak, and slowly, oh so slowly, a crack forms. Beady, dark eyes peer at me through that gap.

"Who are you?" a woman's sultry voice hisses at me.

The air thickens with magic, a palpable force that brings a smirk to my lips as I stare into those malevolent, far from human eyes. "Are you threatening me? If you are, you'll need a lot more magic than that."

"Who… *Are*… You?" she repeats, drawing out every word, her patience growing thin, but mine is far thinner.

"I believe the proper way to greet your prince is, 'How may I help you, Your Majesty.' Is it not?" I rock back and forth on my heels, one hand still in my pants pocket, the other on the golden hilt of my sword, as I wait for her response.

The woman straightens, seeming taller through the slit of the door as a deep voice sounds behind her, "What is the banished prince doing on our doorstep?"

The word *banished* seems to echo in my bones, turning every vertebra in my spine to stone. Of all times for that word to hit me… I refuse to show it though, having schooled my features into a mask of disdain.

My chin tucks toward my chest, jaw tense as I glare daggers into the woman blinking at me. “I believe you have something of mine. I want it back. And gods have mercy on your souls, if a single hair on the duke’s head is so much as mussed. He is a member of the court of lords, and therefore, is under the crown’s protection.” Clearing my throat, I stand straighter, mental claws feeling in the depths of my awareness for the threads of magic piecing together the wards of the house. “More specifically, he’s under *my* protection.”

The woman flinches as if my words have physically struck her but doesn’t relent or open the door. “The person you seek is not here.” Her colorless eyes drop from mine and she creaks the door closed, ready to shut me out.

Without hesitation, I grip the edge of the door, talons bursting through my fingertips to embed themselves in the wood, stopping it from closing without a second to spare. “Lie to me again and it will be the last thing you do.”

I push the door wider, revealing more of the woman hiding behind it. Her dress is torn, the opened fabric revealing the places where blood magic took its price from her living flesh instead of that of a sacrifice. Lesions ooze black goo, and I have to fight down the bile burning my throat.

The woman’s lips part as she staggers back, then chairs are scraping wooden floors. Voices carry through the halls of the mansion, echoing off the drab walls. I barely hear the shouts as I shift, letting my demon form take hold. My obsidian eyes stare back at me in the reflection of her’s.

One foot straddling the threshold, I search that hidden dimension of our world where magic wriggles and weaves, looking for the thread that will send the wards toppling. The woman's backing away, spinning on her heels as she sprints deeper into the house, knowing exactly what I'm looking for.

Golden translucent strands span in every which way, woven and knotted and tangled. They're a mess, a conglomeration of layers upon layers of wards placed over lifetimes. Then one string catches my eye, glowing brighter than the rest.

"Found you," I whisper to myself. My eyes honed in on the origin strand gleaming at me.

I push through the threshold, expecting my magic to fizzle out, for my demon form to retreat, but the wards don't phase me. Furrowing my brow, I look around the space one more time, finding most of it dust-covered and empty. Only this time, chanting swims in my ears. The wards weren't to keep others out; they were to trap creatures in.

10

Asmodeus

The woman who met me at the door smirks, arms crossed at the end of a long hall leading off the foyer. A dark-haired man is beside her, sweat beading on his brow as his voice carries, chanting in a melody that would sound like music to the unknowing ear.

"What do you think? Will the Lord of Solaria agree to a meeting now? Not only do we have his son, but the king's traitor brother, too." Her grin pulls wider when I step toward the hall, only to find an invisible wall rippling there, keeping me from coming any closer. Trapping me.

"Please." I scoff. "No one is going to listen to a blood witch, high on their thirst for power. My brother would sooner chop off your head and the queen? She'd level this mansion to ash with all of you in it. I wouldn't try her. She tends to see flames when her family is messed with."

The glamour making the woman appear mostly human vanishes in a flash, becoming rotting skin and brittle bones. Black ooze drips from every orifice of her face as she steps closer, the patchy bits of hair on her head flowing in the breeze she creates. Though, the moment she's before me, not even the barrier between us can hinder the stench that has my stomach roiling violently.

"Hold your tongue, or I'll remove it for you," she seethes through toothless gums.

"I'd like to see you try, *witch.*"

She leans back, her narrowed eyes widening just a tad. "Strong words for a caged creature."

"Caged?" I say, my lips twisting into a toothy grin. "Who said anything about being caged?" My power answers me in eager anticipation, and that dark part of me… It's been twisted to crave the bloodshed, the screams, the *vengeance*. It's almost therapeutic to me now.

I crook a claw around that tangled mess of an origin strand, slicing it in two and the wards trapping me within this room come crashing down. The witch inhales sharply, staggering back, but she's not fast enough.

Within a blink of an eye, my poisoned dagger is embedded in her friend's eye and my taloned hand is around her throat. Claws break the gray, lifeless skin there, and I anchor her wretched body to mine.

"Do you feel that?" I whisper, taunting the witch in my arms. "That's your pulse against my fingers. One noise, one glimmer of magic, you bleed out on the floor, got it?"

Her form flutters between the old haggish creature I grabbed and that of the cherry-haired young woman I met at the door. Throat bobbing, she gives a slight nod, hands curled around my forearm as if she could hold me there.

"Good, now where the fuck is my nephew." She doesn't answer right away, and my hold tightens just a tad.

She raises a gnarled finger that looks as if it's been broken and healed wrong too many times. "Through there," she whispers, and my eyes linger on the door near the end of the hall that she suggests.

The scent of decay grows stronger the farther we move down the hall, the woman's body stiff in my arms. She takes tentative steps as we pass the mage lights flickering on the walls, repeatedly dimming only to blaze a second later, as if someone has channeled the flames themselves. When we reach the designated door, the witch opens it, and no sooner do I hear it click free from the jam, my boot collides with the wooden slab, throwing it open.

Five witches, as close to death's doorstep as the woman in my arms, jump up all at once. They whirl to face me, eyes widening at the sight. The woman's warm blood slips between my fingers, running down my arms and dripping onto the dusty floor. Though, where it used to hold a crimson hue, it's onyx now, polluted by blood magic—by death itself.

"What is the meaning of this?" One of the witches has yet to stand. Instead, she's seated on what looks like a throne made of dark twigs and bones. Unlike the others, her skin is flawless, her blonde hair rolling over her shoulder in smooth waves. Icy cerulean eyes narrow into slits as she regards me, not bothering to lift a polished fingernail from the arms of her makeshift throne. "First, you strip my house of its wards, and then you think it wise to sink your talons into one of my mages? That's quite the entrance. Even for you, Asmodeus."

"You didn't exactly welcome me inside, and at this point in my life, I've grown tired of pleasantries." A quick glance around the room has my heart sinking into my stomach. "You lied," I whisper into the witch's ear, trying not to breathe in the pungent odor rippling off her.

Her spine goes rigid, her breath quickening. "If I'm to die, I'll do it with dignity. Not by giving the Harbinger of Death what he wants."

"My name is Asmodeus, and you lost your dignity the moment you touched one of those blood grimoires and chose to serve her." I lock eyes with the woman on the throne. Calliope. She used to be one of the mad king's favorite mages and somehow it doesn't surprise me that she's developed a love for the darker forms of magic. She was always a bitch.

"Where is he?" I demand, earning a look of triumph, like she knows something I don't.

"Oh Griffin, darling," she calls, twisting her wrist in the air.

The wall behind the throne ripples and waves until the magic falls away to reveal a large cage made from iron bars that meet the ceiling in the otherwise decrepit space. Within, Griffin is clad in nothing but a skin-tight strip of fabric that only covers the bare essentials. Long, thin straps loop over his broad shoulders and he leans nonchalantly against the barred door, arms crossed.

"Has the mistress returned for round—" He cuts off, meeting my gaze. "Asmodeus!"

A thick black collar is snug around his neck, a leather leash dangling freely from the clasp, swishing at his hips as he pushes off the cage wall. His stark white hair and bright blue eyes stand out against the dimly lit room, and the druidic tattoos trailing down the centerline of his body seem to pulse with a life of their own.

"Am I glad to see you," he breathes, dragging a hand through his shoulder-length hair. "You're going to love it here. They've been so nice, and don't even get me started on the orgies—"

"Glad to know you've been enjoying yourself," I say, cutting him off. Retracting my claws, I release the woman I've been holding hostage.

Her dark blood spills from the wounds on her neck as she staggers away from me, applying pressure as if she'll heal. She's far beyond that. At this point, the only thing keeping her soul tethered to her practically undead body is magic.

My eyes lock on Calliope's. "Release him. *Immediately.*"

"Or what? He deserves to be in a cage and even if I was to let him out, you'd be *delighted* to find he won't want to go with you." Her voice drops like she's cooing a pet cat as she reaches between the bars to stroke Griffin's sharp cheekbone. "Isn't that right?"

"I will serve on my knees, Milady. Cross my heart."

Gods spare me. "What did you do to him?"

"It's just a little spell. So long as I live, he'll love me," she says, scratching under his chin like he's a dog.

"Very well, then." My mind was already made up before I came into this room. Before I even crossed the foyer, really. Everyone here shows signs of blood magic use, except Calliope. Though, I'm sure she's having the others do her dirty work for her.

The witches in this room should be killed as an example for daring to hold Griffin against his will alone… even if he's saying otherwise now. The spell has him talking nonsense, but there's a glint in his eyes that tells me he's still in there, fighting to get out. That, and the fact he hasn't insulted someone or made some snide remark in the last five minutes is proof enough that he's not in his right mind.

Inhaling deeply, I feel the magic build between my fingers. I hear it sing in my veins, vibrate in my bones. Smoke coils around my hands in an instant, heeding the call. Curling my clawed fingertips toward my palm, the blood witches glaring at me from the shadowed corners of the room evaporate into ash. All but Calliope.

Granted, she likely should've seen that coming. She knows about my magic, that I command death itself. If she hadn't sucked her minions dry, like the leach she is, maybe they wouldn't have been on the brink of death.

"Oops," I muse, enjoying the way her eyes burn.

Even the mad king took issue with the morality of blood magic, and the man tortured his children and countless others. There wasn't a need for a trial. Nor was there a need to involve my brother or Alice. The evidence of blood magic condemned these creatures. It convicted them for taking innocent lives for the sake of magic.

"I suggest you run," I say, picking the witch's blood out from beneath my nails.

"Run?" She snorts, but I catch her eyes scouring the room for exits. Calliope might be bitter and cold and inhumane, but she's not an imbecile. She knows better than to try to face me on her own.

The queen might've wanted me to refrain from making an enemy of this clan, but can they be an enemy if they're all dead?

Besides, not punishing them would only send the wrong message to the other ruthless creatures in this realm. Some might believe the crown is weak and incapable of controlling its people. It would open up the door for others to dare worse acts and push the laws that keep this land peaceful… *mostly*.

"Have it your way," I say, rolling my eyes. A flick of my wrist has her clawing at her throat and her feet inching toward me step by step. I match her pace, meeting in the middle, avoiding Griffin's wide-eyed stare. Though, I hear him snarl deep enough to rattle my bones. "Down boy." I lace the command with power and force Griffin to sit cross-legged in place, my attention never leaving the cold, menacing blue eyes of the witch before me. "Now, what were you hoping to negotiate with the Lord of Solaria? You know I'm a man of my word when it suits me. Play nice, and I'll make it quick."

She swallows thickly, her shoulders squaring as if my magic isn't coiled around her body like a snake. Griffin thrashes against my thrall, the snarls and snaps growing louder as he transforms partially into his beast. Though, his claws shred the vacant air as I pin him in place.

"We wanted…" She starts, sending a worried glance toward Griffin.

"Don't look at Griffin." I pinch her chin, forcing her stare back to mine. "Keep going, or I'll feed you to him."

"The elves wanted us to secure the ports around Solaria. Promised us control over the outer realm if we did." I let her face go, holding her still with my magic as I mull over what she's admitted.

The elves? Alice had mentioned stirrings, that some of the lords were worried they might be planning something. If they wanted the blood witches to secure shipping ports, then it's proof of treason.

I don't bother asking another question, I simply twist my wrist and Calliope's head whirls in a sharp jerk, until it's facing the wrong way. Her body goes limp and falls to the ground the moment I release my hold on her.

Griffin roars, then stills. His beast alter ego retreats until the man regains control, blinking rapidly and squinting as if the light is too bright in the dim room. It's like he's been held in a dark dungeon for days and is just seeing the hell flame for the first time. Slowly, his gaze travels down his body, taking in the outfit that leaves little to the imagination. "What the fuck am I wearing?" His head lifts, his eyes veering from me to the body at my feet and the ash piles scattered about the room. "Oh gods," he whines, buckles and heaves the contents of his stomach onto the floor.

With a snap of my fingers, Calliope's body is gone. She should be landing in the dungeon below Hell Hold any second now, but at least he won't have to look at her any more. Stepping forward, I rest a hand on his shoulder, but he bats it away. "What took you so long?"

"That's an odd way to say thank you." I arch a brow as he glares up at me from the floor.

"I might've said thank you three days ago. Do you have any idea how many witch toes I've had to suckle since then? We're long past thank yous." He grimaces as if he's given himself a mental image.

"Well, maybe next time you'll choose your *lovers* more carefully." I pull him to his feet. "Let's get out of here."

Griffin jerks his limbs away from me. "Oh no. I'll walk."

My face falls. He hates teleporting, but I command him with my power anyway, dragging him closer, and threads of shadows and light spin around our joined bodies, whisking us through the folds between worlds. Then as the magic fades, we find ourselves in front of Grim's Keep. "Welcome home."

"Home? You're kidding me, right?" Griffin stalks after me as I start toward the front door, wondering if Valeria has risen yet. Not that I expect her to. She needs the rest.

"Alice's words, not mine. Trust me, I'd love nothing more than to send you back to your father's castle."

He's nipping at my heels now. "What does my mother have to say about this? Did Alice even ask her?"

"I don't know. What I *do know* is, whatever spell Calliope used on you will take time to fully work out of your system. She knows more about what the elves are planning and my brother can pluck those details out of her mind. She's not a blood witch *yet*. Her soul is still intact and as a mage, she has spare lives. She'll come to within a prison cell, but when she does, the spell on you will take hold again."

Griffin snorts, stopping in the foyer with his hands on his hips. "Then what was the point of saving me?"

"The keep is warded. As long as you stay within the stone walls in the forest, she can't control you. Step outside, you might as well get the collar on your neck bedazzled. Understand?"

Pursing his lips, he nods, but the muscle in his jaw ticks, giving away his disdain for the situation.

"Good. Now, for the love of all that is sacred, put some clothes on." I spin on my heels, but stop short of taking a step. "And the top floor is off limits to you."

"Why?" It's not the question he asks that bothers me, so much as the intrigued tone of his voice.

"Would you like me to toss you over the wall?" I arch a brow at him, glancing over my shoulder. He tilts his head as if weighing his options, a curiosity burning in his otherworldly blue eyes. Then he shakes his head no. "Then don't ask stupid questions."

11

Asmodeus

The fresh air hits me the moment I step out the back door of the keep and I don't wait around for Griffin to clean up. After being in that mansion, that grove, breathing in the sour decay of that witch, I need this. I need space.

My muscles are tense, the adrenaline still pumping through my veins as I ease onto the bench that overlooks the garden. It's beneath one of the twisted trees near the base of the gigantic stone walls, blooming with vibrant purple flowers.

It's hard to believe I planted them here long ago. They all but tower over three stories high. My mother's favorite... When I was young, I wanted something to remind me of her, even if she was the reason I grew up in this place instead of the castle in Hell Hold. The reason Grim was more of a father to me than my own flesh and blood.

It seems dumb now.

Picking up the flower that has fallen from the branches above, I circle my thumb over the soft petals. I breathe deeply, the scent of pine and wet earth grounding me, reminding me of a world that thrives on simple, uncomplicated beauty.

Then there's a thunk followed by a string of curses behind me.

Griffin.

"That was fast." I drop the flower onto the ground.

"Yeah, well, excuse me for being eager. I'd like to forget about the last three days as quickly as possible." Griffin plops down into the seat beside me, wearing his own clothes.

"I see you managed to summon your things." Sometimes it's easy for me to forget that he's not just fae but half druid. He lets his beast side show often, but I've hardly ever seen him use his magic.

"It only took five tries, but yes." Legs wide, he leans back into the stone seat. "Thank you."

"For?" I tease, my lips pulling up at the corners ever so slightly.

"You know what for," he scalds under his breath.

Before I can taunt him further, he stiffens, and those cerulean eyes of his flare bright, his beast skimming just beneath the surface.

"What is it?" I follow his gaze, drifting from the meticulously kept gardens to the wild, untamed forest that skirts the keep's boundaries.

"Something is out there."

I squint harder, standing from the bench and venturing a couple steps forward, deeper into the garden in an attempt to see or feel what he has. Reaching out with my magic, I search the courtyard, then push my awareness deep into the forest that surrounds us. My magic creeps over the ground, pulsing into my fingertips and down through the earth beneath my feet, scouring for movement, but coming up empty-handed.

Checking my palm, I stare at the dark circle tattooed there. No lights gleam around its inked edge, and the enchantment is strong. I'd cleared the woods here mere hours ago. If something crossed that wall since, I'd know.

"Are you sure?" I ask, turning in place until Griffin's far too pale face comes into view. He nods silently. I huff out a breath, shrugging out of my tunic. I already need to wash witch blood from the cuffs. Might as well not add more. I toss it next to him on the bench and he gives a startled jump, ripping his eyes from the forest for the first time. "Stay here." It's not a question, but a command. And whatever is lurking in those woods… It scares him enough that he doesn't argue.

Wandering out of the iron gate of the courtyard, I venture toward the forest. The heat of the hell flame radiates down upon my bare torso, warming my blood. Something shifts in the shadows of the trees, catching my eye. It's fleeting, a mere shimmer that could easily be dismissed as a trick of the light. But there's a tug in my gut, an inexplicable pull toward that glimmer. It's as if the darkness that lives within me recognizes it somehow or can see what my eyes can't.

Without a word, my strides lengthen, eating up the space between me and the forest. I tread softly, my boots barely making a sound against the grass, the world around me holding its breath. There's something there… Something bright—*glowing* even.

How did I not feel it?

My heavy exhale mists into a white cloud as I near it, the drop in temperature making my skin pebble.

Odd… A second ago, I was on the verge of sweating and with the hell flame high in the sky, the air shouldn't hold the icy chill it does now. It's not until I'm feet away that I experience what Griffin did, a whisper of magic that curls around my senses like smoke, filled with *emotion.* So strong, it nearly takes my breath away. It's raw menacing pain, followed by the urgent need to laugh and cry and *flee* as if I'm being hunted by a creature that could devore me.

I peer down into the brush, nestled around the base of a large tree. There, the mesmerizing glow shines bright. So bright, I can't make out what is creating that light. Gently, I reach for it, but it lurches before I can make contact, shooting deeper into the dark woods.

I straighten, blinking in the direction it took off. The sound of a child's laughter clinging to the breeze rustling the treetops, the pitch of it sends a chill down my spine.

It's a spirit… a soul, lost in the forest.

The branches above creak and groan against the wind whipping through the valley, and as intrigued as I am, I'm not sure I have the heart to go after it. I should… It's lost. This forest is known for trapping souls within it. When living things die, they must find their peace, accept their death. Then, a pull guides them to the River Styx so they can flow into the Soul Well to be reborn. However, the magic that comes from these trees interferes with that *pull* and causes souls to wander in circles for all eternity.

Some go mad, become poltergeists, and shred their souls apart, piece by piece. Others, slowly forget themselves, and simply wither away into pure energy. Which seems to be what's happening to this one.

It no longer has a shape, a body, or a face.

If I could catch it, I might be able to guide it out of the forest, but the closer I get, the more it seems to elude me. The glimmering ball of bright blue and silver darts away before my fingers graze its ethereal light. I push through the thick undergrowth; the branches scratching at my bare skin. It leads me deeper into the heart of the forest, where the hell flame struggles to pierce the dense canopy above.

Then the humming hits my ears… The same child's voice as before, but this time, I recognize it. It's a song I've heard countless times. I've listened to that same tone-deaf voice humming in the kitchens of the keep for years, prior to being banished to the Realm of Monsters—before someone destroyed the place I called home.

It can't be… A wave of catastrophic horror strangles my voice, clutching me so fiercely, I'm rendered speechless. My blood becomes ice, crystallizing my veins, and the word fades away. I can still see the forest before me, but not really.

The day I was freed from that wretched prison world, I'd tried to see Grim. Except, he never came. I thought he was angry at me for leaving this place unprotected, abandoning it without warning, even if it wasn't my fault.

I have seen none of those I grew up with since being freed. Not the servants, not Grim's second, none of them. But that was hundreds of years ago… I'd just assumed their mortal lives had ended naturally. But hearing that voice, *that song…* I don't know when I started to pace, just that I'm doing it now. Spiraling, I bury my fingers into my dark hair, pulling at the root as I close my eyes.

No… No, no, no, no… they couldn't have. I wasn't even there. Why would someone hurt them when my mother had already locked me in the Realm of Monsters?

There were no bodies in the keep when I arrived. Though, Valeria might've buried them somewhere when she made the ruins her home. Still, despite the place being destroyed, there was no evidence that the people—that my friends and those I'd once called family—were killed in the keep.

My heart pounds, my breaths so shallow the world spins. The emotions… The magic derived from them builds beneath my skin, burning through vein after vein. In seconds, I feel as though my blood has become liquid fire. My eyes belong to my demon half, the threads of life—of existence—stringing through the air, connecting every tree within this forest together, like one entity.

Minutes pass before I can snuff the demonic side of me out. My claws disappear from my fingertips and finally, I can take a simple breath.

I have to know. There's no way around that. The possibilities will eat me alive if I don't get the answers to all the questions raging through my mind. As much as the truth might hurt, *I need this.*

Collecting myself and steeling my gaze, I turn in place, searching for that light. It's nowhere to be found. Deep within the woods, the only glowing colors come from the mushrooms and bioluminescent foliage that carpets the forest floor. But if I'm right, I know where the spirit darted off to.

I make way for the cavern just inside the wall that circles Grim's Keep. It was his favorite place. The forest seems to disappear around me as my mind swirls with memories. I'd just been given lordship over Grim's Keep, barely twenty-five years old and green and magicless still. It was before the spellbinding my mother placed on me broke, before I'd taken dozens of innocent lives. Before I became a monster.

The chef's son used to poke at the piano keys on the second floor, and thanks to the open spiral staircase, his unseasoned songs would float right up to the third story and into my room. It was always the same song, the same tune he tried and failed to play. It's the same one being hummed within this forest now.

Reaching the cave, I bend to peer inside. It's barely tall enough for me to crawl into on my hands and knees if I wished. However, for a little boy, this place was a hidden fort—a hide out to escape shoes that seemed too big and heavy to fill. At least, it was to me. It was my sanctuary and as I got older, I passed it down to him.

Inside, that glowing light shines, painting the rough stone in shades of blue and silver. Tears sting my eyes at the confirmation of my greatest fear… That more innocent blood is on my hands. I haven't worked through the guilt from the stains I already knew were there.

"Hello." It's the only greeting I can think of, let alone force out over the swelling lump in my throat. All I can hope is it won't scare him away. "You might not remember me, my face has changed a lot since I knew you, but I remember your song."

The floating orb doesn't flee and I take that as an invitation to continue, plopping down onto the mossy ground, crossing my legs. For a moment, I simply hum the verses, proving that I know the rest of it and not just the chorus the boy was humming. As if approving of my song, the orb grows into a silhouette of a child and sits at the mouth of the cavern in front of me, mirroring my position.

"I heard you poke the tune of that song on the piano for months, every day before your father served dinner. You were just a boy and I remember thinking that I couldn't listen to those choppy notes any longer. My mate, Jade, convinced me to teach you to play piano and night after night, just before dinner, you'd sit on my lap. Your little hands would sit on top of mine, and I'd play it for you until you picked up on the chords and learned to play it yourself."

Locking my jaw, I quickly wipe at my eyes, brushing away the tears, threatening to roll down my cheeks. The boy hums that melody, but this time, his rounded arms morph until little hands shape the ends of them and his fingers move as if he's pretending to play the chords, an invisible piano between us.

"It was almost a year of playing with you every night that I finally learned why you loved that song so much." I mirror him, breaking to hum the tune as our fingers dance in the air. "You'd lost your mom before your father became the keep's chef. You never told me, but I figured you enjoyed this song for the same reason I planted those trees in the courtyard, because you wanted to be closer to someone you loved and lost."

I don't stop the tears as they slide down my cheeks, dripping off my chin and jaw.

I did this.

I'm the reason this little boy is dead.

My existence has cost the lives of so many, but this one might hurt the worst. I took this boy's life away. He never got to know love, never got to become himself or go after his dreams. He died here before he ever truly started living.

When I look at him again, that silhouette has become a glowing translucent boy. His bright blonde hair is shaggy, his dark eyes full of hope and love and innocence. That same crooked, mischievous smile paints his lips, nearly bringing a grin to my own.

"Do you know who you are?" I ask, thankful that those memories still exist in my mind, that they could make him remember.

The boy shakes his head no before tilting it, his eyes alive and curious.

"You are Chester."

"Ches… ter." His voice is rough and graveled as if his vocal chords have been dormant for far too long, shedding the mummified stone encasing them.

His soul, his ghost, becomes brighter as if saying his name has made him whole again. "Chester Wesbroke."

I huff a short laugh, wiping at my cheeks. "Yes. Yes, you are."

"And you're Lord Asmo."

"Just Asmo." I give him my best smile, reaching out to grip his hand, even though I can't touch him physically. Still, I hope the gesture is as comforting as if I could.

Suddenly, his gaze becomes grave as he stiffens. Those dark eyes meet mine. "I was supposed to find you."

"Find me?" I shake my head, not understanding.

"I'm supposed to tell you what happened."

My heart plummets into my stomach. "And?"

"The rest of them roam the woods. A few have moved on. The day you left, Lord Elcrys came with his men under the king's orders to seize you. None of us knew where you were, but they didn't believe us. They slaughtered us one by one if we refused to talk. It wasn't until half of us were gone that a messenger came and told Lord Elcrys you'd been imprisoned. He destroyed the keep and killed the rest of us, anyway." The boy lifts his head, tilting it back to reveal the jagged line across his throat where someone had drawn the edge of a blade.

Fury sears through me, my eyes flickering between man and demon. Lord Elcrys still serves on my brother's court. He didn't need to kill these people, but he'll die for his crimes. His blood will be spilt on the very grounds of my keep. He'll plead on his knees and my face will be the last thing he sees before I'll end him, the same way he did Chester. By the gods, I fucking swear it.

A hand settles on my shoulder, ripping me back to reality and I twist to peer up at Griffin. "I'd told you to stay put."

"And you took too long to come back." His eyes flick from me to the boy. "I'd thought you were dead, that something had finally got the upper hand on you. Turns out, you're just wiggling your fingers at a five-year-old."

"Six," Chester corrects.

"Same thing." Griffin's eyes roll in their sockets as he crosses his arms.

"It's good you're here. I'm going to need your help." Twisting, I purse my lips. My eyes lock onto a pebble on the ground and I pinch its rough surface between my fingers. "I have an idea."

"Oh… Great. Because your ideas always end so well."

I glare up at him. "What does that mean?"

"The last idea you had killed someone."

Pausing to double-check my memory, I shake my head. "No. That man died of natural causes. I didn't lay a hand on him."

"Oh, okay, so what about the criminal who tried to poison Alice? Hmm?" Griffin crosses his arms, arching a white brow at me. "He just jumped from that tower window all on his own, did he?"

"Last I checked gravity was a force of nature." Weighing my head from side to side, I frown. "He might've thought he could fly. It's not my fault he believed something so absurd."

"It is when the thought you pushed into his head was accompanied by magic. You *made* him believe that."

I shrug. "Good riddance. He tried to hurt Alice."

"And was being tried for it. Hell, he was already set for execution. Why not let him die on the block?"

Because I wanted to be the one to kill him. Because he tried to hurt someone I love and deserved it.

When I don't answer aloud, Griffin sighs. "Tell me what you need. But just so you know, we're even after this."

"Fine. I need the blood grimoires Calliope used."

Griffin's face falls as he takes a step back, the blood draining from his face. "I'm not going back there."

"You don't need to. Just tell me where to find them."

12

Valeria

Oh gods . . . I need a priest.

There's something wrong with me. Dangerously so if I'm dreaming about demons. Well, one demon in particular.

The hours have blended together and I'm not sure how long I've sequestered myself within these strange walls. Those odd floating symbols languidly spin around where I lay on the bed, anchored in place by my own mind.

I haven't dared to leave the room. Not even when I heard the sharp click of Asmo's door, or when I heard the sound of his boots gliding down the stairs, both of which made my heart beat as fast as it had in my dream. A dream where he had a starring role.

I barely know the man, yet I've already dreamt of the ways he could defile me.

Voices carry through the ancient stone walls and my stomach grumbles, rattling my ribs as I stare at that glass dome above my bed. If not for the berries I had stashed in my cloak, I might've starved in here, thanks to my self-imposed exile.

Sure, I know where the kitchen is. Having lived here for weeks, I know every inch of this place, at least what it used to be. And even though the walls are prettier, the layout is still the same. It wouldn't have been difficult for me to scavenge what I'm sure are plentiful cupboards for something to eat, but that would've meant leaving this room. It would've meant the possibility of coming face to face with Asmo and I'm not ready for that. Not after the dream I had.

There are pretty men in Vanderlyth. Elven men, with their ethereal grace and sharp, arresting features, have always embodied a beauty that seemed unmatched by any other creature I've laid eyes on. The only demons I know of are lords on the king's court, but even then, I've never truly met them. I've seen them from a distance, dressed in the finest linens, but they pale in comparison to the elves.

At least they had…

The sight of Asmo covered in blood splatter, sword in hand, redefined my elvish definition of beauty entirely. It was savage and wild and something I never thought I'd witness. It's something I should not want to witness again, yet that's exactly how he appeared in my dream. He'd knocked on my bedroom door and smirked roguishly when I'd answered.

He houses enough power to snap me to pieces should he want to, and that should terrify me. All he'd have to do is mumble a word, and I'd be nothing more than a riddled pile of discarded bones, and what could I do to stop it? Become invisible? Because that worked so well last time.

But I wasn't scared. I was *fascinated.* Still am, in a way I've never been before.

He moves with graceful fluidity, commanding the very air around him. It's almost a divine experience to be in the near vicinity of him and it makes me feel like I've completely lost my mind.

Now, every time I close my eyes, it's not my dream of drowning I see, but one of him that resurfaces. My consciousness is consumed by that sight of him in the woods. It's blissful torture and all too vivid, like I could reach out and touch his scar-ridden chest, feel the pulse of his heart beating against my fingertips.

I'm not sure I can face him in reality. Not after imagining those dark amber eyes staring up at me from between my legs. My body hums at the idea of those rough, ringed fingers sliding over my skin, of hearing my name rolling off his tongue… Clearly, I've been alone too long, or maybe there's something about his magic that completely garbled all sense of my sanity, or perhaps I was just sleep deprived. No matter the reason, leaving this bedroom, seeing him after the things he did to me in my mind, sounds like damnation.

But I can't stay hidden away up here forever. Asmo said we'd have company at dinner and judging by the noises circulating outside my door, that time is coming sooner rather than later.

The morning light filters through the gossamer curtains draping around the terrace doors and through the glass dome in the ceiling, casting a warm glow over the room as I reluctantly rise from the bed. Giving my enchanted closet a go, I start with the basics, summoning a tunic that clings softly to my form, woven from the finest threads of silver and moonlight.

The neckline is open, revealing a bit more than I'm used to. The glossy fabric is intricately embroidered with patterns that speak of ancient magic, common symbols in the Elven Islands, specific to the original families and the blessings the furies and old gods gave us. It's as if the closet knew of my heritage or sensed my tastes somehow.

Slipping on a pair of skin-tight pants, I tuck the dark fabric neatly beneath the knee-high boots I lace up my calves. It's an elegant look, but not as formal as wearing a dress would be. And seeing as I've yet to see Asmo wear a proper shirt without blood on it, I doubt anything more than this is necessary.

After a quick look in the mirror and a moment to comb my hair, I quietly leave the room. Overhead, the blues, silvers, and whites swirl over the map of the Seven Realms, casting everything in a gentle azure glow. No one is up on this floor from what I can see, but a quick glance down the open center of the stairwell reveals a man with striking, white hair that swishes gently over his shoulders with every jerk of his head. He wears a dark tunic, leather pants with half of his hair tied up into a knot on top of his head. As if sensing me, the knot moves and his chin tilts up toward where I'm gawking over the banister.

The man double takes, catching me spying and his lips stretch into a toothy, up to no good grin. Crystal blue eyes, so vivid I can see the turquoise hue of them from two stories up, stare into mine and I jolt away from the rail.

"Awe, come back. I don't bite," he says, a humorous ring to his otherwise tenor voice. He sounds young. Looks it, too. I'd be surprised if he's older than me, maybe early twenties. But that hair...

It's not common for creatures within the Seven Realms to have pure white hair like his. Not even our most pure bloodlines do. Our original families have silver.

The color of his hair alone names his heritage without me needing to put much thought into it. He's of the Midicious bloodline, descending from the gods and druids of old. A line which descends from the mad king who once reigned over the Realm of Monsters, otherwise known as the prison realm that collapsed and released the wicked beasts on our world.

Though the mad king is long dead, a handful of his children have carried down their vivid white hair, and only one male has been born to that line. The Duke of Solaria.

"Oh, Asmo," the man sings as I descend the steps. "It would appear your lady friend has risen. I don't think she likes me much." There's something knowing in his voice, like some secret meaning hides in those words.

"Her name is Valeria." I'd recognize that voice anywhere, especially the snarl in it. "And *friend* is a stretch."

Reaching the first floor, I find the white-haired man grinning wildly, arms crossed as if awaiting my arrival. His dimples flash as he turns his attention from me, down the hall, where I find Asmo *shirtless*, and standing over a table he's pulled out of the apothecary. The dark wooden surface is covered in a thin layer of old, leather-bound books.

I've got this.

Asmo rakes a hand through his dark hair, pushing it out of his face before flipping the time-withered pages of the book open in front of him. I take a solitary step before he leans over, brings his lips close to the crease in the binding and blows a stream of air through that crevasse. A plume of dust spills around him and I swallow hard.

The act shouldn't be arousing, but it has a memory storming my senses no less. The image of him in my dream, after he dragged the tip of his hot, wet, tongue down my body, from my collarbones to the juncture between my thighs. He followed that trail with the warm air of his breath, and as if he's done it just now, the centerline of my body turns both hot and cold.

A shiver rolls through every limb of my being and I shift my weight to my other foot, clearing my throat as if it will shake me from the trance I've fallen under.

I don't got this.

For a moment, I forget to breathe. It's not until amber eyes pool into mine that I jerk my gaze away. My spine rigid, I shift my weight from foot to foot, crossing my arms to pretend like I wasn't gawking at Asmo. Willing my face into a mask of emotionless stone, I clutch my crystal pendant, letting the hum of magic there soothe my far-too -maginative mind.

"What's with all the books?" I ask, clearing my throat.

"They're grimoires and I'm looking for something."

That's a vague answer if I've ever heard one, but it's clear by the tone, he has no desire to elaborate on the matter.

Here I thought we'd moved past the power play, that we made a truce, signed and sealed with our blood. For a moment, I saw a possibility of us becoming, dare I say, *friends* when he showed me around my new home, and it seemed like he wanted to. Why else would he invite a woman who stabbed him to live in his home? Perhaps, the peace I sensed was merely a dream. It was likely me just scrounging for a place in this world that I belong, where I'm needed or wanted, rather than being a nuisance for existing.

Trapping my lower lip between my teeth, I breathe in deep, letting the fresh air push away the thoughts swirling my mind. It's far too imaginative indeed.

Asmo closes the grimoire and the slap of the book coming together, sends a jolt through me. With a sharp pivot he faces me, arching a dark brow and crossing his arms over his bare chest. It's like he's waiting for me to apologize. For what? Interrupting him?

"My nephew will live here for the foreseeable future. However, you have my formal permission to ignore the bastard as you see fit. The gods know I find it hard to entertain the likes of him. If he annoys you, you can lock him outside. Perhaps we'll make him a doghouse."

My gaze shifts uneasily from Asmo to the duke, and the scowl on his ethereal face. There aren't many fae in the Seven Realms, and though I've never seen one in person, I've heard stories. They're supposed to be beautiful creatures, far too beautiful to be mortal. And looking at him now, the stories are true.

Asmo flicks his wrist in Griffin's direction. "This is Griffin, the son of Lady Eva and Lord Finn—"

"I've gleaned as much," I say, cutting him off dryly. Doing my best to paste on a smile, I bow my head respectfully to the duke, as if he's a lord himself, deserving of such an honor.

"It's the hair, isn't it?" Griffin grins a bit too widely in my direction as I right myself, his blue eyes dragging down my frame at a snail's speed, as if I'm something he could swallow whole.

I take a hesitant step forward, glancing between the two men. I'm not sure who in this room is less of a threat, the fae with hungry eyes or the grumpy demon who's scrutinizing every move I make.

"Well, it is rare," I say, politely. "There's only one family line with hair like yours and only one male born to it. It was an easy guess." Griffin all but beams, like he's reveling in the fact I've heard of him. "So, why exactly are you living here? Shouldn't the duke live in the lands of which he is the duke of?"

"Unfortunately, it wasn't his choice." Asmo pushes off the table. "Seeing as he allowed a witch to put him under a love spell, and the keep is warded against such magic, he'll remain here until it..." Asmo trails off, clearing his throat. "He'll stay until it wears off."

"What he means to say, is I'll be pussy-whipped until the bitch is dead," Griffin says in a melodic voice that makes my insides explode with butterflies. I was taught that his familial line descends from Aphrodite and I can see why. Not only is he beautiful, being in his very presence is like chugging faerie wine. "More importantly, I'd love to know why you're here." Griffin is closer now, so close, that he glides the tip of his index finger along the shell of my pointed ear. "And my… What sharp ears you have."

"Don't act like you've never seen an elf before." The snarl in Asmo's voice has me sucking in a sharp breath. "As for why she's here, well, she is the Lady of Grim's Keep and you'll treat her with some respect, not like one of your many conquests."

Griffin whirls, the motion so fast and fluid that it sends wild tendrils of my dark hair flying into my face. "The *lady?* Since when are you involved with someone?" His white eyebrows practically disappear into his hairline.

"Involved? No. Suffering the presence of? Yes. It'll be your job to protect her. Whatever she needs, you do. Her life has been tethered to mine, so you'll ensure she doesn't kill us while I'm away." Asmo pauses, his eyes rolling up at the ceiling for a moment before he taps a finger in the air. "Climbing trees in particular will be off limits."

"Tethered?" It takes me a moment to realize that I didn't just think the question but snapped it out loud.

"How else did you think our deal would work? You die, I die, and vice versa." Asmo closes the distance between us in leisure, hands in his pockets like he owns the very ground he walks on, though I suppose he does. My ears twitch as I glare daggers into him, my frown deepening when his sensual lips curve into a wicked smile.

"Now, now…" he coos, tipping his head to the side. "Don't be angry, Starlight. It was the insurance policy we both needed, yes? The moment we can trust each other, we'll break our deal. And considering who's more likely to die in this scenario, I'd say you got the better end of it."

Heat floods through me, burning my face, making my ears feel like they're on fire, and I storm across the hall, eating up the ground in seconds until I can poke a finger at his chest. "You tricked me."

"I did no such thing. If I had, I'd admit and gloat about it with pride. You would've known the moment you agreed to what I had asked of you."

I don't waste a moment to think about what I'm doing. I simply plant my hands against his solid chest and push with every ounce of strength my body possesses. However, he doesn't move an inch. The sheer force sends me falling backward, and before I can hit the ground, he's yanked me toward him by my wrists.

"Careful. You don't heal like I do. Your head smacks that marble and we're both done for." His eyes are dark, the amber rings almost nonexistent as he glares down at me. "I'm beginning to regret this."

"You're despicable. Am I to be trapped in this fucking house, too?"

"You're free to come and go as you please, though I wouldn't. At least not until you learn how to properly defend yourself first. And until our deal is broken, you'll need to take someone with you if you intend to cross the wall. Griffin won't be able to, so unfortunately, you'll be stuck with me if you want to adventure." He rights me, and though he lets my wrists go, he makes no effort to move away. I've never seen someone look so menacing, yet touch so gentle as he swoops a chunk of my hair behind my ear. The timbre of his voice drops an octave as he leans a bit closer, and my breath catches in my lungs, my dream flooding every sense. "There are creatures in the woods surrounding this keep who thoroughly enjoy feasting on pretty things."

My spine goes bone straight and his lips curve. Chuckling beneath his breath, he turns to Griffin, the muscles of his throat flexing. I have the oddest urge to kiss him there, to feel his pulse under my lips, to hear the moan such an action might elicit.

"Griffin would surely get you both killed for beauty alone," he adds.

Griffin snorts, and though I can't see him, I can feel his eyes roll. "Very funny."

"Break the deal. I'll leave now," I say, dragging Asmo's attention back to me.

"Not a chance, Starlight. You're stuck with me. I'm just starting to have fun with you."

"Break. It." I seethe, and when his grin pulls wider, I jerk that little itty bitty dagger out of its sheath on my hip and hold the sparking blade to my throat. "Break it or we both die."

He drags in a deep steadying breath, but his eyes flare, flickering between man and demon. "You and I both know you're bluffing. If you so much as draw blood, I could force you to drop that blade with a flick of my wrist. So go ahead, try me."

I'm not sure what to do. Honestly, I hadn't thought this through. I thought he'd value his life enough to end the deal between us if I threatened it, but clearly, that was a terrible assumption.

I lower the blade, the fight leaving me in seconds.

He pinches my chin, smiling down at me with a feigned sense of affection. "Look at you… learning already."

"Fuck you, demon prick. Find someone else."

"Well, that's an odd way to be propositioned, but bring me flowers and I might."

I tear my eyes away from his in defeat, and he takes a step back. "Now, I'd consider taking a bath if I were you." He returns to his grimoire, thumbing through the pages of scrawled text and drawings.

"Excuse me?" Those two words drip poison stronger than anything his blades are laced with and I grip his arm, spinning him around to face me.

"I'm sorry, let me try that again." He plucks my fingers from his arm one by one. *"Bathe.* As you've so blatantly reminded me, I'm a demon. And putting your lust on display might as well be an invitation to do as I please. So, go to your room and take care of whatever you need to as long as you're quiet, because I'd rather not be privy to your *needs* while we dine." Choosing to not give me a chance to reply, he snaps my fingers and the darkness and light spools around me until I drop in a heap of flailing limbs straight into a bathtub, filled with steaming water.

Worse, I don't need to look down to know there's not a shred of clothing on my body. They're gone, lost to the ether, and the warmth caresses every inch of me.

"Asshole…"

13

Valeria

Griffin is slouched in his chair, idly spinning a silver fork between his fingers, the last rays of dust bathing the dining room in a warm glow. His azure eyes, twinkling with mischief an hour ago, are now thin slits, an air of annoyance clinging to him as he stares absently across the room.

It's not until I step through the arched doorway that I see what he's glowering at. A young boy with messy blonde hair stands near the far wall, except every inch of him is covered in a blue sheen, glowing as if he's translucent.

A ghost.

"I wasn't aware the place was haunted," I say, moving closer to take a seat at the table across from Griffin, blocking his view of the lad.

"It is now." He snorts, dropping the fork on the table with a clang.

Ghosts aren't an uncommon occurrence in the Seven Realms. In fact, we have a holiday that honors those who are stuck on our plane of existence in the elven islands. It's dedicated to helping them find their peace so they can move on to what comes next.

I glance at the ghost boy. If it weren't for that ghoulish glow, I'd think he was a guest, ready to join us at this table, *alive* though every piece of me knows he's not. It's a good thing, though. It means his spirit is whole, and not so far gone that he could reach between planes of existence and cause harm.

Most spirits, like the boy, can't interact with our world, and simply exist in the space between. However, those who don't return to the Soul Well go mad eventually and tear their moral compass to shreds. Poltergeists, I believe, is the proper term—vengeful spirits, void of the ability to tell right from wrong. And as a result, they feel with such raw, unchecked emotion, that they can reach through the planes of life and death and do unspeakable things.

It's why we have our holiday, to prevent such creatures from ever existing.

This boy isn't a threat yet, but it doesn't mean I like the idea of spirits lurking around the keep. Griffin must be on the same page since he's still shooting disgruntled looks over my shoulder, as if he's silently willing the boy to disappear.

Skimming my fingers over the intricately carved edge of the long table, the wood is cool to the touch, almost as frigid as the air in this room. My breath mists, Griffin's too, and icy lines seem to creep up the pillar candles flickering along the center of the table. The empty plates in front of us transform, and in an instant, they're brimming with food.

I'm not familiar with the kind, but I know it's meat of some sort, with veggies and fresh bread. Whatever it is, it smells delicious and my nostrils inflate as the scents of garlic and rosemary flood through my senses.

Beside me, there's a third place setting at the head of the table that matches ours, but Asmo is nowhere to be seen. *He can't still be leaned over those books, can he?* I didn't see them splayed out on the table in the foyer. *Maybe he's putting them away in the library?*

An awkward silence fills the air, only made more so by the boy floating forward with hungry eyes. He bends over Griffin's plate, and the fae goes statue still, blinking in rapid succession as the boy inhales deep, oohing and awing as if he can smell the food, too.

"Did he just…" I trail off, unable to form the words. I tilt my head to the side, feeling my ears twitch.

"Get—*get back.*" Griffin shoos him away with his fork, his frown deepening. "If you want to sniff food, go sniff that one—" he nods toward Asmo's plate. "Keep your little greedy nostrils away from my steak."

I have to resist the urge to laugh, resting my head on my joined hands, elbows propped to hide the smile that creeps over my lips. Griffin sighs deep, shaking his head as he cuts away a small chunk of meat, seemingly tired of waiting for Asmo to join us. Despite his impatience, and his attack on the ghost, his manners are impeccable. I suppose being raised to reign over a realm one day, like I have, will do that to him.

"Where the hell is Asmodeus?" His icy blue eyes pin me, as if I have something to do with the man's absence. I don't reply, just arch my brows in silent question. "Don't do that. Surely you know where he is."

I breathe out a sharp, "Hah," adjusting the spacing between my silverware before lacing my hands together, without a single care given to my elbows being propped on the table. "When would I have had time to look after the *Lord of Chivalry?* Hmm? If you're forgetting yourself, he unceremoniously teleported me into a bathtub last I saw him."

A smile cracks his stoney, beautiful face. "Right…" He lifts the goblet of wine in front of him to his lips, as if to hide it. The ghost boy's hollow eyes track our every move as he continues sniffing Asmo's plate. The sound is obnoxiously loud, but I do my best to ignore it.

"I suppose I have you to thank for the food?" I stare at the steak, looking at it down the bridge of my nose, wondering if it's poisoned. Though, our deal should protect me. What would be the point of poisoning me if *Sir High and Mighty* died too? So, *it must be safe, right?*

"Unfortunately, no. As much as I'd love to hear your praise, the queen is responsible for that. Until Asmodeus can get a staff for the keep, to run the kitchen and such, she's offered to send us meals. She'd never let Asmo or her favorite nephew starve. Gods bless her." Griffin pops a bite into his mouth, chewing with the grace reserved for a king.

"She seems to be *invested."* I bounce my brows, then dig in myself. Letting the flavor of garlic veggies steal me away for a moment. After scavenging for weeks, this is heaven on a plate.

"Is that jealousy I sense?" The excitement in Griffin's voice cuts down to the bone.

"No. Curiosity. Asmo hasn't told me much."

Griffin nods, his brows lifting ever so slightly. I swear a purr comes from his chest as he eats, like the fae beast inside of him is pleased. "Well, let me put your mind at ease. There's nothing there. The queen and Asmodeus are strictly friends. Though they'd go to war for each other if necessary." He tips his glass, swirling the crimson liquid around. "I almost pity the person who comes between them. They're both rather hot-headed when it comes to those they love."

The boy lets out another long string of sniffles, then leans his head back as if he's in pure bliss.

"Are you going to mention the ghost in the room? Or am I supposed to pretend he's not there?"

"You can ask Asmodeus whenever he finally decides to grace us with his insufferable presence."

"Glad to see you get along," I say, taking another bite.

"He's my current jailor, so I don't have much of a choice." Across from me, Griffin leans back in his chair, white hair glinting in the firelight. A sly grin spreads across his face. "Though, I'd be lying if I said I wasn't curious… What are you to him, anyway?"

"Nothing." I take a long gulp of wine. Seems like I'll need it to get through this dinner. I resist the urge to roll my eyes. Just as I'm about to elaborate, a shadow falls over the tabletop beside me.

"That's not true." Asmodeus rounds the table, every step crackling with power, making the air in the room electrify with his presence. As he takes his seat, dark amber eyes meet mine, a silent challenge in their fiery depths. I hold his gaze, refusing to be the first to look away.

"Then what am I to you, *my lord."* I say the term of endearment he hates like it's a dirty phrase one would whisper in the ear of a lover, but the disapproving look I give him is enough to make him shake his head.

For a split moment, I think I made him blush, but if I did, it vanished just as quickly as it came. More than likely, it was nothing more than the firelight dancing off his sharp jaw and strong cheekbones.

"You are the Lady of Grim's Keep. That was our deal. Make of it what you will, *my lady."* The purr in his voice… The way his eyes darken as he leaned forward and named the title he's blessed upon me… I can't help but swallow, taking another sip of my wine to cover up the way his words have affected me.

Curse that damn dream.

A long silence passes, no one daring to break the silence as we eat.

Then, as if sensing I've finally grown comfortable, Asmo clears his throat. "I see you bathed."

I nearly choke on a vegetable. "It's not like I had a choice in the matter." My voice is harsher than I intend it to be, but he did undress me and toss me into a bathtub, so sympathy isn't something I'm capable of right now. "It would seem you and your ghost child have more in common than you think. You both continually put your noses where they don't belong."

The ghost boy sniffing Asmo's plate stands upright, his wide translucent eyes bouncing between us. All while Griffin sputters, slamming his cup down on the table as he beats a fist against his chest. It takes a moment for him to stop coughing, but Asmo doesn't move a muscle and I don't dare look away from him.

"I take it all back," Griffin says, waving a hand. His eyes water and he clears his throat. "I want to stay. Nothing this interesting ever happens in Solaria."

The ghost boy moves in my peripheral, attempting to take a seat next to Griffin at the table, but the chair goes through him, and he falls to the floor. I'm not sure why he can touch the floor and not other objects, but if I understood how the universe worked, I probably wouldn't have gotten onto that ship. I wouldn't have been stranded here or made a deal with the demon staring at me.

Tension fills Asmo's shoulders, his jaw working at the hinge, then he looks away, taking another sip of his wine while the ghost, yet again, falls through the chair.

"For the gods sake, *stop it.* You won't be able to sit until we get you a body, all right? Just have some damn patience." Griffin growls, shaking his head as he takes a bite.

The boy scowls at the fae, then glides from the room without a word.

"You could be a bit nicer. He's just a boy," Asmo says, his movements smooth and skilled as he cuts his food. It's the precision of someone used to handling knives and blades. But, then again, everything about him—even the bloody, carnal side of him—is graceful. It's mind boggling to think someone could be so composed, so refined when I can sense the barely leashed power thrumming through him. It's like a current roving over my skin, beckoning me to give into its thrall.

It's *maddening*.

Asmo catches me staring, a smirk already pulling at his lips. I swallow my bite, then say the first thing that comes to mind, anything to explain why I've been gawking at him like an uncivilized idiot. "I see you're wearing a shirt."

Asmo snorts, dabbing at his lips with the fabric napkin. "Yeah, well, as I told you earlier, I'd rather not have you—" He rakes his eyes over me, something dark lurking within them that's unreadable. *"Worked up,* at my table."

Apparently, what they say about demons being able to sense things is more true than our teachers in Vanderlyth suggested. They forgot to tell us that demons could smell you and know exactly how you're feeling—fear, lust, all the above. It would've been nice to have a heads up, but I'm a quick study, and now I know. Now, I can be prepared.

Though, there's only two ways forward in this conversation. One, apologize for something that's completely normal. Something I shouldn't be ashamed of. Or option two, own it and make him swallow his words.

The latter sounds like the winner to me.

"I believe the word you're looking for is horny." This time, they both choke. Asmo on his wine that he's already refilled once, and Griffin on a bite of his steak.

Griffin tosses his napkin on the table. "It's fine. I'll just starve." He stands from his seat, and for the first time, I realize how tall he is. He's not lanky, despite being at least a foot taller than me, but from where I sit, he's positively imposing. "Let me know when you're ready to look for bodies."

I snap my head to the left, meeting Asmo's stare. I'm not sure how long he's been watching me. "What bodies?" I ask.

"The boy's and the people who used to live in the keep." He lets out a long exhale. "Turns out, in my absence, they were murdered by Lord Elcrys."

I stiffen at the mention of my father, darting my eyes away. "I see… Why would he do such a thing?"

"He was trying to find me. It was a long time ago, but when he came to the keep and I wasn't here, he tortured my people and killed them all." Asmodeus gives a lazy shrug, long fingers toying with the buttons of his shirt, but the muscle feathering in his jaw tells me he's not as calm and composed as he's trying to appear to be.

For the first time, I'm not sure what to say. Sorry doesn't feel good enough.

The only thing I know for certain, is I did the right thing withholding my last name. If he didn't already hate my father, I'm sure learning that made him.

Perhaps I could offer help instead of an apology…

"What bodies, exactly?" I ask, glancing between him and Griffin.

"Humanoid bodies," Griffin says, a sarcastic ring to his voice.

"Obviously, but where? I found bodies in the keep when I arrived. I buried them in the woods."

Griffin's little tilt of his head, and the flirting smirk at the corner of his lips, causes an unsettling whirl in my gut.

"You buried them?" Asmo asks, his voice hardly above a whisper.

"Was I not supposed to?" I stare at him, brows drawn together, trying to read his expressions, but he gives nothing away. Most of the time, he seems to keep his emotions so locked down that it's hard to draw lines.

"Can you show me where?" Asmo sets his napkin on the table, rising from the chair.

"Sure." I suck in a breath when he pulls out my seat, not expecting it. *I guess we're going now.*

The ghost boy floats back into the room, gliding through the air like a leaf in the breeze. His clothes are nothing more than tatters, stained with blood from unseen wounds. Even in death, he's chosen to wear them still, instead of imagining himself in something less gruesome. Dark, sunken eyes peer at us from a gaunt face and I can't imagine what it must be like to be lost and kept from finding peace for so long.

Asmo's lips curve into a sly smile. "He won't hurt you."

"I know." I ignore his outstretched hand, standing as I smooth the front of my tunic.

"Then why the face?"

"I'm just wondering why you need their bones."

As we turn toward the archway, leading to the foyer, his hand rests against my lower back, not pushing, but there. And if I had any thoughts of turning around, or refusing to tell him where those bodies are, that hand tells me there's no choice but to show him.

"We're giving him and the others still wandering the woods a second chance at life."

I halt, but his hand urges me on. "You can't bring back the dead."

"I can, and I will." There's not an ounce of hesitation in his voice. He truly believes it.

"You'll be messing up the balance. A life given is a life owed." I would know. My mother gave up hers for me.

"In most instances, yes. However, in this, they're not fully coming back. They'll be given bodies, and their undead souls will be tethered to this plane. Thanks to my magic, there's a chance that that boy and the others could exist like the living within the keep's boundary wall. They'll still be able to move on if they make their peace, but until then, they'll stay sane and live well."

I tense. "What do you mean *your magic?* You're a demon. No demon can manipulate the fabrics of life and death." Stealing a glance over my shoulder, there's such hope in that boy's eyes, enough that it gives me pause. *Do I have the right to deny him this? This life?*

"You mean she doesn't know?" Griffin chuckles under his breath, having taken the lead. "Oh, this just keeps getting better."

"Know what?" Unease stirs within me as I meet Asmo's knowing gaze. This night is shaping up to be far more complicated than I imagined it would be when I made our deal.

Still, he doesn't answer, just nudges me along.

14

Valeria

I chew my lip. This is blood magic, and it goes against every waking instinct in my body. "Blood magic is forbidden for good reason," I begin carefully. Asmo merely lifts a brow, amusement dancing in his eyes. I press on. "There are always consequences, often deadly. You could lose your soul if you don't sacrifice an innocent life to power the spell. I know you mean well, but…" The words die on my tongue, my eyes widening at the realization that *I'm innocent*. I've harmed no one, and until recently I've obeyed the rules. He's going to sacrifice *me*.

Suddenly, it's hard to breathe. My breaths are short, shallow, and far too quick as lights burst in my vision. "I understand you want to bring them back but our lives are tethered. I die, you die." I'm rambling, but I don't care. My feet are rooted to the floor as I reach for my crystal pendant, feeling it hum at my touch. I'll fight if I have to. I'd rather die doing so, than be offed like some lamb. "Sacrificing me will—"

Asmo whips me around to face him. "I'm not sacrificing you. Okay? Now breathe before you pass out."

BREATHE. Something dark wraps around the edges of my awareness, encroaching and growing thicker, repeating the command over and over until I have no choice but to comply.

As if the thought was my own, my lungs expand, and I drag in a deep, steadying breath. It takes me a moment to realize that I didn't make the decision to calm down. Nor did I tell myself to breathe.

"You just spoke in my head." I blink at him, my knees becoming weak as I struggle to understand what just happened.

"No, I pushed a thought into your mind."

"That is… That's not okay. You have no business being inside my—"

He silences me with a pointed glare. "I can't read your thoughts, nor would I, even if I had that power. The only thing I can do is push my own voice out or speak commands into your head and it's not something I do lightly."

Is that all? Though, he has had countless opportunities to control me. If he wanted to make me into an elven puppet, he would've by now. Yet, that was the first time I've felt such a thing.

He leans forward, his voice low and earnest. "I can perform the magic needed, safely. I would not jeopardize both of our lives if I thought it wouldn't work. Griffin is fae and blood magic works differently for them. No one is dying, and no one is losing a soul… at least not for long."

I nod, aware of every place he's touching me. The rough calluses of his hand stroking down my bare arm, squeezing my hand. The way his gaze seems to caress me, to hold me in some mystical trance. Even the air between us seems to vibrate, reveling in the shadow of his power.

For the first time, I understand why people used to throw themselves at the feet of the old gods. *Fuck*, I might've too just to bask in their grace. It's magical and tantalizing, and the warmth of that power on my flesh… I've never felt more safe. Yet, everything I've been taught about demons, about people like Asmo, says otherwise.

Ripping myself from the trance, I met Asmo's amber gaze, a hint of concern lurking there. So little, I almost miss it. "Even fae blood won't completely prevent the drain upon your spirit. You'll have to anchor yourself to something or someone on this plane..." I trail off, realization dawning. *It's me. I'm not the sacrifice. I'm the anchor.*

Did he know about these ghosts before our deal? Was that why he was willing to spare me?

Asmo pinches my chin, lifting my face as if he's about to kiss me. "And that's what I have you for, Starlight. You'll get to lead me back from the brink of death."

"You barely know me. What if I don't want to help you?"

His breath is warm against my cheeks. "You don't have a choice."

He could command me. Maybe that's one of his exceptions for using his gift to push thoughts into people's heads.

"Let's go, love birds. We have things to do and graves to rob," Griffin yells, and the term *love birds* has something stirring in my gut. Something bad.

Asmodeus doesn't let me go, just continues to study my face a moment, his expression unreadable. Then, slowly, he releases me and inclines his head. "You'll have to trust me, for now."

"I don't even trust the man who gave me life, and yet you want me to trust you?" I lose a breath.

"Try."

My mind turns over endless possibilities and pitfalls that await us. A mad feeling has settled into my very core as we leave the keep and travel through the dim forest, but there's no turning back.

The graves are tucked away just past the wall and when we reach the stone boundary, Griffin hangs back. Asmo grips my hand, the shock of his skin touching mine stealing my words, and before I know it, shadows and light fold in around us and we're on the other side.

"You didn't think I was going to let you climb a tree again, did you?" He smirks down at me, his hand lingering a bit too long. I pluck his fingers off my arm, using the minimal number of digits necessary for the job.

"Don't worry, I'm laughing on the inside." Rolling my eyes, I search for the tree I marked, finding it off to our right. "It's that way."

"What I want to know is how did you get them over the wall? I saw how gracefully you crossed on your own. You expect me to believe you dragged multiple bodies over that and lived?" He points a thumb over his shoulder at the boundary.

"The wall wasn't spelled when I was here, and I made a door. Had you let me, I would've shown it to you." Crossing my arms, I twist my lips.

"Hmmm, I see." Something tells me he doesn't believe me, but I'd rather not waste my time.

"Do you know your ears twitch when you're frustrated?" He cocks his head, his eyes drifting back and forth over my face like he's reading something written there.

I don't answer.

Of course, he'd point that out. As if I haven't been teased about it my entire life. No one else's ears twitch. Why the hell do mine? And worse, no matter how hard I try not to, it always happens.

Fingers curled into fists at my sides, I lead Asmo through the trees, our footsteps soft against the carpet of fallen leaves. The cool night air has goosebumps forming along my bare arms. Then, as if sensing my need, something warm settles over my shoulders. Fur brushes against my neck and I pause.

"Were you in my head?" I ask, staring at the thick leather coat, the neck lined with silver fur.

"No, I can hear your teeth chattering from here. I don't need magic or power to be annoyed by it." A dark brow arches in my direction as he huffs, then proceeds to try to put my arms through the jacket sleeves.

"I can dress myself." I push his hands away.

"Then do so." He waits. Slowly, I shrug it on and he motions for me to continue into the forest.

"Are you always this pushy?"

"No, but I did warn you what happens when I get bored."

"Oh, right. Murder. How could I forget?"

He chuckles behind me, the deep sound of it sending a shiver up my spine.

I spot the trees I marked, symbolizing the corners of the makeshift graveyard. Not realizing he's following so close, I bend without notice, ready to brush away the leaves that cover the little headstones I made.

Before my hand can connect with the ground, Asmo barrels into me from behind.

"What the—" The words die in his throat, lost as my weight is launched forward.

My arms flail, ready to catch myself before I hit the ground face first, but his hands grip my hips, forcing my bottom backward to steady me. I jerk the moment my ass connects to his… his… *Gods, spare me.*

"You can't just stop like that," he growls.

Said every unsatisfied woman ever.

It takes me a moment to remember I have limbs, that I'm still bent over, ass to his rather extraordinary *appendage*, as if he's about to take me here and now.

As if someone resumed time, I jerk away from his hold and stand up straight, dragging my fingers through my hair the moment there's a safe space between us. "Well. That was unexpected."

He arches a brow, lips parted. His beautiful face is painted in tans and shadows and bright silver, the scar running through his eyebrow and cheek almost glowing in the light of the moons. He's breathtaking.

As if this moment can't become any more awkward, my brain has lost all sense. My mouth speaks the first thing that comes to my mind, and it's not becoming of a lady. Not at all. "I didn't expect to get bent over by a demon in a graveyard, but here we are."

Oh no… no, no, no. I should smack myself for saying that.

Gods look at him. He's speechless.

Then the furrow between his brow lessens. His eyes grow wider. The icy mask he's so good at hiding behind melts away, and the laugh that leaves him sounds *divine*. It's hypnotizing, and I've never heard a more heartwarming sound.

"Don't laugh at me," I say, blinking. I'm not really sure if I want him to stop, yet I'm worried I truly might've broken him at the same time.

"I'm sorry, I just…" He explodes in another fit of laughter, eyes clouding with unshed tears. "I just didn't expect that, either." He clears his throat and clasps his hands together. "Okay," he breathes out a deep exhale, stilling himself. "Graves. Dead bodies. Ghosts."

"Are those your affirmations, or…?"

The corners of his mouth tip up, a sharp puff of air leaving his nose, but he quickly presses his lips together to hide it. “No. Where are they?”

“You’re standing on them.”

He pales, his head jerking as he glances down at the leafy ground, then points at his feet. I nod and he quickly hops a foot or so to the right.

“They’re there, too.” He frowns, but doesn’t say anything. “You’re already planning to dig them up. I don’t think stepping on their graves can be much worse than that.”

“Thanks… because that’s going to help me sleep tonight.”

I grin. “Glad I could help.”

Asmo brushes away the leaves, revealing the wooden signs I made to mark each body's grave. I didn’t know who they were when I laid them to rest in this grove, but I tried to imagine each of them a backstory, to give them a name based on the things they died with.

"Well, isn't this delightfully creepy," he says, then brushes off another.

15

Asmodeus

A whispering shroud of mist curls around our feet like possessive fingers as we move through the rows of graves. Some are still buried in the leaves, but those I've managed to uncover are all marked with withered wood plaques. Names have been scratched into them, and verdant moss clings to the wood grain, like the ground attempted to swallow those make-shift headstones.

I stoop to reveal another headstone. "Who's Riddick the Brave?" Brushing aside the moss, I trace a finger over the lines she carved, as if they were drawn with a piece of white stone.

She doesn't answer, and I glance up at her. The silver fabric of her tunic swishes around her thighs as the breeze sweeps through the forest, shaking the leaf canopy above us. Lips twisted and vacant eyed, she's present, but somehow not.

"Starlight." My voice is a bit louder, but my nickname seems to grab her attention.

Valeria's lips twitch as those emerald eyes fly to meet mine. "I'm sorry, what?"

"Who is Riddick?" I hold up the wooden board, name faced toward her.

"I found a broken bow next to his bones. It seemed fitting, and everyone deserves to be remembered."

Something warm blooms inside my chest, and I knead my palm over my sternum, desperate to send it away. Of course she would name them all. Somehow, that doesn't surprise me. If she felt strongly that she carried their bones out here to bury them, naming them seems so… simple.

I didn't think elves held any sort of compassion for demons. They always have looked down on just about every other creature in existence except for the dragons they worship. Yet, Valeria buried demons she'd never met, never had a reason to care for.

The act alone cuts through any of the remaining regret I've held on to for allowing her to live in my keep. Since I made that deal, I've worried I've made the wrong decision. Especially with Griffin living in the keep now. Our deal doesn't protect him from her, like it does me.

Something about her is different, though, and despite Valeria stabbing me upon meeting, I knew it then. I saw it in her eyes. Just wasn't sure of what until now.

Where the elves couldn't care less about others—unless they were of pureblood, fury marked, or moon blessed—she cares. Valeria *feels*, unlike the emotionless, high and mighty elves I'm used to associating with. And although we are different species, in this graveyard those differences fade away. We're more than just the flesh on our bones, our magic or gifts and abilities. We're people with empathy for life.

It's too bad someone like her couldn't lead the elven realm. Things would be very different, and we certainly wouldn't be on the brink of war. Had someone with her ability to see past the species lines that divide us sat on the throne in Vanderlyth when Jade was alive, maybe she wouldn't have been cast out.

Jade was highborn, but not pureblood. She was a result of an affair. She descended from one of the original family lines of elves, yet due to her father being a shifter, Jade was considered a half-breed and sold as a servant slave to the highest bidder. Luckily, my mother sought to end such things and would buy any children sold into the trades. It's how Jade came to live in Hell Hold, and how I met my mate.

We were so young then… But had someone with Valeria's compassion ruled over the elves, Jade might've never been sold, we might've never met, and I might've never killed her. She'd have lived a long and happy life.

Sucking in a breath and pushing up from the ground, I drag my fingers through my hair, drawing the dark, blue-black strands away from my face. "Well, we should get to it then, huh?"

With a flick of my wrist, two shovels spring forth from thin air. Handing one to her, we begin to dig. For a long time, there's nothing but the rhythmic sound of metal against soil that passes between us. It's not until I find the first body that I dare break the silence.

It's wrapped in fabric. As I brush away the dirt, my fingers glide off the remnants of wax drops, like a candle had been tilted over it, like they've been blessed the same way elven royalty are laid to rest. Pulling the wrapped bones from the grave, I can barely make out the design on the fabric. It used to be curtains, and she must've forged it from the ruins to ensure they were put in the earth properly—as her people believe—and that only makes me appreciate her more.

Stealing a glance in her direction, I watch her dig, hands caked with dirt. Smears of it line her brow. She took care of my people and buried them with such love, like one would a family member…

A silent thanks sits heavy on my tongue, but I don't know how to voice it. Instead, I set the bones aside and start on the next, and the next, until all twenty-six graves have been dug up and the bones collected.

Placing all the bundles in two large canvas bags, I lift the first and toss it over my shoulder, hearing the clack of bone on bone as the weight settles.

"Careful," Valeria snaps. "How would you like to be tossed around? It's bad enough you're disturbing their rest, and if this works, then great, but you can at least try not to break them any more than they already are." Her tone is sharp as she glares daggers into me, crossing her arms. Her ears twitch and I can't help the faint hint of a smile that slips past my defenses.

It stirs something within me—something I have no desire to explore but enough sense to acknowledge. "Yes, Your Highness."

Rolling her eyes, she waves me on and we trek back toward the boundary wall where we left Griffin.

When we reach the wall, she feels the stones, sleeking along the mossy surfaces until one gives away. From there, more come apart until a hole large enough for us to crouch through forms. One at a time, we push the canvas bags through, and before Valeria can crawl through the opening, I set my hand on her arm, stopping her.

"Before we go back, I wanted to say thank you," I say, my voice low—quiet—as if some part of me doesn't want Griffin to hear it. Or maybe I just don't want to admit to myself that I'm thanking the woman who stabbed me.

"For what?" Her emerald eyes blink at me, confusion lacing her brow. "Digging?"

"No." I pause, the words tumbling out with more honesty than I intend. "For honoring them."

Understanding dawns in her emerald eyes, and she gives me a smile brighter than the hell flame. "The honor is all mine."

"IT'S ABOUT GODSDAMN TIME you two showed up," Griffin calls out, leaning against the trunk of a thick oak tree with a lazy grin. His white hair gleams in the dark forest like a beacon, making it impossible to miss him."I was certain you'd been eaten."

"Me? Never." I pause, looking Valeria up and down. "She's who you need to worry about." I set the canvas bag down at my feet as we near him.

"I'm just glad you both are in one piece. I debated playing hero for about half a minute and decided the two of you weren't worth becoming that witches fuck toy again." He crosses his arms, eyeing my bare chest with a white brow lifting in silent question. Though, when he scans Valeria, he seems to settle on the idea that nothing beyond digging happened. "I see you've lost your clothes again."

"You dig up over two dozen bodies, then you can tell me how hot it gets." I roll my eyes, pulling my shirt free from where it's looped through my belt. Wiping away the sweat beading on my brow, I meet his false, all-knowing eyes again.

"Don't lie to me. You'll find any excuse to not wear a shirt. I think you just like to show off your scars." Griffin tsks his tongue, shaking his head. "I bet the ladies swoon for those."

"Or, I just got used to being on my own in a realm where everything can fucking kill you and no one gives a shit if you're clothed or not. If anything, some of the more civilized creatures left me alone when they saw my scars. It's a survival thing really, if you think about it." I tick my head, as if giving the thought my stamp of approval, then get to work dragging out bundle after bundle of bones from my sack.

Valeria is already beating me, seeing as hers is half emptied already. "You were in the Realm of Monsters?" she asks, eyeing me over her shoulder.

"I was. Yes." Dropping my gaze to the task at hand, I busy myself. Everyone's expression is always the same when they realize I was in the prison realm, and after everything today, I'm not sure I can stomach her gawking at me. Not in the way that says I'm a monster. I hear it enough from everyone else.

"Were you born in there, or were you thrown in?" Judging from her voice, she's moved closer. Hell, she might even be right behind me but I don't have the heart to look. It's not something I want to go into right now, but after the way she's treated my people, I can't tell her no.

She deserves to ask her questions, to judge me. I'll give her that for what she's done for them.

Griffin, however, beats me to it. "He was pushed in there by his mum."

"You do not speak for me." My nostrils flare wide as I breathe in deep, locking my jaw until the muscles in my cheeks twitch. I do my best to tamper down the anger roiling through me, but it's easier said than done. I can still hear it in my voice when I finally dare to speak. "But he is right."

"I'm… I'm sorry." Valeria sets her hand on my shoulder, but when I don't look at her, she crouches down beside me. "I didn't mean to upset you… I didn't know."

Setting bundle of bones out, I blink long and hard before meeting her gaze. I expected her to be afraid, to scent it in the air, to have her jolt away from me now that she knows—just like everyone else does. Only, she doesn't. The only thing I see in her eyes is concern. *For me.*

There's no one else alive that's ever truly been concerned for me, except Alice. Not even my brother. He's sort of just assumed I can take care of myself. Yet, it's so blatantly there in her eyes… I can't look away.

"It's okay," I say, standing up before I can act on the need to put my hand over hers, to solidify that I'm not just saying I'm fine to ease her nerves, but that I mean it.

I start spreading out the bundles into a wide circle, while Griffin and Valeria get to work turning those bundled bones into skeletons laid out on the forest floor. Something burns in my chest, searing through the stone I've wrapped around the most vulnerable part of me. I hate it. I shouldn't feel it.

Dammit, Alice… She just *had* to bring up the idea of me moving on with someone else. I wasn't even considering it until she brought it up. And I'm still not, but now the idea is floating around and making me feel things I shouldn't have any interest in.

"Careful with that femur," Griffin quips, his voice light. "Wouldn't want our friend here to limp into the new life."

"Very funny," Valeria retorts without missing a beat. Her focus never wavers from the skeleton taking shape under her skilled hands. Her ears twitch as she continues.

It doesn't help that Valeria has some of the same ticks Jade did. The adorable ear twitches for one. It cracks open my chest, revealing a part of me I don't want exposed. *Ever.*

As long as it's sealed away tight, no one can leave me. No one can trick me into a prison realm, and certainly, no one else can die because I couldn't save them. Or worse, at my hands.

With Alice, it's different. She's immortal and we've literally had a trial by fire, having to rely on each other while in the prison realm. I trust her because she's had every opportunity to betray me and hasn't. How am I supposed to love someone again, when not even Alice has been privy to parts of my past, and she's the person I trust most in this world?

I shouldn't feel comforted around the woman who stabbed me. Yet, Valeria, and that godsdamn hand…

I hate myself.

I shouldn't feel anything, not *a fucking twinge* for someone else. Not after what I did to Jade. Not after letting down countless others whose lives depended on me to protect them… I don't deserve it.

Summoning salt bags from the storage bays in Hell Hold, I tear open the corner and start to draw a large circle in the middle of the ring of skeletons. This is where I'll sit. Then, one by one, I connect each of the deceased to the middle ring with a chalky white line of salt.

When I'm finished, I take my spot, cross-legged in the center of that middle ring, just as Griffin and Valeria finish preparing of the skeletons. Her dark hair tumbles over her shoulder, the wispy tips sweeping over the leaves on the ground as she bends over. Weathered skull in hand, her slender fingers aligning it with its spine.

Pausing, her lashes flick up, cheeks flushing when she notices me watching her. "Sorry, I didn't know you were waiting on me."

"I'm not," I say, a smirk coming to my lips when that flush deepens.

No. No, no, no… I look away. *This is for the best.* Maybe, this spell is a blessing. It'll rob me of my shadow temporarily, which is the part of the soul that allows one to feel emotions. Maybe being emotionless for a bit, will let my head clear and whatever need for companionship that Alice seeded into my mind to die.

"Um, I am. I'm tired and it's been a long day for me, being saved from the blood witches and all. So, if we can get on with it before I grow old, I'd be grateful for at least two minutes." Griffin's angelic, yet self-absorbed voice seems to slice right through me.

He's said things far worse, and it's likely due to the pent-up animosity that I shoved away earlier for him bringing up my mother, but before I can stop myself, my eyes become demonic, leveling him in an instant. "You will have patience."

"Patience hasn't ever been my thing. So chop chop, death lord." He claps twice.

"I have over two dozen graves dug, all of which are ready to put your body into. I'd planned to save them for the Elf Lord and whatever men he's with, but I'm happy to spare one." Clenching my hands into fists, I try to force back my demon half, put it away, but the smirk he gives me is making that hard.

He bows sarcastically. "Please forgive me, *Your Grace*. I did not realize I was in the company of the Prince of Death tonight. I merely thought I was helping my uncle bring back his people."

"Prince…" Valeria whispers, and I swallow hard before glancing at her from the corner of my eye. She's so pale. I'll be surprised if she doesn't faint.

"Yes, Valeria, Darling. He's been tip-toeing around the title all day. Asmodeus *Morningstar* is the Prince of the Seven Realms, the Harbinger of Death, the Master of Necromancy. He's the Devil's first-born who was banished to the Realm of Monsters, but has since regained his title and his throne. And, most importantly, he's also my uncle, and if Alice knew you were threatening to put me in a shallow grave, she'd take our beloved Asmo's balls and he'd earn another title as the royal eunuch."

Well, so much for suppressing it. My demon side has been fully unleashed. The magic coursing through the air around me streams like their threads of fate. Griffin himself almost glows, thanks to his fae blood, and I snarl, so deep, it rattles my chest when he steps closer. My incisors, along with the teeth surrounding them have formed points, and talons now rest against my knees.

With a clench of my fist, Griffin is on his knees.

Valeria's voice slams into me like power itself. "Let him go!"

My nostrils flare as ragged air invades my lungs. Griffin gasps, tapping the ground in a silent surrender. I don't notice the twig soaring through the air until it's too late. It slaps into my arm, bouncing off onto the ground. My magic dissipates in an instant.

"What is wrong with you?" Valeria snaps. "So he said something you didn't like. It doesn't give you the right to attack him like… like some savage beast." Her narrowed eyes pin me in place, rage burning in those emerald rings that I didn't even know she was capable of.

"You threw a stick at me, like some dog." I gesture to the evidence on the ground.

"Stop acting like an animal and I won't treat you like one." She crosses her arms and I rub at the place it hit.

"Enough!" Griffin's chest heaves. "I'm sorry. I shouldn't have brought it up."

"You can make it up to me by filling this," I say, summoning a chalice into my hand and holding it out to him. To my surprise, it's not talons wrapped around the sturdy stem, but my fingers.

"You want me to fetch you wine now?" Griffin's eyes go wide as he leans back on his hands, his mouth dropping open a smidge as his brows furrow.

"With your blood, Griffin." I shove it out again. "I have to consume it so it'll regenerate my shadow. Or would you prefer me to live without that half of my soul?"

He shakes his head. "Gods no. You're already a murder muffin with it. I'd hate to see *soulless Asmo*. He sounds like a real bastard."

"Then come on. Fork it over, pup. As you so graciously said, we don't have all night." The scowl has set in, and I fear it might become my permanent face as he clutches his wrists to his chest.

"Excuse me? No. My mom told me to never let someone have my blood, let alone *drink it,* like some sort of *animal."* He snarls a lip in disgust.

"I'm family. And you've already broken that rule, considering how much of your blood the witches were stashing." I push the chalice out again in his direction.

"You're not *acting* like family, asshole." Griffin groans, shaking his head as he rolls up his sleeve.

"Maybe if you learned to keep your mouth shut, I would."

He takes the chalice. "First the bloody witches and now you." He frowns, shaking his head again before gripping the dagger sheathed on his hip. With precision grace, he slices the blade over his wrist, holding it over the chalice and letting the crimson liquid flow off his wrist until it's two-thirds of the way full. "Here. Apparently that's all I'm good for."

I take it, recoiling in an arc to keep his blood from sloshing over the rim.

"Well, go on. *Drink.*" He waves at me, the line he sliced already healing.

16

Asmodeus

Seated within the salt circle, I close my eyes, letting the hushed silence of the forest seep into my being. The crisp night air chills my skin as it caresses my face, carrying the earthy scent of damp leaves and pine. I feel every limb, every nerve within my body, moving from head to toe. My pulse beats steady and slow, as energy kindles deep within me, growing with each inhale until my veins burn with power.

I plunge my hands into the soft ground, burrowing through the leaves until my fingers can curl into the dirt at my sides. The elements embrace me, and as I breathe deeper, they ground me to this plane of existence, creating a bridge between life and death.

My exhales become frosty plumes, chilling my cheeks as the air turns frigid, laden with the sweet taste of magic and something ancient that's woven the realms together. Power surges through me, scorching my veins until I fear I'll burst. My mind stretches outward, probing the darkness as I unleash the energy in a demanding tide. It roars through the silent forest, beckoning to lost souls, looking for my friends.

Whispering their names loud enough that only I can hear them, I envision each set of eyes, each smile that graced the halls of my keep so long ago—the servants, the guards, the kitchen staff, the gardeners, each and every one of the people I knew when I lived here. As I open my eyes, spirits swarm me in a shimmering vortex, their essence caressing my skin with a gentle glow.

They spin so fast, my hair whips in every direction. All I have to do is remind them of who they are, like I did Chester. I'll relive our shared memories to stitch their souls back together. Brows drawn, the world around me disappears until I'm reliving those moments along with the spirits.

Tears trace hot trails down my cheeks as visions of bittersweet days gone by flood my mind. Laughter in the kitchen, dancing under the stars, lessons in the training yard… each recollection a shard of glass in my heart.

With an agonized gasp, I wrench myself back to the present. The glowing orbs screech to a halt, hovering in the air around me, no longer orbs but people. Ghosts.

They stare at me, confused no doubt. Then a woman drifts through the crowd, and the sheer sight of her threatens to shatter me.

"What are you doing, sweet boy?" she asks, voice achingly tender. Settling in front of me, she reaches a glowing hand out, attempting to wipe away the tears streaming down my cheeks.

I lean into her touch, even though I can't experience it. "I'm fixing this," I choke out. "None of you should've died."

Mirella was the head of the staff in Grim's Keep all those years ago, and a mother to me more times than I can count. She filled the void my own flesh and blood left, and showed me what it should feel like to be loved.

Her voice is so soft, such a contrast to her strong features. "This…" She gestures to the air. "This isn't the answer. You can't do this to yourself. You made us whole, let that be enough."

"I can do more." Burning with determination, I summon the Book of the Dead, one of the grimoires I'd stolen from the blood witches. The leather-bound tome appears out of midair, falling into my lap, open to the spell I need to turn the bones into gargoyle bodies.

I mumble the incantation, one hand outstretched toward the body, the other toward the first ghost. With a deep breath, the stones around his skeleton grow in size, sliding toward the bones and wrapping around them until not an inch of ivory can be seen. The stones swell until they form a body that's a spitting image of the ghost before me. All except for the large, webbed wings that span from its back.

An agonizing scream cuts straight to my core, but I can't break my focus to see who it's coming from. Though, the pitch alone already gives me a good idea. Chester.

No one said this process wouldn't hurt. As the spell sears through my veins, I take the boy's pain as my own, guiding his spirit into his new body. Teeth grinding together, my heart flutters in a rapid cadence, my head pounding as if it's being crushed. Then the scream is snuffed out and I release the magic, unable to look away from the body I just created.

Move... Come on... MOVE. A stone hand slides just an inch—the first sign of life—and slowly, ever so slowly, the boy rises, stretching his new wings.

One after another, I repeat the process until it's a struggle to hold up my head, to lift my arms, to breathe. Blood spills from my nose, my demon half taking over when I become too weak to suppress it. The magic consumes me, the ravenous energy gnawing at my very essence. Pain lances through my middle, but I grit my teeth harder, determined to see this through, for them, for all we've lost.

I can do this. One more body. One more soul.

Just as the darkness threatens to overwhelm me, a speck of light glows on the ground near my legs. It pushes and pulls like blown glass, stretching into a tiny dragon made of light, prancing along the length of my thigh. The magic seems to sing a melody, so pure that I know exactly what kind it is without looking up. It's elven magic. *Valeria's.*

Something flutters inside me at the sight of it. A bead of sweat traces a path down my brow, along the length of my nose, until it drips away, lost to the ground below. The creature nuzzles against me, pushing me as if it's real, but for a moment it takes my mind off the pain. It gives me the strength to finish this.

My soul quivers. My awareness shrinks as my head spins as I channel every ounce of my shadow into the spell. It's more tasking than I predicted, and that knowledge has my gut clenching tight. To control the dead is one thing; to bring souls back, to reunite them with bodies made of stone, is to venture into uncharted territory. Yet I'm teetering on the edge.

I should've broken that deal with Valeria before doing this; I shouldn't have risked it. I'm immortal which means I'll come back, without a soul albeit, but I'll be alive. However, with my life tethered to hers, Valeria might not be so lucky. It's never been tried. And though I could do this same process for her, there are rules. These people will never be able to leave the grounds of Grim's Keep. To do so, would rip their souls from these new bodies and shred them out of existence entirely.

I shouldn't have chanced this... But being tethered to Valeria is the only shot I have of saving my soul after this. It needs something to cling to while Griffin's fae blood heals it. Otherwise, the fragments that will be left when the spell is over will fade and be long gone before his blood has a chance to piece it back together.

It had to be this way.

The little dragon purrs like a cat as it climbs and curls into my lap, and I trace the edges of its wings with my gaze, letting the spell steal what it needs. With a final agonized cry, the last spirit stirs to life. Its gargoyle body lifts from the dewy ground and the magic in my veins sputters and flickers out, leaving me gasping. *Hollow.*

Pressing a gentle hand to my aching chest, a void spreads there, a darkness so deep, that no light can reach it. Reserves dangerously depleted, my strength gone. I stagger, climbing to my feet, and meet Griffin and Valeria's worried glances, the small dragon fizzling out at my feet.

"See, and you were worried. Piece of cak—" My knees buckle, every muscle going limp as the world spins. Griffin catches me, using his beast's speed to cross the space before I can slam into the unforgiving ground.

"Damn it, Asmo." He growls, lowering me into his lap.

"Is he going to die?" Valeria's voice is so calm, so warm, so *near.*

"No. I'm just hoping what I gave him was enough to regenerate his shadow."

I stare up at Griffin, too weak to speak, head loll back against his leg.

He shakes his head, lips pressed into a firm line. "Better safe than sorry." With a sharp jerk, he unsheathes his dagger and opens a vein. Without time to process what's happening, his wrist is pressed to my lips, the warm crimson liquid pouring into my mouth. I try to jerk away, but he holds me there, and I'm incapable of fighting him in this state.

His blood has a strange sweetness to it, clouding the metallic tang that it's usually accompanied by. It's an odd flavor that's distinctly fae, full of magic—of power. It makes my tongue tingle as it slips down my throat. Reluctantly, I give in, doing my best to tell myself it's wine. I can smell the crisp scent of his cologne, mixed with the earthy musk of the leaves the spell stirred along the forest floor.

Griffin brushes my hair out of my face, but his hand is so small, so *dainty*. Peeking an eye open, I find Valeria staring down at me, cradled in Griffin's lap. It was her hand I felt. Every place her fingers touch seems to vibrate with some sort of laden energy, and that smile…

Valeria's voice breaks through my fading consciousness. "You did it, Asmo," she whispers, continuing to brush the hair from my face. "You just have to hang on. Please don't kill us both."

A chuckle rumbles from deep within my chest, my head lolling with the effort of laughter. "Calm down, Starlight," I rasp, my voice barely audible against the deafening roar in my ears, the darkness closing in on my vision. I grip her hand as if it were my lifeline. In many ways, it is. Our blood bond pulsates deep in my middle, beckoning me to cling to it with every ounce of strength I have left. "It'll take a lot more than this to kill me. Monsters don't die so easily."

My eyelids flutter closed, tired of fighting. I should've broken our deal before I started the ritual. I shouldn't have risked her to save my soul, but a dark, twisted piece of me feared she'd leave, and I'm just starting to more than tolerate her presence.

A soft, angelic voice is in my ear, the warmth of her breath dancing over my face. "That's because monsters don't risk their lives to bring people back from the dead."

Her fingers stroke over my cheek, causing my heart to beat a smidge faster.

Then my consciousness slips away.

17

Valeria

Sitting here, in Asmo's room, the silence is thick, suffocating even. The domed glass ceiling over his bed reveals the dark night sky, riddled with twinkling lights of the crystals that hang up there, like stalactites off the ceiling of our world.

I'd never expected to see this room. Especially not alone with him, but the only thing filling that stagnant silence is the faint whispers of his snores.

At least he's breathing. No doubt about that.

It's a brutal reality that I've become entangled in somehow. All by living in an abandoned keep. Two days ago, I was worried about what I was going to eat, since I'd picked the berry bushes in the nearby woods dry. Now, I'm worried the man I've tethered my life to might kick the bucket.

Things have escalated far too quickly, and I'm not sure if I should be relieved to not be alone any more or worried I've gotten myself in over my head.

He's the Prince of Death… He was banished for killing everyone inside an entire castle. We're not talking about dozens, but hundreds of lives. Gone. Poof, like they never existed.

The velvet covered bench I dragged from the footboard to sit next to his bedside creaks as I shift my weight. I'm not even sure if I need to stay in this room, to stay near him, but I don't want to risk doing my job as the tether wrong. So, I've sat here, alone with my thoughts, staring at his beautifully masculine face for the better part of two hours. It's as if I've convinced myself that being here can prevent his soul from slipping away into the veil, like I have a say about it.

His lashes, dark as midnight, cast soft shadows on his cheeks. The steady slow rhythm of his chest rising and falling is hypnotic. I can't help but wonder what else about this deal he's kept from me or skillfully worded to hide the true implications. Our bond the deal made is invisible, but I can feel it every time I touch him, as tangible as the bench I'm sitting on. Though, it's oddly satisfying to be linked to the deadliest man alive. Mostly, because he has to ensure I stay this way, because just as I'm at his mercy of death, he's at mine. It's a feeling of safety that I'm not sure how to process.

Even in the woods, when his eyes turned to obsidian voids, I'd felt safe. The last time I'd seen him like that, it couldn't be more the opposite. I'd been pinned against the wall of this very keep, heart thundering in my chest. Scared enough to stab him.

I'd never done such a thing in my life. But in those woods, as he embraced his demon half to breathe life back into those lost souls, all I felt was a deep, gnawing need to ease his pain, to help him.

Griffin slips into the room, drawing my eyes. The door closes with a soft click behind him. There's a mischievous glint in those turquoise eyes of his, but I'm more concerned about the bucket in his hand. "Well, everyone is settled in, though it would appear being reborn had a bit of an effect on the ghosts' psyche. But the bright side is, I managed to summon that water you asked for."

"What do you mean?" I find my voice, returning my gaze to the steady rhythm of Asmo's chest. If this was all for nothing, I have a sharp, persistent feeling that he won't take it well when he wakes.

"Most have to learn how to speak again, but some are even having trouble understanding me. I've resorted to stick figure drawings for the last two hours." Griffin places the bucket of steaming water and the washcloth down beside the bench, then finds a seat in the upholstered armchair in the corner of the room, facing me.

I chuckle to myself. "It's better than it could be." I grab the rag, dipping it in the water and wringing it out. "Thank you for this. I doubt he'd appreciate waking up caked in mud."

Griffin raises an eyebrow, a smile playing at the corners of his lips. "You can play nursemaid if you want, but there's no way in hell I'm touching his little piggies. I've seen enough feet to last me a lifetime."

I give him a look, one eyebrow raised in silent question.

"The witches who kidnapped me forced me to do… *obscene* things. Let's just say they had peculiar tastes."

"Ah." I drag the cloth over Asmo's hand, wiping away the dirt from his skin. "So, this summoning thing, do you just make stuff with magic, or—"

"You have to know it exists. Think of it as calling an object to you, or teleporting to it. Only one creature in existence can make things out of nothing and that's the queen," he explains, leaning back in the chair. The druidic tattoos on his arms and chest glow faintly in the light of the moons. It's just barely visible from beneath his shirt, but those on his arms are impossible to miss. They're delicate swirls and symbols that weren't there earlier, as if they're only able to be seen in the moonlight.

Tilting my head, I dip my rag in the bucket again. “So, you happened to know exactly where a bucket of warm, clean water and rags was sitting? Where did they come from?”

“Solaria.” He cringes. “My dad takes a bath everyday around this time. He’ll be rather pissed to find it gone, but it is what it is.”

I pause, looking up at Griffin. "You stole your father's bath water?"

“He hadn’t got in it yet… I don’t think.” He pops his lips. “Regardless, all fifty gallons of it is currently in the bathtub downstairs.”

I can't help but laugh. "Only you could get away with stealing the Lord of Solaria's bath water."

“He’ll be mad but if he knew what it was for, he would’ve offered it willingly. My dad has a hero complex and despises the fact I don’t.” He smiles coyly, an amber bottle of wine appearing in his hand. Griffin uses his teeth to dislodge the cork.

“Well, you were a hero today.”

“Hah! I watched. If watching is a heroic act, then I should get that embroidered on a pillowcase.”

I snort, shaking my head as I clean Asmo’s face. “Please do.”

“So, you never told me the story,” Griffin prods. I’ve only known him for a day, but I’m already beginning to get the sense he enjoys gossip and putting his nose where it doesn’t belong.

“What story?” I feign ignorance, knowing damn well he’s referring to the conversation we started at dinner. Dipping the rag, I wring it out, the slosh of dirty water filling the silence around us.

“Of how you two met.” He nods towards Asmo.

"I um… I was stranded here and stumbled upon this place. Though, it didn't look anything like it does now. It was mostly destroyed, but it was a roof, and the wards kept the creatures in the woods away. The wall wasn't spelled, so the creatures that lived in the forest kept hunting me. I'd been here for a few weeks and Asmo just kind of showed up."

"Oh, and I'm sure he took having pests in his castle well," he rolls his eyes, his smile sincere yet tinged with the shadow of humor.

"About as well as he took to you mentioning how he ended up in the prison world."

"He hurt you?" Griffin's brow arches, his gaze drifting from the sleeping Asmo back to me.

"No. He demanded answers, and I was worried he would. In the elven islands, we're taught that demons are pretty much savage brutes without a shred of conscience. He'd ripped my necklace off my neck." I clutch the red crystal pendant, turning it over in my fingers. "I was powerless and panicked."

Griffin gives me a knowing smirk. "What did you do?"

"I stabbed him with his own dagger and ran."

Griffin tosses his head back, a laugh as divine as if it came from a god leaves his mouth. "You *did not.*"

"I did. A few hours later, he found me in the woods. I was going to steal my crystal back. To my surprise, he wanted to make a deal with me. I thought for sure the moment he caught me that I was dead. Of course, at the time, I didn't know that the deal consisted of tethering our lives. I thought we just couldn't kill each other without consequences. Even if I'd known, I might've still taken the deal he offered. I needed a place to live, and I was out of options."

"Well, it's been an eventful few days for you too then," Griffin observes, as matter-of-factly as one commenting on the weather.

"I suppose." Twisting my lips, I eye Griffin. He's examining his nails as if he was the one digging up bodies. "Though, my last few days didn't consist of doing obscene things with witch feet. That sounds sadistically worse." Unable to stop the smile from reaching my face, I watch him tense, then press his lips together and nod, as if he's giving me deserved credit.

"Ya, I suppose you're right." He lifts the bottle of wine to his lips, his Adam's apple bobbing as he takes a deep swig.

I turn my attention back to Asmo, dabbing gently at his face with the rag. "Will his shadow be okay? You're fae, you should be able to sense that, right?"

He scoots the chair closer, grabbing Asmo's hand and closing his eyes. "It's there. Weak as fuck, but there."

"It'll come back then?" My voice barely hides the worry as I clean Asmo's bare chest, the rag gliding over his numerous scars there.

"I hope. Asmodeus is more familiar with fae magic than I am. He's seen their magic up-close. I'm just sort of following his lead. My fae blood comes from my mom, but she doesn't have magic, just her beastly alter ego. So, everything I've learned has mostly been through him or trial and error."

"What about your dad? He couldn't help you?"

"He's a druid, so the magic is different."

I nod, dropping the rag into the bucket with a wet plop. The rest of the dirt will have to wait until Asmo wakes.

"What happens to demons that lose their shadow?" The question slips out before I can stop it, revealing a fear I didn't realize I've been harboring until now.

Griffin's eyes darken, his mouth twisting. “They lose the ability to feel emotions, and the idea of someone like Asmo losing the ability to feel is bloody terrifying. So, let's hope for all of our sakes, he doesn't.”

“What? You think he'll be evil or something?” Leaning against the bed, I prop my elbow on the satin covers and rest my head in my hand.

Griffin shakes his head, white hair falling over one eye. “Not evil, but after living in that prison realm and serving my grandfather, he's been forced to do some wretched things. Things that broke the part of him that determines right from wrong.” His eyes take on a distant glaze. “Eventually, you kill enough that the value of life becomes non-existent. Sometimes I think the only reason he thinks twice is because Alice will be mad at him.” He flexes his eyes as if to emphasize his point. “He cares about what she thinks of him. Without emotions, he wouldn't.”

Alice. The Queen of the Seven Realms. I've heard of her dozens of times since I've been here, yet barely anything about the demon king.

“Why is he so close to her, but not his brother?”

Griffin's eyebrows furrow. “What makes you say that?”

“He's mentioned her, so have you, but not really anything about him.” I don't dare meet Griffin's eyes. Earlier, he was convinced I was jealous. And maybe he's a tad bit right. Not jealous that he's close to her, but because I yearn to be close to someone like that, to have someone care about me wholeheartedly, the way he does her.

“Asmo and Alice were trapped in the prison realm together for a time. She went there to save my father, and the two of them worked together to survive. He's trusted her with his life ever since. He didn't even meet his brother until after they both escaped. By then, he'd already forged a friendship with Alice."

"Yeah, but the boundary around the prison world came down two hundred years ago. I've only been alive for twenty-two years and I've formed friendships." *Sort of.* As much as one can while being the Duchess of the Elven Islands, and the daughter of a dictator. "Asmo's had time to do the same with his brother."

Griffin snorts. "In case you haven't noticed, he prefers to be alone or with the dead. The only living folk he claims to stand are Alice or children. With everyone else, it's like he doesn't know how to socialize with them. You'll see what I mean at some point if you stay here."

"He attacked you in the woods. I hardly think that's someone you leave unattended with your children." I scowl at him.

"I've done far worse to him." Griffin traces a jagged scar slicing down Asmo's chest.

I follow his finger down a jagged scar, spanning from the base of Asmo's throat down his sternum and across his lower rib on his right side. It's wide and raised in stitch marks but everywhere the thread touches his skin is melted like the sutures were on fire.

"You did that?" I ask, unsure if I want the real answer, but needing it nonetheless.

"Unfortunately. My beast took control for the first time and Asmo was the only one brave enough, besides my very pregnant mother, to follow me into the Enchanted Forest. It takes a special person to stand up to a fae beast."

I shudder, picturing the gruesome wound. "Surprised he lived. It looks deep."

"It was. I flayed him wide open and can still hear his wail, from when it happened." Griffin twists his lips, trapping them between his teeth a moment before continuing. "Remembering that sound is what has allowed me to control the shift, to return to myself at will when my beast seems insistent on being in control and it's what brought me back that day. I'd used my magic to sew him up," he says, tracing those melted marks.

"I can't believe that didn't kill him." It looks like it was deep. Then again, most of his scars do.

"It did. I was in the woods for hours, bawling my eyes out before he came back. I'd thought I ended the fool for good." A brittle chuckle escapes him as he glances up at the domed glass ceiling. "So, if he can deal with my outbursts, I'll happily deal with his. I'll be whatever he needs, because he's always there for me." He smirks, a light returning to his eyes. "It doesn't mean I won't give him shit for it, though."

"It sounds like stupidity, more than bravery to me." I chew the inside of my lip, fidgeting with the fabric of Asmo's blanket.

"This is the mainland, pretty girl, where monsters, demons, and all the creatures that go bump in the night, exist. Sometimes things are out of our control, and we need those we love around to bring us back to reality or save us from ourselves."

18

Valeria

The soft glow of the hell flame casts flickering shadows across the room as I lie curled up on one side of Asmo's bed, my body cocooned in rich, heavy blankets. The world's deadliest demon sleeps soundlessly beside me, his chest rising and falling in a steady rhythm.

It's been three days. And the only reason I know is because it was dark when Griffin laid him in here, and the hell flame is losing its glow, meaning it will be night soon. And night only comes once every three days in this realm.

Has it truly been that long?

All that time and Asmo hasn't even twitched a finger. I've had to check to ensure his heart is still beating in that scarred, thick chest of his, and if it weren't for the faint hint of his snores now, and the deep rise and fall of chest, I likely would again.

I don't know what will happen if he doesn't wake up, or worse, *succumbs*. Will my light simply go out? Will I be torn from my body and dragged into the veil with him, or will I spontaneously combust?

For that alone, I haven't left his side. I've lived in this room, breathing the same air. Griffin has brought me food and books to keep me company, but the more time passes, the deeper the worry settles into my bones.

I can't even be mad at him for attempting such a thing while my life is tethered to his, because he saved all those people. People my flesh and blood killed. They deserve to live and if it means my life ends along with him to right the wrong my father has committed, then so be it. It's still scary as hell, though, and all I can hope for is my end to be painless.

"Valeria," Griffin calls softly from the doorway, his voice soft and by far the quietest I've ever heard it before. "It's time to get up."

A reluctant groan escapes my lips as I rise to a sitting position in the bed, dragging the thick blankets around me to stave off the chill that wraps around my arms the moment they're exposed to the morning air. Ears twitching slightly, I rub the remnants of sleep from my eyes. "I can't leave. If I leave, he might not get his shadow back."

"Trust me," Griffin says, strolling into the room to stand next to Asmo's side of the bed. He reaches out, fingers brushing Asmo's hand as he closes his eyes in concentration. "His shadow is regenerating. He'll be whole again soon."

"But why hasn't he woken up?" My voice is barely above a whisper, my throat constricting and managing to become even drier than it was a second ago.

If it's not his soul keeping him comatose, then what is?

Griffin shrugs, the action far too casual for the gravity of our situation, but then again he seems to be casual about everything. "Why does Asmo do anything?" He sighs deeply, sinking next to me on the bed. "This kind of magic doesn't just harm the soul; it drains your body and pushes its limits. He's healing internally, but he's very much alive, just needs time."

"You know that for sure?" Griffin's eyes dart away from mine. *I didn't think so.* "How much time?" I search his face for answers, but he's schooled it, revealing nothing.

He weighs his head side to side. "I wish I knew." Slapping his hands on his knees, he stands, offering me a hand, a silent demand for me to heed his earlier order to get up. "What I do know is that bathing, changing your clothes, and eating a proper meal won't kill him."

Casting one last glance at Asmo's sleeping form, I reluctantly place my hand in Griffin's, but I make no effort to get up. "I don't want to leave him. He shouldn't wake alone."

"He'll be fine, Valeria. He likes being alone." Griffin squeezes my hand reassuringly, then jerks me from the bed. "Let him rest, but in the meantime, you need to take care of yourself." He leads me from the room, my feet fumbling to keep up with his long legs and fast pace. It's like he knows I might change my mind and barricade myself in the room if he wastes a single second.

"A bath and some fresh air will do you some good." He opens my bedroom door and pushes me inside. "I'll meet you downstairs for breakfast." Griffin props his hands on his hips. "Now, can I trust you to take it from here, or do you need me to watch?" His eyes drop down my body, a wicked smirk tugging at the corners of his lips. "I'm not opposed to it."

"No, I got it," I say, resisting the urge to look through Asmo's doorway. It doesn't feel right to leave him, but if Griffin says it's safe… He knows more about this than I do.

He clasps his hands together, a mischievous glint in his eyes. "Good girl, now hop to it. The chef has prepared a meal."

"The chef?" I ask skeptically.

"Indeed," Griffin nods, the corners of his mouth twitching like he's tampering down his amusement. "As it turns out, one of the ghosts Asmo brought back was the chef here, and he might only be able to communicate via charades, but he seems to know his way around the kitchen."

Before I can respond, he's halfway down the spiral staircase, and I resign myself to getting cleaned up. Entering my room, I find a gargoyle woman clutching a broom, her movements jerky and uncoordinated as if she isn't quite used to her new body. She nearly drops the broom at the sight of me, her stone eyes wide with surprise. For a moment, we simply stare at each other, blinking, unsure how to proceed.

A strange sense of unease settles over me as I study her, spotting the simple apron wrapped around her rocky body and her stone features resembling what I assume was her human face.

"Um, hello," I say, stepping closer with caution. "Thank you, but I don't need a maid. I can clean up after myself," I tell her, trying to sound polite and attempting to give her a smile, but finding it harder than it should be. I can't seem to muster the energy.

Maybe Griffin was right. I need to eat something more than the small snacks he's brought upstairs—a real meal.

The gargoyle woman continues to gawk at me, then utters a single, unintelligible, "Eep."

"Is that your name?" My brows furrow together.

The poor gargoyle woman looks like she wants to flee, but instead, offers an uncoordinated shake of her head, the stones of her body rattling and grinding from the movement.

"I'm not sure I understand."

"EEEEp," she says again, dragging it out this time.

All I can do is give her a blank stare.

The gargoyle woman huffs, seemingly bored, and says it again as if the third time's the charm. Except it's not, and she juts out a stone tongue at me, fast and sharp, like a lizard catching flies.

I suck in a breath, put my fingertips over my mouth to hide my surprise. For a moment, all I can do is lean in, then out, and in again, attempting to make sense of what the hell just happened.

This must be what Griffin meant when he said some are having difficulty communicating.

"Okay, let's try something else," I suggest, racking my brain for an alternative approach. The gargoyle woman taps her foot, crossing her thick arms, her impatience growing more apparent by the second. After several failed attempts to act out that I want her to leave, I give up.

With a sigh, I give her a wide berth and shuffle towards the bathroom. After bathing and changing into a comfortable yet elegant dress, one that billows in the sleeves and shoulders, the length stopping just past my knees, I reluctantly make my way downstairs to join Griffin.

Stepping into the dining hall, I find him lounging at the table, the same spot he sat in before. Only this time, he has a pipe in hand, his feet propped up on an empty chair, and he's focused on the book in his hand. There's a steaming cup of coffee before him, and another waiting for me across the table.

"Ah, there you are," Griffin says, taking note of my presence. He whistles appreciatively, his eyes trailing over my body, but it's not a hungry gaze. It's more clinical, like he's evaluating my well-being. "Asmo is going to regret not seeing you like this. I bet if you waltzed into his room and spun around a few times, he'd miraculously rise from his coma." He pauses, eyeing me one last time before returning to his book. "I would, that's for sure."

"Thank you." A blush creeps up my neck and floods through my cheeks.

Griffin arches a white eyebrow skeptically. "For what?"

"Your compliment. It's nice to feel pretty for a change, especially after the last few days."

"Pretty?" Griffin snorts, clearly amused. "You don't get complements often?" He chuckles, turning the page. "I highly doubt that."

"No," I admit, dropping my gaze as I find my chair. "In elven culture, dark hair is frowned upon. Silver is a sign of pureblood and being highborn."

Griffin tsks his tongue, shaking his head. "Well, just another reason to hate them, then." My smile falters, but I can't argue with him.

Since coming here, I've felt more included than ever before. I haven't been shunned to exist in my rooms away from where the public can see me, nor have I been grimaced at, like I'm something foul. I'm beginning to question if those in the Elven Islands were ever truly my people or just a place I was born into. Ever since my mother died, since she brought me back and my hair turned dark and my eyes green, the elves haven't exactly been accepting of me.

Carefully, I grasp the warm coffee cup, savoring its rich aroma. For a moment, I allow myself to enjoy the simple pleasure of it as it warms my throat, my chest, my stomach.

Griffin looks at me over the edge of his book, pipe smoke coiling from his lips. "You know, you don't need to dress up to be pretty. Here, we don't care what color your hair is. You were beautiful yesterday, even in dingy clothes you exhumed bodies in, just as much as you are now."

I don't know how to react. For a moment, I don't think I breathe as I let his words sink in.

"I'm just saying, if wearing frilly dresses makes you feel beautiful, then go for it, but don't feel like you have to. I'm still going to enjoy the view, and so will Asmodeus, except he'll be more secretive about his gawking."

A smile pulls at my lips, and I do my best to hide it with my mug. "Well, thank you for clearing that up."

"Don't mention it," he says, grinning as he swings his feet off the table. "Now, let's see what culinary delights our ghostly chef has prepared for us." Flexing his brow he sets his book down. "The good thing about rock people is I can hear them from a mile away."

The doors to the dining hall swing open, revealing the gargoyle chef followed by two more stone people carrying covered silver trays. The scent of roasted meat wafts toward us, and my mouth waters involuntarily.

They place the trays before us, and I can't help but wonder if these ones can speak. Slowly, they lift the silver covers with a rusty, stone-grinding flourish. I brace myself for something bizarre, but instead find an artfully arranged plate of what looks like a scone and a whole, uncooked potato.

I glance at Griffin and smile, trying not to giggle at the way the stone people strut from the table, toward the chef. It's not something that should be funny, but their movements are so stiff, like stone soldiers.

The chef speaks, hands laced behind his back as he looks between us, but there are no true words that leave his mouth. Instead, I hear a string of random sounds. "Eep, mag, dedoo, baa." It's utterly incomprehensible. My brows furrow as I stare at him, desperately trying to make sense of it all.

The chef turns to Griffin and flaps his bent arms like a bird taking flight, then pecks the air before pretending to take a bite out of an imaginary apple.

Griffin clears his throat. "I think it's chicken of some sort, and I'm not sure about the rest, but he wants us to eat it." With that, the chef leaves, two other gargoyles following behind him. The one leading up the rear trips into the other, who tumbles into the chef and a string of sounds follow, and I can only imagine them being their version of curse words. I stifle a giggle as they scramble to leave.

Griffin and I eye our plates warily, poking at the scone only to find meat and other not so normal things inside.

I grimace. "Do you think it's safe?"

Griffin lifts what looks like a wing or a leg to his nose, sniffing it before frowning. "That's a good question. He hasn't cooked in over two hundred years, so..." He trails off, still scrutinizing the whatever that is he pulled from his scone. "I'm going to say no."

I bark out a laugh, quickly covering my mouth to smother it. Without looking, Griffin summons two apples out of midair and hands one to me.

"It's the thought that counts," I say, trying to defend the chef's efforts.

Griffin gives me a look, silently stating that he begs to differ. "Until it ends with food poisoning and praying to the porcelain god," he retorts.

"The *what?"* I give him a weary look, poking my fork at the raw potato.

I've never heard of one of the old gods being made of porcelain, and certainly not one that had divinity over it.

"I mean the toilet, love," he sighs, rolling his eyes. "But we're at a table, and I'm trying very hard not to be vulgar."

Pursing my lips, I nod, then a bite of the apple. It's crisp and juicy, a far cry from whatever monstrosity lies on my plate, but it'll do.

19

Valeria

I stand beside Griffin, arms crossed as I watch the three gargoyles attempt, yet again, to communicate their request. So far, it's been a mix of stuttering words and animated gestures.

Two days have passed since Griffin convinced me to eat breakfast with him and leave Asmo's side. To my luck, it hasn't made his condition any worse, but he hasn't changed much either. The most we've seen from our darling lord is a subtle shift of his head.

"Is it… dancing?" Griffin guesses, scratching his chin thoughtfully as he observes the stone creatures gyrating and hip-thrusting with surprising enthusiasm.

"I don't know if that's what I'd call dancing," I say, unable to suppress the giggle that bubbles out at me as the stone men grind on one another. "It is… Well, you know." I bounce my eyebrows.

"What?" Griffin gapes at me. "Do you mean sex?"

I give him a slight nod, cringing as the gargoyles keep going at it.

"Well, is she right? Are you fools wanting to get laid?" Griffin visibly cringes, his eyes dropping to their naked stone bodies. "I think the three of you are lacking the necessary parts for that."

The stone men groan in unison, one palming his face hard enough to chip his eyebrow.

“Not that then,” I say, pursing my lips. “Could you write it?”

Griffin shakes his head. “Tried that the first day. We’re out of pencils. Their meaty hands broke them all.” He glares at them as if it’s their fault.

“All right, then try again.” I wave them on, pulling out a chair from one of the various round tables in the throne room and taking a seat.

The gargoyle chef shakes his head, then waves to the other two, as if he’s telling them to assume the position. Though the gargoyles have tried to get better at speaking and have impressively improved their charades game, it’s still painstaking to communicate.

Don’t even get me started on Eep, the one I’ve all but dubbed my lady’s maid since she seems to only be interested in cleaning my room. I’ve learned that arguing with her gets nowhere and have settled on letting her do as she pleases.

The gargoyles jump around, the marble floors shaking from the movement, then two of them proceed to tango, while one steals Griffin’s wine bottle out of his hand and dumps the crimson liquid all down the front of him, since he can’t swallow once his stone mouth is full.

"Wait! Is it a party?" Griffin jumps up, eyes bright.

The gargoyle chef nods vigorously, his stone features contorted with relief. He leans against one of the round tables as if all of this dancing has taken it out of him and the wooden surface tips under the strain of his weight.

"Well, why didn't you say so?" Griffin grins, waggling his eyebrows at me. "I'm always up for some good shenanigans."

“I’m sure you are.” I roll my eyes and point out the obvious. "It's not a good idea to invite company here when the Lord of Grim’s Keep is in a coma and the only other high standing individual can't leave the boundary wall."

Griffin's smile falters, and he concedes with a nod. "I suppose you’re right. We can be ready for it when he wakes up, then.”

I hesitate, considering it. When I can’t come up with another excuse to say no, I nod slowly, giving in to Griffin's infectious enthusiasm.

"Perfect," Griffin declares, a mischievous glint in his eyes. "We'll be ready with libations and the chef can make all the food, so the others can sniff their way into heaven and happiness." He pauses, jumping up to his feet for dramatic effect, "We can have live music and dancing in this very throne room."

I hold up a hand, stopping him. "Asmo doesn't like people. The last thing he'll want to do after waking up from a coma is cater."

Griffin snorts, unfazed by my objection. "Who said anything about people? These are gargoyles.” He pokes the chef in the stomach.

“I mean it. No one besides those living inside this keep or those that sleep in boulders in the front lawn comes,” I say, putting my foot down.

"Great! No problem." Griffin grins from ear to ear. "If anything is worthy of celebrating, it's Asmo's awakening." The gargoyle chef gives him a pointed look, and Griffin quickly adds, "And the ghosts coming back to life, of course. Being dead for two hundred years is no easy feat."

With a flourish of his hands, Griffin conjures a large wooden crate in the middle of the throne room.

I jolt as it slams into the floor, eyebrows furrowed. "What the hell is that?"

"My party supplies," he answers nonchalantly. "You know, the basics: booze, drugs, streamers, some flutes…"

I gape at him, wondering what kind of parties he's been attending—or throwing for that matter. But instead of dwelling on it, I join him as he begins hanging up decorations in the throne room and delegating tasks to the gargoyles of the keep.

"Okay, I'll admit it," I say as we work side by side, a smile tugging at my lips. "This might actually be fun."

"See?" Griffin grins. "I knew you'd come around."

HOURS LATER, THE PLACE has been fully decorated, complete with long tables that the chef can fill with food, the piano from upstairs placed in the corner of the throne room, and all the various instruments that came in Griffin's box beside it.

Griffin reaches into his box, grabbing two large bowls out. "Here, pour these in one and the other will be for punch. Put them on the long table."

"You could say please," I say under my breath, doing as he suggests. "What is punch?"

Griffin stills as if I offended a god. "It's like wine, but more of a community thing. Everyone can fill up a goblet, and sometimes other things are added in."

"Like what?" I ask, trying to figure out what you add to wine.

"Well, if you ever go to a celebration in Hell Hold, never drink the punch. Lust, one of the demons there, likes to spike it. That shit makes you go mad and next thing you know you're naked in an orgy and have no idea how you got there." Griffin shivers as if ridding himself of a mental image.

"I see… Isn't lust a sin demon?"

"Yes." He doesn't look at me while he takes up his make-shift sign. In large bold letters, he's painted the words, 'Welcome back from the dead' on a banner he made from a spare sheet.

"I thought sin demons can only force the sins they embody through their tears." I pause, refraining from looking over my shoulder at him, even though it's taking him an awfully long time to answer.

"You'd be correct," he finally says.

"So, you're telling me lust is crying into the punch bowl at these social gatherings?"

"Yes. Sometimes he does it on purpose, or others someone has coerced him to. You'd be surprised what mentioning dead hellhounds would do to the man. Blubbers like a baby every time."

I turn, hands on my hips. "Please tell me you didn't make the man cry to start your *shenanigans.*"

"My lips are sealed, but it's okay to say the word sex you know. You don't have to be a prude about it."

"I am not a prude."

"You didn't say the word earlier, when the gargoyles were all but humping each other. You didn't say orgy now. That sounds an awful lot like prudish behavior."

"Think what you want," I say, pouring the silver packets into the bowl. "What are these?" I grab one, holding it up at eye-level for a better look. It's silver and square, though something round is inside of it.

Griffin is beside me in an instant. "Come to think of it, I don't think those will be needed here. I doubt gargoyles can procreate." He steals the bowl from me, popping it out of existence. I don't have to say anything. My thoughts must be written all over my face because Griffin groans. "Must I explain everything? They're condoms. They keep you from creating little yous when you have sex. See? This is exactly what I meant." He mouths the word *prude* and twirls away.

"We just have magic," I say with a shrug. "Every woman and man drinks a potion when they come of age and until you go through marriage nuptials, it makes it impossible. At least that's how it is for highborn elves. I'm not sure about the rest."

"Must be nice," Griffin says, attitude lacing every word. Though, when I turn around, I find him seated on a gargoyle's shoulders, trying to secure a corner of the banner he couldn't reach from the table he'd been standing on a moment ago.

"Griffin," I snap, watching him teeter precariously on the gargoyle's broad shoulders. "Get down before you end up in a coma, too."

He gives me a lazy look over his shoulder. "You wound me—" The boulder-like creature he's sitting on whirls to face me, the movement so abrupt that Griffin nearly loses his balance. He clings to the gargoyle's round head. His turquoise eyes widen as he stares past me, raising his arms triumphantly in the air. "The lord has risen!" he shouts.

Confused, I scowl at him, face scrunched. Slowly, I turn around to find Asmo leaning against the doorframe of the throne room, looking very much alive. My heart leaps in my chest and relief floods through me. Over the last week, I've gotten close enough to Griffin that I wouldn't hesitate to hug him if he had been the one in a coma. But with Asmo, I'm not quite sure how to react or what's acceptable.

"Just so you know," I say, pointing a thumb over my shoulder at Griffin, "all of this was his idea."

Asmo smirks, pushing off the doorframe and sauntering into the room. I can't help but study him, basking in the sight of him awake and well. His dark amber eyes are filled with amusement. Asmo's smirk widens as he takes a step into the room, his eyes flickering between Griffin and me.

"I see you two have grown closer," he says, damp strands of his blue-black hair clinging to the nape of his neck. He must've bathed before coming out of his room to find us.

"I tolerate him, if that's what you're asking," I tease, glancing at Griffin who wobbles precariously on the gargoyle's shoulders. My heart skips a beat when he jerks, clinging to the stone man's head again. When I turn back, I find Asmo still staring at me with those warm, entrancing eyes. "What is it?" I pat my face, wondering if Griffin had managed to stick something on it during their party preparations. "Did I have something—"

Asmo chuckles, shaking his head. The sheer sound of that laugh makes me freeze in place. "No, Starlight. It's just nice to see you smile."

My cheeks flush and I dip my head. "Well, it's nice to see you out of bed."

Griffin snorts from his perch. "Just wait until you play charades with your ghost friends. It's a blast."

Asmo's brow furrows, and as if in answer to his questioning stare, the gargoyle Griffin is sitting on tries to say *party* but fails miserably, resulting in a series of P sounds and clicking.

20

Valeria

Asmo's eyes flicker toward the banner behind me, and his face falls into that emotionless stone. Even the gargoyles with their animated statue faces show more expression than he has right now. My stomach drops, worry settling deep, an iron weight settling on my shoulders.

No… Gods, I knew I shouldn't have entertained this idea.

He doesn't want a party, and I don't blame him, but I didn't realize how much I was looking forward to it until now. Seeing his face… I shouldn't have gotten my hopes up. Judging from the dark circles beneath his eyes, I'm surprised he's not still resting. He might've woken from days long slumber, but he looks like he hasn't slept a wink.

"You're throwing a party? For me?" His voice carries a note of surprise, mingled with a reluctance that makes me want to blurt out an apology.

I don't, though.

Griffin's face falls too, likely noticing the same shift in Asmo I have, but the disappointment etched in his normally bright eyes has me straightening my shoulders. Standing up tall, I plaster on my biggest and brightest smile. Maybe I can save this—for both of them. For me.

"Yes, we're throwing a party. Just us and the gargoyles. No company. Griffin has been preparing the keep like a madman, trying to ensure every twinkling light in this place sparkles just right for when you woke up. And now you're here, so…" I trail off, turning in place to eye the chef. "I think it's time you shuffle off to the kitchen and prepare that spread you talked about. All the food you and your friends desire to sniff." I lend Griffin a hand as the gargoyle sets him down. "And you, better get to work on that punch."

Griffin's face doesn't change as his eyes meet mine. He knows as much as I do that Asmo isn't interested in a party and it guts me straight to my core. He put in all this work, but I won't let it be wasted. That's a hill I'll die on and I'll save it myself if I have to.

Elves are known for their parties, though in our culture, it's usually ball gowns and wine, and noble families meeting so the younger, available suitors can promenade. And seeing as I'm the only unmarried female born to the original families at the moment, it kept me busy. Though I enjoyed the dancing and singing and music, it'll be nice to do so on my own terms and not because there's a line of people waiting to talk my ears off.

It never really made sense to me, seeing as my father had the final say in who I was to marry. He never once asked if there was someone who interested me, so they should've been trying to swoon him, but those parties were some of the few times I was allowed to leave the left wing of the Vanderlyth castle.

I'd begun to look forward to them, and though most of the conversations were filled with lies in an attempt to make my knees weak, it was socialization—*civilization*—that didn't just involve the maids and servants. Especially since, in recent years, they often got in trouble if I distracted them from their work. I didn't want them punished for my sake and decided to leave them be.

So, my days were filled with learning magic and everything there is to know from the books in the castle library. It's not like I was imprisoned, but I knew the likelihood of me getting to see the world was slim. If not for my father being embarrassed of me, then because my future husband would be the Elf Lord some day. He'd be the next in line and therefore, neither of us would be allowed to leave the islands. It protected the succession of our family's position.

Those parties were the only thing I was allowed to attend for that reason alone. My brother is dead, and I was the only heir. Losing me would put our entire family's legacy at risk.

Call it what you want, but a small part of me is glad they think I'm dead. Being sealed away like some breakable doll, having to be perfect all the time to make up for my pitfalls, isn't a life I want to live.

And since washing up on that beach, my life has been nothing but eventful. I survived with knowledge I'd learned in the library, stabbed a demon lord, helped bring back the dead…

I deserve this party. Griffin deserves this party, and Asmo might not think so, but he damn well deserves this party, too. The hell if I'm going to let all this work go to waste.

"I'm flattered, truly, but—" Asmo starts, but I hold up a hand, silencing him.

"No buts. This is happening. You can attend, or you can sleep, but this isn't just for you. You're just the excuse we needed. The gargoyles are alive because you brought them back. They want to celebrate that. So, let them celebrate you."

His gaze lingers on me, then shifts to Griffin and the gargoyle chef. I don't think either of them blink as they patiently wait for a yes or no.

"A celebration of life, then," Asmo says, more to himself than to us. "It's been a long time since there's been anything resembling a celebration here." There's a wistfulness in his tone, a longing for a past perhaps not as burdened by the weight of his responsibilities. Or maybe his actions and convictions… I can't tell.

Griffin jumps, fisting the air as he flashes a smile that's all teeth—pointed fangs and all. "That's what I said!" He gestures broadly, to the gargoyles who had assisted in the preparations. "But it was their idea. We just assisted."

Asmo's smile is slow to return, but when it does, it's hesitant. "You best make that punch strong then," he concedes, his gaze sweeping over the room's transformation. "And I won't promise to be down here long."

Stepping closer, I'm acutely aware of the tension that lines his frame, the rigidness that's overcome his spine, the flutter of the muscles in his jaw as if he's grinding his teeth, though his tone suggests otherwise. "No promises necessary. You do what you can and if you're still tired, we understand," I say softly, hoping to reassure him. "The Lady of Grim's Keep will ensure the rest is taken care of."

There's a moment, brief and fragile, where Asmo's guard seems to lower, his eyes meeting mine with a vulnerability that takes my breath away. "I suppose I chose well then," he says, bowing his head as if he's in the presence of royalty. "I'm holding you to that, though."

Griffin claps a hand on my shoulder, drawing Asmo's eyes. It's a welcome reprieve from the intensity of the moment. I'm not sure how I would've responded, anyway.

"Let's get this party started!" Griffin claps his hands and the instruments in the corner rise all at once. With an elegant twirl of his wrists, they begin playing all on their own, a melody of violins and flutes, upbeat but still classical enough to formally dance to if one wished.

"We're doing this right now?" I arch a brow, dropping my gaze to the floor. I should change into a ball gown, maybe put my hair up but that would take at least an hour and I'd likely have to convince Eep to help me lace up the back of my dress. It's the only pitfall of my closet and I was lucky enough that the corset strings were in the front of the dress I learned that with. Maybe I could get it to make one with the corset in the front—

"Stop overthinking it," Griffin says, playfully tugging on the braid in my hair. "Gods, with the strength of the anxiety wafting off you, I'd think you were the queen."

I force myself to meet his gaze, unsure of how long I've been zoned out on the floor, letting my mind spiral. "I should change." Brow furrowed, I mindlessly spin on my heels, ready to head upstairs, but he grips my elbow and tugs me back before I make it more than a step away.

"No, you don't. Remember what I said the other day at breakfast?"

I pause, letting the conversation return to the forefront of my memory. He'd told me I don't need to dress up to be pretty, but this is different. This is an occasion—even though no visitors are present—that a duchess, much less a lady of the house, should be dressed up for.

Nodding, I drag in a deep breath, trying to steady myself before I have to speed change.

"Good, then you'll understand when I say that you look fine. It's just your friends here." He arches a white brow, crossing his arms.

"Sorry..." I'm not sure why I apologize. He's the one putting his nose where he shouldn't.

Griffin pats me on the cheek, then bobs his head to the beat of the violin, high stepping backward. "Now, if you'll excuse me, I have punch to make, and Asmodeus owes you a dance considering you all but starved yourself living at his bedside the last few days."

No... Why did he have to put it that way?

"Please tell me he's lying." I can feel the power rippling off Asmo, though the currents that slide over my skin aren't as strong as they usually are. Another sign he's still healing and likely should be in bed and not feeding my insecurities, let alone my desires of feeling normal.

Clenching my teeth together into an awkward straight-lined smile, I go stick straight, turning in a tight circle to face him. "I wish I could."

"Why? I would've been fine." His brows knit together, and he's close enough that I can see the faint wrinkle that forms between them.

"You told me I was the tether. I knew you would survive, but I didn't want you to lose your soul because I didn't stay close enough." Now that I've said it out loud, to him of all people, it sounds stupid.

I expect him to tell me as much, but instead, the corner of his mouth ticks up and he mumbles a simple. "Thank you."

"Er... Um... You're welcome." I curtsey, remembering who he is.

I just demanded the Prince of Death—the Prince of the entire fucking Seven Realms—to attend a ball. I've had days to wrap my head around who he is, ever since Griffin spilled his secret during the ritual. Yet, as I stare at his beautifully lethal face, he doesn't look like royalty. He looks like a man who's seen some shit and is in desperate need of a nap… and possibly an extra large glass of wine.

Asmo offers a nod, the shadow of hesitance still present but tempered by a glow in his eyes that seems so much brighter than I remember it being. They're vibrant amber, like flames have been trapped inside them, flickering and licking and dancing in the light. Beautiful isn't a strong enough word for what he is. I'm not sure a word exists to describe him.

He takes a step forward, the smirk on his face growing wider. "Well, then… Would the Lady of Grim's Keep offer me a dance?"

Reality crashes into me. "You want me to ask you?"

Asmo presses his lips together, ducking his head a bit. It's a look a child would use to get out of trouble, and something tells me, he's used it hundreds if not thousands of times. "If I'm honest, you terrify me, and I'm not sure if you're the kind of lady who wants to be asked to dance, or if you're the kind of lady who prefers to do the asking."

"The Prince of the Seven Realms, scared of me?" I can't help but smile, holding a hand over my heart as if I've been wounded.

"You did stab me, if I recall."

"Oh, right…" I drop my hand, casting my gaze away as I purse my lips.

His finger crooks beneath my chin, his boots heavy against the marble floors as he steps closer, tipping my face up to his. "Don't look sad about that. It's a compliment. I can't say there are many alive that have managed to nick my skin, let alone wound me. It was impressive."

"Impressive? Lucky is more like it. Surely, you were distracted, and I just happened to act at the right time. I don't know the first thing about using a dagger or sword or any weapon, really. I'm not even sure I could punch someone if my life depended on it." With a scoff, I attempt to turn away, but he drags my face back to his.

"I was distracted," he says, his eyes flicking over my face. "But we can work on the rest of that. The Lady of Grim's Keep should know how to protect herself, in case I'm not around to do it for her. And let's be honest, Griffin is deadly in beast form, but I'm not sure how great he'd be under pressure. If the place was under attack, he'd go for the wine cellar and barricade himself inside."

I chuckle, Asmo echoing me.

The music plays even though Griffin has left, the chef too. We're alone—though, it won't be for long. If I believed the things I was taught, I'd be trembling in the spot beneath the gaze of the deadliest demon to live, but it's not fear that has me shaking. It's nerves.

My body is teeming with them, vibrating with spark after rogue spark. It's like every piece of me is panicking at the thought of him hovering so close, with his lips mere inches away from mine and the desire to know what they feel like. What they taste like. To know if I was right in my dream.

"So, will you dance with me?" His breath blankets my cheeks, and I'm suddenly aware of every rise and fall of my chest—of his.

"I... Yes, I'd like that very much," I say, my voice steady despite the rapid beat of my heart.

Asmo takes my hand, threading our fingers together with such gentleness that I'm in awe of the contrast between that touch and the firmness of his hand sliding over the small of my back, bringing my body to his.

The hesitance, the unsettled restlessness that I saw in him earlier is long gone, replaced by a man so warm, with a smile that's kind and sincere. It's a smile I'm beginning to enjoy more than I care to admit, that makes my heart flutter every time I see it.

The gentle glow of the orbs overhead, mixed with the ambient light Griffin arranged around the throne room, casts beautiful shadows over his face, highlighting every feature, from his strong, sharp jaw, to the beautiful curve of his eyebrows, and the amber eyes they frame.

"I wasn't sure about this… about any of it," he confesses as we sway gently to the music. "But I find myself grateful for the distraction, for the chance to forget, if only for a moment."

His honesty, raw and unguarded, strikes a chord within me, a pang of curiosity filling my mind in seconds. "Forget what?" I ask, my voice barely above a whisper.

"The things I saw while I was asleep. It was odd, like dreaming but so lifelike. It took me a while to realize it wasn't reality, but a nightmare." Asmo squeezes our joined hand a bit tighter, and where my hand rests near his neck, I have the sudden urge to play with the loose strands of his hair, to comfort him in a way I don't understand.

"What was the nightmare of?" My heart leaps the moment the question leaves my lips. He probably doesn't want to talk about it. I shouldn't have asked—

"Of being back in the Realm of Monsters. In my dream, I was still the dungeon warden in Solaria, serving the mad king. It's odd, even now I can still feel the weight of the enchanted cuff he forced on me. It drained my magic, so he could take and give whatever he pleased. He never let me forget that it could kill me in the span of him mumbling a single word." His eyes drop, staring at the slim space between our bodies as we sway.

"That sounds terrible." I shake my head. "I can't imagine what that must've been like. I'm sorry you had to relive that."

He lets out a "Hah," and traps his bottom lip between his teeth a moment before meeting my eyes. "It's not my ideal dream." A silent moment passes before he says, "Did you sleep in my room, too? In my bed?"

I stiffen, my feet ceasing to move, but I don't back away. "I um, I did. Yes. The chair is comfy, but I nodded off in it and it hurt my neck. I didn't think there was any harm in laying in the bed, so long as I stayed on my side."

His smile grows wider as his eyes narrow. "And did you? Stay on your side, I mean?"

Swallowing the lump in my throat, I drop my gaze. "Why are you asking?"

"Because I remember being deep in that nightmare and suddenly feeling warm—held—like I was safe. And I'd like to know if that feeling was random or because a lovely, little elf woman decided to cuddle my comatose body in the middle of the night."

I don't dare look at him. The heat in my cheek, in my ears, is a dead giveaway. Though, he deserves the truth. "I um, woke up that way. I hadn't intended to do so, but must've been cold, or something. I'd made a pillow barrier the next night to ensure I didn't violate your personal space, if it makes you feel better."

Asmo chuckles, pressing a bit harder on my back, urging me closer. "You didn't *invade* anything. You were asleep. And it helped."

I breathe, letting the air I'd trapped in my lungs out in relief. At least he's not mad.

Desperate to change the subject, I clear my throat. "I wouldn't have expected you to enjoy dancing." It's not a lie. His steps are fluid and graceful, like he was born doing it.

"Yes, well, I'll have you know, I'm a fantastic dancer. Though, I like to keep my skills to myself and usually only do so in the privacy of my room." He lets go of my back, lifting our joined hands and beckoning me to twirl under his arm. The moment I do, he stops me mid spin, his body warm against my back, his breath hot against my ear. "I know I told you not to bug me the first night you were here, but I want you to know, if you're ever cold, I'm more than happy to fix that."

I tilt my head, slightly looking over my shoulder. "Are you inviting me to your bed?"

"I'm inviting you to snuggle. It never has to be more than that. And only if you want to." He spins me again, bringing me face to face once more.

What if I want it to be? I find myself holding my breath as I gaze into his eyes, eyes that give absolutely nothing away. "You want to *snuggle me*?"

He slowly, unabashedly, took in every line, every curve of me. "I do. And I promise to be the perfect gentleman."

Caught off guard, I fumble for a response, the blush deepening in my cheeks until they feel like they're on fire.

Everything my people taught me about demons is so obnoxiously wrong. They claimed everyone but the king and queen lived in dungeon-like homes, ate creatures raw, and picked their meat off the bone like savages. I'd believed that demons were bloodthirsty killers incapable of emotions or empathy. They were supposed to be monsters, not snugglers.

Asmodeus might be the first demon I've met—that I've talked to for more than five words—but he's nothing like I'd expected. I don't doubt for a second that he's deadly. I've seen him covered in blood, just as I've seen his magic. He's capable of things beyond my imagination, but he's also the man with a map on his ceiling so he can check on those he loves. He's the one that created bodies for people who were wronged, all to give them a second chance at life, and nearly lost his shadow in the process. He's no villain—not like my people have made it out to be.

"I owe you an apology."

He raises his eyebrows as I meet his gaze. "For what?"

"I was deeply misled about your kind. The elves are taught that demons are despicable creatures, but you and Griffin—" I shake my head.

"It's okay." He tucks a chunk of my hair behind my ear. "I'm glad you saw otherwise, that you were open enough to make your own assumptions, but I don't blame you for believing what you were told."

I haven't had time to think about what comes next for me. We'd made a temporary deal—a truce that helped us both. Though, the longer I've been here, the more I see what could be. The truth is, every time he calls me the Lady of Grim's Keep, my heart glows. It's like I have a purpose, a meaning. I'm not just a pretty woman on some man's arm. I don't have to sit on a throne and smile and wave to those who visit while my husband does the talking.

If I wanted to change something, I believe Asmo would listen. He'd hear me out. I have a say here and can make a difference. The staff could use some culinary training and direction, but they're more than just servants or subordinates under Asmo's rule, they're treated like living beings, with just as much respect as Asmo and Griffin give each other.

Sure, their dynamic can be weird, but there's an undying love there that I yearn to have with someone someday. To have someone care enough about me that they'd face my fae beast to bring me back.

I wouldn't have had that in Vanderlyth. I would've been married to a high-horsed, womanizing, narcissistic asshat who only cared about gaining my last name and the title it comes with. He'd have shoved me back into that gods forsaken wing, raided the whorehouses, and only come knocking when it was time for an heir.

The man left me for dead.

I have no desire to go back. Every living, breathing part of me wants to stay here. With him. Whether that's platonic, as friends, or if this becomes more… I don't care.

Asmodeus interrupts my thoughts. "What are you thinking about?" *How long has he been watching me think, guiding me around our make-shift dance floor?*

I can sense the uneasy change in him, like he's worried that offering to snuggle with me somehow will have me running for the hills, when in reality, it's the exact opposite. Reaching up, I do the only thing I can think of to comfort him, to sooth the worry he must be feeling. His face is so smooth against my hand as I cup his face, my thumb absently stroking over the indentation of the scar that cuts through his cheek.

"I'm glad you found me in the keep," I confess, smiling up at him, that trembling nervousness returning. No matter how hard I try, I can't push it away, not when he's this close. Not when the only thing I want to do is drag his face to mine and kiss him until he smiles again. "I'm glad I've had the chance to meet you."

Asmodeus arches a brow, leaning a bit into my touch. "Why do I feel like there's a 'but' coming?"

"No buts," I assure him with a laugh.

His eyes drop to my lips, then his gaze returns to mine. I can't look away. I can't breathe.

Kiss me. Please kiss me.

He leans forward as if he can hear my silent plea. My breath catches when he pauses, so close… I push up on my tippy toes, needing to close that gap, but something sizzles in the quiet, and I'm not sure how long it's been since the music stopped playing.

Asmodeus lurches back, hissing out a curse. He shakes his hand in the air, then brings it up, looking over his palm.

Did I do something? Did I burn him somehow with my magic? I didn't touch my crystal or cast. I look over my own hands, as if I'm scanning for evidence.

"What? What is it?" Griffin's voice carries through the throne room, and I look over to find him pushing off the wall.

How long has he been there?

He winks at me before turning his undivided attention to Asmo, who's gawking at his hand as if it's predicted someone's death.

"What is it, Asmo?" Griffin repeats, his voice holding a growl that wasn't there prior.

Asmo lifts his face, his eyes finding mine, then Griffin's. "Someone's crossed the wall."

21

Valeria

"What do you mean someone has crossed the wall? How would you know that?" I glance between them, urging them to elaborate, to give me some kind of context.

Asmo holds up his hand, revealing the dark, inky circle on his palm. I traced its smooth outline easily a dozen times while I waited for him to wake up. "It's the boundary wall in the forest—" He points to the pin-point of light around the rim. "And this means that someone touched it. Someone who's not of my or the queen's bloodline."

I drop my gaze, head twisting to the side as I process what he's admitted. "But it would have a light for me, wouldn't it? I'm not your blood relative or the queen's."

"The deal we made linked your life to mine and therefore the wall now recognizes you as me. Griffin's mother is my biological aunt, so we share blood. The ghosts are tethered to the boundary itself." He examines his palm, probing that light. "For this to happen, something else is out there."

That's how he knew I'd crossed that day, when I'd fallen out of the tree.

"So, what do you want to do? Go see who it is? We can't just wait for them to knock on the door. It might not even be a person." The echo of Griffin's boots against the stone floor fills the room as he crosses it in five long strides.

"That's exactly what I plan to do." Asmo twists his lips, his eyes becoming vacant as he retreats into his mind.

"You're healing. Do you even have magic right now?"

Asmo jerks his head up, the gentle, sweet demon I'd just danced with gone. It's been replaced by his scowling, deadly alter ego. The man I met when he first came to this keep. Only this time, I know he won't hurt me and for that alone, I refuse to cower.

"Don't look at me like that," I snap, crossing my arms over my chest, lifting my chin. "It's an honest question. You just used blood magic to raise the dead. And this time yesterday, you didn't even have a shadow. So, if you want me to be okay with you going out in the woods to hunt down whoever crossed that wall, you better fucking show me."

Griffin's eyes widen, revealing more white around those bright blue eyes than I've ever seen. As for Asmo, he doesn't seem to even blink, but the scowl relaxes just a bit.

"Careful, Starlight, I might start to think you care."

I grip my crystal pendant, feeling it thrum against my skin like the beat of music. My senses explode as magic tingles in currents over my arms, up my throat, ready to obey my command. For now, it simply gives me strength as I storm forward, closing the distance between us. "Of course I care. You tethered my life to yours. Magic or not, I die if you make a mistake. Now, show me, or Griffin and I will go investigate while you tell the gargoyles the party is off."

Asmo inhales deeply, his chest rising. Without looking away from me, he lifts his hand and flames burst to life, forming a circle around us. Griffin jumps back just in the nick of time. A sword materializes out of thin air and he quickly fastens it around his waist before discarding his shirt and handing it to me in a balled-up heap.

My breath catches at the sight, whether from the spontaneous flames or sheer astonishment, I'm not sure. But I choke it down and force my eyes to narrow into lethal slits as he clears his throat.

"If you'll excuse me..." He trails off, stalking through those flames as if they're nothing.

I know they're real. I can feel the heat radiating against my calves. They're not some optical illusion conjured by him. He's immune. Not even his clothes catch on the flames, as if protected by magic.

"They'll go out in a moment. Stay here and keep everyone inside," he says without a glance back.

"It's not like I have much of a choice, do I?" I call after him. Griffin turns to me before following Asmo out the doorway, mouthing an, "I'm sorry," and leaving me alone in the circle of flames.

As promised, they don't last long.

They burn out right as some of the gargoyles enter the throne room, the scent of various foods mingling with the earthy tang of soot that now mars the marble floors. Not wasting a second, I sprint past them and crouch under trays to avoid crashing into them. But as I reach the front door of the keep and stare across the clearing, scanning the forest edge, Griffin and Asmo are nowhere in sight.

I want to chase after them. Part of me believes my gift, my ability to bend light, could make us all invisible as we go to see who crossed. Despite Asmo's sudden shift in attitude, I know why he wanted me to stay. If I had gone, I'd likely be another person he has to protect—a distraction.

Ultimately, until I learn how to use my magic to protect myself, I'm far more useful here. If for some reason whoever crossed got past Asmo and Griffin, I might be able to hide the gargoyles by disguising a doorway. If all three of us went, we'd be leaving the people he nearly died to resurrect defenseless.

Though, I wish he'd just said that instead of becoming grumpy again. I've never seen someone flip so fast before.

Just as I'm about to go back inside, a voice comes from behind me. "Don't worry, my lady. He'll be fine. They both will."

I spin around, my eyes widening in shock as the dry air stings them. Leaning effortlessly against the doorframe, one of the gargoyles smirks at me—a man, younger but obviously older than me based on the creases in the corners of his stone eyes.

"You can talk…" It's not a question. It's a fact.

"I can, but that secret should stay between you and me."

I blink, almost certain I'm imagining things. "Can the others?"

He shakes his head, making stone grind like the way a pestle works herbs into a mortar. "A few, but most can't." Pushing off the wall, he holds out a large hand. "My name is Xren, and it's about time we've been introduced."

"Valeria," I say, hesitating a moment before taking his hand—or rather his thumb, seeing as it's the only part of him I can wrap my hand around—and awkwardly shaking it.

"Well, Valeria, we should probably go inside. Let the prince do his rounds and ensure the keep is safe. And should something manage to get past him, I'm sure myself and the other guards who used to look after this place, will gladly pick up a sword." He beckons for me to step inside and with a huff, I do.

"So, you were a guard?" I ask, trying to shove away the feeling that I'm once again told to stay out of sight and out of mind while the important people do as they please.

No... This is different. I can protect them. I'm just as important staying here as they are going into the woods. No one has shoved me away into a wing of the castle because I'm useless until I'm married. I'm staying behind because I'm needed here.

"I was. I was the prince's personal guard before..." Xren trails off and I regret bringing up something that made him think about his death.

"I'm sorry, we don't—"

He holds up a stone hand. "Nonsense." His lips pull into a gentle smile. "I was his guard until he snuck out to meet his mother. He never came back and the next day, the elves came. I'm glad he wasn't here. I don't think even his presence would've been enough to stop them."

My father and his men would've likely killed Asmo. We don't have prisons on our islands, and from what I understand, the bounty on Asmo's head at that time was dead or alive. The thought alone has my stomach flipping, to know my father would've done such a thing—*has* done such a thing.

"I'm terribly sorry for what happened to all of you. It never should've and I truly hope you find justice one day." We enter the throne room, finding most of the gargoyles gathered around that long table, bent at the waist and sniffing vigorously at the food laid out there.

"It's been years. I've accepted my fate, and now—" He twirls in place, hands outstretched. "I have a second chance." Despite the weight of his words, there's a glint of hope in his eyes that sparks something within me.

We make our way further into the throne room and I can't help but notice the subtle changes in the gargoyles as they catch sight of Xren. It's a difference that speaks volumes about his role among them.

"They respect you," I say, nodding to the group of gargoyles now staring at us, having forgotten about the spread before them.

"I suppose they do." Xren chuckles, a rumbling deep enough to echo off the walls.

"They've known me for decades—*centuries*. We lived and died together, and that makes our ties go beyond mere loyalty."

"Why haven't you talked to Griffin? He's struggled for days to take care of the needs of your people. You could've helped him," I say, smiling at one of the gargoyles that's making their way toward us. I recognize her as the chef's wife, the one who'd spoken to Asmo during the ritual. In her hand is a cup and she extends it out to me without a word.

"It's punch," Xren says, urging me to take it. "She says that the chef would like you to taste it. He's made some adjustments to what Griffin prepared."

"How do you know that?" I turn to him, scrutinizing his features. *Can he read her mind?*

"Yes." His voice sounds inside my head and I gasp.

"How…"

"It was my gift, and it appears that when Asmodeus brought us back, that carried into my gargoyle form, too." He smiles, his stone lips cracking a bit to reveal carved teeth.

I give a polite curtsey to the woman and take the cup. "Thank you, tell the chef that I'm sure it'll be lovely."

She bows her head, and the stone floor rattles as she returns to that long table, the others already devouring the scents of the food there again.

The moment she's out of earshot, I turn to Xren. "So, you can translate for them?"

"I can. They might not be able to speak, but their thoughts are pure." He watches me intently, as if he's waiting on me to drink, but something feels off about this.

"It doesn't explain why you didn't help Griffin."

He huffs, rolling his eyes as if he's growing bored with our conversation. "If he knew, I would've spent my first days alive at his beck and call. Beyond that, I don't know him, and it was far more interesting to watch him struggle."

As I gear up for the argument I'm about to start, that things would've been better for him and his people had he just fessed up to his ability, a soft rustling catches my attention. Turning towards the source of the sound, I spot Griffin slipping back into the room. Asmo strides in behind him, both of their expressions grave. They're unscathed, from what I can see, but there's tension lingering in the air. It's a sense of urgency that shoots down my spine like a bolt of electricity.

Something is wrong.

"We have company," Asmo announces to the room, his voice cutting through the silence like a blade. Squaring his shoulders, he continues, "The queen will be joining us this evening."

The queen? Is that who he sensed? I thought she helped place that boundary. *Why would she set it off?*

A ripple of gasps sweeps through the room, each gargoyle turning to face Asmo with bewildered faces. Behind him, a flash of red hair peeks through the door and the sound of stone grinding erupts as the gargoyles bow.

After a moment, I do too, staring up through my lashes to see the queen stand next to Asmo, her hand resting on his shoulder.

The mere sight of them shouldn't claw at my gut. Griffin has assured me twice now that they're only friends, not that I should care if it weren't true. However, there's something about them standing together that burrows deep inside of me, turning my blood into sweltering iron.

Why? Why am I reacting this way? He was on the brink of kissing me until we were interrupted. But maybe that's just it... It's not their familiarity with one another that unsettles me. It's the stolen moment that had been ripped away, leaving me here to brood and steep in my jealousy.

"Oh, please don't..." The queen lets out a deep breath, closing her eyes as if the respect she's been given is an irritation. "All rise," she says, her voice flat.

Heeding her command, we all stand, and the room resumes its idle chatter. My eyes connect with Griffin's in a silent plea to tell me what the hell is going on, and he shoots a glance at the queen and Asmo before scurrying across the room. When he reaches me, he grips my shoulders, leads me away from Xren and positions me so my back is toward everyone.

We stand side by side, facing the wall as he whispers, "Something has happened."

"Obviously," I say through gritted teeth, resisting the urge to smack him with the back of my hand. "What?"

"We were supposed to attend a family gathering tonight, but seeing as I was kidnapped when it was planned, I didn't know. And Asmo was—Well, you know."

I wave my hand in a circle, telling him to get to the point.

He huffs but skips to the important part, anyway. "She came looking for us. Her familiar set off the wall. I guess one of the villages along the sea border was attacked, and she worried that Grim's Keep had been too."

"Attacked?" I turn to face him.

He grips my shoulders and spins me back toward the wall. "Keep your voice down. We don't want to cause a panic."

"Who?" I'm not sure why I insist on asking. I know who. I was supposed to be the distraction for it… But that was weeks ago. Why would the ships that broke off on the way to have my wedding blessed wait until now to do something? Were they instructed to, in order to ensure me and my *betrothed* returned before they opened fire? Did something come up, or is this separate, altogether?

"It was the elves. Apparently, they've officially declared war."

My heart ceases beating in my chest, the blood draining from my face. "Are you sure?"

"As sure as I can be. I mean, the queen said as much. I guess dinner turned into an urgent court meeting. They convene in the morning which means—"

I finish the thought for him, "That Asmo has to be there."

"Not just him," Griffin says, looking me up and down from the corner of his eye. "All lords and *ladies* of the court will need to be present. Just as both my father and my mother attend, you will need to accompany my uncle and officially establish yourself as Lady of Grim's Keep."

I steal a glance over my shoulder, finding Asmo's eyes pinned on us from across the room. If I didn't know any better, I'd think he could hear us. "Does he want me to go?"

"What do you mean *does he want you to go?* You're the lady, are you not?"

"I mean, he calls me that, but I'm not sure it's an official thing," I admit, feeling my cheeks flush when I look again and Asmo is still staring. Only this time, he looks ready to murder someone. I just hope that someone isn't me... Surely, he wouldn't randomly start to hate me for my ears, right?

He might change his mind about trusting me, maybe... But what deserved a look like that? Unless it's not aimed at me, but at Griffin for spilling the news.

"Do you want to be the Lady of Grim's or not?" Griffin turns toward me, crossing his arms over his broad chest. I glance up at him, unsure of how to answer.

"I mean, I do, but I'm not expecting anything. If he wants me to go, I'll go. If not, then I understand."

Griffin relaxes his shoulders, but as he opens his mouth to speak, he double takes on something behind me. "Whatever you do, I said nothing."

"I'll take your secret to the grave," I say, spotting Asmo on a warpath across the throne room.

22

Valeria

“I’d like to introduce you to someone,” Asmo says, reaching for my hand while glaring at Griffin.

“Oh, um—” The words are lost to a gasp as he tugs me away, toward where the queen is grimacing at the gargoyle’s sniffing antics. It takes me three steps to catch up to him, but I spot the tick in his jaw, the irritation feathering there. “Don’t be mad at him.”

“And why shouldn’t I be?” he says, his voice barely audible over the hushed whisper of nearby conversations. It’s as if he’s worried someone will hear us.

“He was just trying to stop me from worrying.” I tighten my grip on our laced fingers, hoping my touch will soothe his nerves.

With sudden abruptness, Asmo halts and whirls me around to face him, his grip firm on my hand. “You think I care that he told you about the wall?” He scoffs, leaving a bitter taste in my mouth as he continues, “I’m upset that he’s the reason I had to re-enchant it. He told the blood witches where they could find abandoned magic. The wall around our keep, remnants of the boundary that used to surround the realm of monsters, the tree of life—a place that was sacred to my mother—and they siphoned the magic out of it to help the elves destroy a village.”

The venom that drips from his eyes, from his tone, has a knot forming in my stomach, but I don't look away. "The elves would never work with blood witches. They're abominations to them. As for Griffin, you and I both know he was under a spell and wasn't in his right mind."

"That's just the thing, Valeria. He never thinks through the consequences. He saw a pretty woman and wanted to bed her. I doubt he thought for a moment how unsafe it was to ditch his guard and go off alone with a stranger."

I cross my arms, feeling a chord struck somewhere deep within me. "That's easy to say for someone who grew up without a guard following you every second of every day. People need their space or they do irrational things."

He cocks his head, eyes narrowing on me. I can hear his teeth grinding as he pushes the words through them. "And I suppose you would know what that's like, huh?" The hostility seeping from him was palpable—so much so that I felt it coiling tightly around my heart, threatening to wring it dry.

Shit.

"No, but I can imagine. Growing up a duke, knowing you'll rule over a realm one day, has to be a lot of pressure. Everyone is terrified that their only heir will get hurt, so you're placed in a bubble. You can't eat, sleep, or breathe with someone there, watching. It's lonely, and the silence is deafening. Sometimes, you need a reprieve and just to crawl out from underneath the weight and responsibility of it, to remind yourself what it's like to live."

Asmo's eyes toggle between mine, but he makes no effort to speak or move. Though, the frown on his face has softened a bit and that muscle in his cheek has calmed.

"At least, that's how I'd imagine it being," I add, clearing my throat and looking past him to nod toward the queen. "Shall we continue?"

For whatever reason, he doesn't press me any more on the subject and the death glares at Griffin stop as he leads me to the infamous Alice Morningstar.

"I'd like you to meet someone," he says to her as we near. "This is—"

Alice locks eyes with me, her face falling as she cuts him off. "Valeria, right?"

"Yes, my queen," I bow my head respectfully.

"Of course you'd already know her name." Asmo scoffs, shaking his head. "You have to stop scrying or you're going to lose an eye. You know how hard it was to get mine back. Do you want to go through that?"2

The queen's lips tip into a smirk as she pivots her gaze from me to him. "I do remember, but it's also the only way I can keep an eye on the elves these days. Had I not scried, it wouldn't have just been Ogre's Landing that burned to the ground, but two other villages, too. Besides, they make stunning eyepatches now."

"Then send guards to protect the villages along the sea border. It's not worth losing you to know the future. Look at what happened to my mother. My father kept her lifeless body in a glass box because she lost her soul. An eye patch is just the start of what could go wrong."

I squeeze Asmo's hand, realizing he hasn't let it go, and to my surprise, he squeezes it back, casting a worried glance my way.

From my studies, I know scrying is like glimpsing the future in a flurry of images. Only witches or those born from the old gods with the gift of sight can access it. And it works by transporting a creature's spirit through the folds of time and into future or past versions of oneself.

Where the shadow is what makes you feel, what gives you magic, the other half of the soul, known as the spirit, makes you who you are. It's what each of the gargoyles are. That half of the soul can get trapped if a creature scries a time where they don't exist. The spirit has nothing to jump into and if not reigned back in, it can become lost to the ether, forever.

I'd never heard of that happening to the late queen. And judging from Asmo's tone, it must've gutted him when his mother passed. Though, I can't begin to comprehend why, seeing as she was the one who trapped him in the prison realm. You'd think he'd hate her for it. Had it been me, I might've even danced on her grave.

The queen's laugh yanks me from my thoughts, so bright, I'd never expect for her kingdom to be at war. "Excuse me, my children need me? Of course they do. But what good am I if my castle falls and the elves kill me, them, and everyone they care about?" Asmo doesn't argue, but the death grip he has on my hand tells me he's anything but calm as Alice adds, "The benefits outweigh the risks."

Choosing to end the argument, I take my hand from Asmo, flexing my fingers a second before saying, "Have you tried the punch? Griffin and the chef made it. I heard it's lovely. Let me get you a glass." Pasting on a cheery smile, I make my escape, weaving through the gargoyles toward the punch bowl, dishing out three cups worth and leaving the one prepared for me by the chef's wife behind.

Something seemed off about it. I haven't tried it, but the way Xren eyed me, like he was patiently waiting for me to take a sip… I'd rather pour my own, just to be safe.

Balancing three cups in my arms, I return to Asmo and the queen. Their voices are no longer edged with tension but still, they fidget in place, like they're unsure of how to interact now that their opinions charge the air.

I'm about to say something, when music hits my ears. The floating instruments have straightened themselves from where they rested on the floor, and now hover as if being held in someone's invisible hands. The violin's sharp strings pull tight, its resonance silencing the room. Griffin holds his arms up like a conductor in the middle of the dance floor, his fingers working the air as he taps his foot and the other instruments join in to the melody.

"We're not dying today, folks. Tonight, we celebrate our friends coming back to life, and we'll dance and drink. So, move your stoney bodies. Chop chop." Griffin sways, and arms and legs gliding in unison as he waves over the gargoyles, demanding they join him.

A smile tugs at my lips as I watch him, his white hair floating on air as he closes his eyes and feels the music, the violins, the flutes, and dances as if no one is watching. "Is he always like this?" I say with a chuckle, leaning in slightly toward Asmo.

"Mostly." Even he can't fight the smile as he witnesses Griffin's suave moves.

"That is you and Finn." The queen gestures to all of Griffin. "I'm not sure Eva was even involved in the making of him."

"Me?" Asmo holds a hand over his heart as if he's been wounded and snaps his head in her direction.

"Yes, you. He's got Finn's no-fucks given attitude and your charismatic charm. Griffin is exactly like I'd imagine you had you not been trapped in the Realm of Monsters. I guarantee it."

Asmo snarls, rubbing at his chest like she's driven a dagger in deep and twisted the blade. "You wound me."

"Wound you? You should be proud. He's happy and alive, and comfortable with himself, beast and all, because of you." She smacks his arm, and it rips a giggle from my throat.

Taking a sip of the punch, I raise my brows. Fruity flavors explode on my tongue, sweet and sour and savory all at once. It's delicious. I quickly down the rest of the glass and return to the punch bowl for more, but when I return, Asmo and Alice are gone from the spot I left them.

Surveying the room, I find them being tugged onto the dance floor by Griffin, his head bobbing to the violin's tune. Asmo grimaces, like he'd much rather steep in the pits of hell than dance, but the queen seems to quickly pick up the beat and grips his other hand. In unison, the two of them tug Asmo along, and they disappear into the group of gargoyles.

The throne room pulsates with vibrant energy, full of hearty gargoyle laughter and light. The gargoyles have become lively, all having abandoned their table of food and now grinding on the dance floor. I lean against the table, sipping my drink as I watch the scene before me, hoping for a glimpse of the three of them, curious to see if they'll ever get Asmo to dance.

By the time I'm four cups deep, the mage lights transform into a kaleidoscope of colors, casting their glow on the merriment of the room. The sweet scent of punch and wildflowers swirls around me, intoxicating in its intensity.

"Why are you still standing here? Get you pointy ears out there!" Griffin grins, grabbing a cup of punch as he takes a moment to catch his breath.

"I'm not really sure how to dance to this," I admit, hiding the flush in my cheek with my cup. "Elven balls are more formal, partner dances. Not so much the jerky hip movements."

"You mean twerking?"

I stare at him, unfamiliar with the word. "What?"

"It's called twerking. It's what the gargoyles are doing. Believe it or not, it's a dance style that's existed for years in demon culture. Though, way back when, in the time of the old gods, the royal maidens would do it to seduce their suitors. Of course, that was prior to the gauntlets and bloodbaths my grandfather replaced it with. Though, I suppose the tradition stuck around in areas like Hell Hold."

I turn my head sideways, watching the gargoyle's carved butt jerk up and down, so fast, the stone nearly blurs. It's an odd dance. It's an odd way to lure a suitor, too.

In our culture, our balls and dances are made to show off how graceful we can be. It's to show that we're pure-blooded and that we've been educated in how to be a lady, that we're esteemed enough to not embarrass our future husbands. But this… I'm not sure what it shows beyond the possibility for spinal issues in the future.

"How does being able to *twerk*, and twitch your hips like that, draw suitors? What does it prove that you can do?" I ask, turning to Griffin only to find him biting back a grin so wide, his cheeks have reddened.

"It doesn't prove much of anything I guess, though when it's ladies doing it instead of gargoyles, it's a sight I have no wants to look away from."

I ponder that a second, still wondering how it narrows down who he'd wish to mate with. "But what specifically makes you decide who's twerk is best?"

Griffin howls out a laugh, then downs his glass. "You just pick whoever you want to touch more. And if they're into you, they might twerk on you laying down."

I try to imagine that, but the only possible theory of how one would twerk laying down makes me think of a fish out of water or a person seizing. Surely, that's not what demons see as sexy… Right? It has to be a misunderstanding.

Yanking my arm, Griffin drags me deep onto the dance floor, forcing me to join the celebration. My vision shifting as if I've drunk cups upon cups of faerie wine.

"What was in that punch?" I ask, yelling over the music.

Griffin arches a brow. "I'm not giving away my secrets. Why?"

My senses buzz with an otherworldly intensity, the room taking on colors so vibrant and bright it puts me in awe. I can see the music, the streams of it glowing as it mingles in the air. "I think I'm drunk," I admit, realizing I haven't let go of his hand.

His laugh hits my ears as he leans in to say, "Not drunk. You're seeing like a fae."

"You can see music, too?"

He nods. "Music, magic, all of it."

Around me, gargoyles bump and grind with abandon, their rocky bodies creating a cacophony of stone-on-stone contact. It's a surprising sight, seeing creatures that appear like statues gyrate with such fluidity. Their movements are bold, exaggerated, as if they're completely unaware of their hardness.

For a moment, I allow myself to get lost in it, closing my eyes and swaying to the beat.

"Hey!" Griffin says in excitement, "Look at you go."

I don't open my eyes, letting the music fill me up, and guide me. Before I know it, my body begins to move on its own accord, lost to the bliss of music.

23

Valeria

I've lost track of time, unsure of how long I've been in my own little world. Opening my eyes, I notice most of the gargoyles have cleared out, except Griffin and two of the lady ghosts.

Asmo and the queen are nowhere to be found.

As I reach Griffin, I barely make out the clacking of stone on stone over the music, drawing my eyes to a pair of gargoyles in the corner. From what I can see, I think they're attempting to kiss in the privacy of the dark. They gaze at each other affectionately, their stone bodies making it difficult for their lips to touch. With an awkward blink, their stone heads connect, and they seem satisfied with their display of affection.

The sight is both endearing and *confusing*, and I can't help but shake my head as I take it all in, returning my attention to Griffin.

"Where did Asmo go?"

His white hair is sweaty, his bare chest gleaming from his efforts. In his hand is a flask; the distinctive scent of whiskey hits me, leaving an anticipatory tang on my tongue despite not having tasted it. "Who knows. Probably off brooding somewhere."

I shake my head as I slip from the throne room, leaving the party behind.

Asmo has to be around here somewhere…

Wandering through the back door of the keep, I step into the courtyard, the light of the moons highlighting every tree and flower, and the mage lights floating throughout the air casting a warm amber glow on the rest.

It's empty save for the queen, gazing at the twinkling night sky above.

"Excuse me, your Majesty," I say politely, "Have you seen where Asmo went?"

She turns her stunning blue eyes toward me, shaking her head. "No, I haven't. But before you go searching for him, I wanted to talk to you." I blink at the queen, my pulse echoing in my bones. After a short pause, she adds. "Alone."

My heart skips, my ribs somehow closing in on my lungs, making it hard to breathe. "Of course," I say, swallowing hard and taking a seat on the bench next to her. *What could the queen possibly want to discuss with me?* "What may I help you with?" I struggle to keep my voice steady. Between the punch and the colors and the worry that seems to seep from every nerve of my body, it's a miracle that I manage to.

"Valeria," she begins, eyeing me carefully, "I know who you are."

"Excuse me?" I say, caught off guard by her statement. My pulse quickens until I have the urge to flee, to sprint into the forest and never look back. The only reason I don't is because I know I wouldn't make it far.

"I know that you're a Nightborn, the daughter of the elf lord." She's watching my reaction closely, reading me like an open book. Lying isn't an option. She'd see right through it. "What I don't know is why you're here and not in the Elven Islands."

Clearing my throat, I turn my spine to steel, meeting her knowing gaze. "I mean no harm to anyone here," I assure her. "I don't support what my father has done. I could never agree with slaughtering an innocent village in the name of war."

"Good," the queen says softly. "But it's not safe for you here, at least not if Asmo doesn't know the truth. Your father has made many enemies and if someone were to find out and you were left unprotected..." She doesn't finish the sentence. She doesn't have to. "I know he made a blood deal with you. If someone hurts you, I lose him. I hope you understand what I'm saying."

"Please," I beg, desperation clawing at my throat. "There's got to be another way. If Asmo knew, he'd force me to go home. He wouldn't so much as look at me without blood rage. My father is the reason this keep was in ruins and why his people died. I can't be sure he wouldn't take it out on me if he knew I'm a Nightborn."

The queen studies me for a moment before asking again, "Why were you on the mainland in the first place?"

"My ship was attacked on the way to be blessed to marry a man I don't love—can't love. He's a narcissist and left me for dead in the water. The only reason I survived is because the reaper took mercy and helped me get to the mainland. If I go back, I'll be forced down the aisle."

Alice nods, her eyes filled with understanding. "For now, your secret is safe with me. But you'll have to tell Asmo eventually." She hesitates before adding, "You should be at the court meeting tomorrow. He's told me that he made you the Lady of Grim's and therefore, there are things you should know."

"Thank you," I whisper, relief washing over me. "I understand."

The queen nods, returning her gaze to the sky. “You know, I saw you while I scried. Though, I never saw your face until today. I suppose it’s for the best. I’ve seen the way Asmo looks at you, and had I known you were the elf lord’s daughter, I would’ve delivered you to the Elven Islands myself. You’d have never met Asmo, which would’ve been a pity, since Griffin claims that my best friend has never smiled at anyone more.”

My cheeks heat, and I pick at the hem of my dress, unsure of how to respond. I’m not even sure if there’s a hidden meaning in her claiming she’d have delivered me to my father. It wouldn’t surprise me if she’d meant in pieces.

“You should know, if you’re here because of your father, spying on us, Asmo would be the first to kill you if he found out. He might like you, but he’d put his own emotions aside to protect his family and those he loves. He’s done it over and over again. So, I hope for your sake, your story is true. If it comes to that, if you hurt him again, it’ll be me you face.”

“It’s true. I swear it,” I say, looking her straight in the eye. I want her to see the truth in my soul. “I have no desire to hurt anyone.”

“Then we understand each other,” she says, standing up. "Now, I should be getting home."

As I stand to escort the queen out of the keep, I can't help but feel a mixture of gratitude and unease. My secret is safe, but for how long?

I follow her, watching her loose red curls bounce with every step, and the gold of her crown catches the light, along with the scales of her leathers. We pass through the front door of Grim’s Keep, but I freeze in the doorway, spotting a monstrosity of a creature bounding through the yard. Its gray and white stripes glisten in the night, its blood-stained ivory teeth gleaming as it snaps at one of the gargoyles.

The stone man sprints with everything he has, barely missing the creature's teeth by the skin of his back. Its golden eyes are wide, revealing slitted pupils, nosing the three large horns on its head at the gargoyle, almost knocking him off balance.

"Luri! Stop that!" The queen yells and the creature slams to a halt, pushing up grass and dirt with its large paws. Chest heaving, the gargoyle swats the creature on the nose and yells, "Mah!" before stomping back toward the keep.

Fluffy tail swishing, the monster cat glares at the queen.

"You can't eat the gargoyles, you asshole. Gods. I can't take you anywhere, can I?" she says as the creature swishes its head and stalks our way, attitude in every powerful step.

As the gargoyle reaches us, his face and features come into view. It's Xren. I fight to hide my amusement, as he brushes past me into the safety of the keep, finding it hard not to laugh at the absurdity of the situation.

"Don't let him be late tomorrow, and the two of you will want to bring a bag. It'll likely be more than one day of negotiations." The queen mounts the cat, her hands gripping chunks of that thick, rather soft-looking, white hair.

"You have my word," I say, bowing my head. Then the queen is gone, having used her magic to transport her and her familiar back to Hell Hold.

As I step back inside, the hint of piano keys sings to me, so quiet compared to the beat coming from the throne room. There's a piano on the second floor. Taking a shot, hoping it's Asmo, I ascend the spiral stairs, the keys picking up again as I reach the floor, peering through the arched doorway to find Asmo sitting on the bench, his brows drawn together as he focuses.

I find myself drawn to that captivating melody, and in awe of the way the mage lights bathe the grand piano and the man playing it in a soft amber glow. Those gentle notes echo through the space, captivating everything in earshot. His fingers dance gracefully across the keys, his dark eyes closed, lost in the emotion of the music.

Leaning against the door frame, I witness him weaving every note into a symphony of pain, love, sadness, and affection. Each chord played sends a vibrant wave of color floating through the air. It tears at my heart, all while making it so full all at the same time. It's as if he's pouring his very soul into the song, and I hold my breath, not wanting to disturb the moment.

As the last note hangs in the air, I clap, gliding into the room. Startled, Asmo's head jerks up, and his gaze meets mine over the piano. A mischievous glint dances in his eyes, and I feel a sudden warmth spread across my cheeks.

"By now, you've likely realized that Griffin's punch isn't just wine," he says, his voice smooth and teasing. "It makes you see like a fae would—all the colors and magic. It’s one of my favorite times to play."

I nod, acknowledging the truth of his words. "I haven't seen anything quite like it."

His lips tip into a knowing smile and as he grips his cup, the crystal clinks against the metal of his rings, and brings the rim to his lips.

"Your music," I say, unable to suppress the awe in my voice, "it's beautiful."

"Thank you." He looks away for a moment, seemingly embarrassed by the compliment. "Music has always been… an escape for me."

"An escape from what?" I ask, my fingers tracing the cool, polished surface of the piano as I near.

"From the world," he says cryptically, his gaze locking with mine once more. Those amber rings dance with mischief as he studies me. "I'm shocked you're up here and not downstairs with Griffin." The corner of his mouth lifting into a teasing grin. "I thought elves loved to dance."

"We do." My voice is barely above a whisper.

"Then why are you still here?" The question hangs in the air between us, charged with the unspoken tension that has built over these past few days.

I hesitate for a moment, unsure of what to say. Finally, I admit softly, "I'd rather listen to you play."

His smile deepens at my confession, and it's as if the darkness in the room recedes ever so slightly. "Do you know how to play the piano?" he asks, curiosity sparking in his eyes.

I shake my head. "Unfortunately, no."

"Come here," he beckons, waving me towards him. "I'll show you."

I finish my cup of punch and slide into the seat next to him on the bench, but before I can sit down all the way, his hand grips my waist, guiding me onto his lap instead. The sudden closeness sends butterflies fluttering through my stomach, and the effects of Griffin's punch make the world around me shimmer with newfound intensity. Every sense is heightened, awakened with such vibrancy, I almost don't want to experience normal again.

"Put your hands on top of mine," Asmo whispers, and I suck in a breath as his lips brush my ear. His breath is warm against my skin, sending shivers through me.

Still, I do as he says and rest my fingers on top of his, aligning them with the keys.

He begins to move, taking my hands with his and he glides across the keys, each note ringing out clear and true. The melody is hauntingly beautiful, and I lose myself in the music, leaning into the warm, sturdy man at my back as my heart beats wildly in my chest.

Time seems to stand still as we navigate the keys, but as the final notes of the song linger in the air, Asmo's movements slow and he laces his fingers with mine, gently stroking his thumbs over the top of my hands.

"See, I knew you could do it," he says, and the sheer pride in his voice has my heart melting into a puddle at our feet.

I glance over my shoulder at him, pulse racing. Our eyes lock, and for a moment, nothing seems to matter but me and him, and I'm aware of every place our bodies connect. The stolen kiss from earlier dances at the edges of my thoughts, and an unspoken desire passes between us.

As if reading my mind, Asmo leans in, his lips brushing mine ever so gently. The sensation is electric, igniting a fire deep within me that spreads through my body, making my breath catch. I can taste the lingering sweetness of the punch on his lips, the faint tang of magic mingling with the warmth of his skin. The scent of him, a mix of nightshade and storm-soaked earth, envelopes me. It's intoxicating and irresistible and so damning.

But I don't want him to stop.

My body has never felt so *alive* before.

I press into him, and he responds in kind, his arms encircling me as he pulls me closer. The kiss deepens, our mouths moving as one in a dance as ancient as time itself. His tongue teases along my lower lip before slipping past, exploring with a hunger that mirrors my own.

Without giving me a chance to catch my breath, to stop my head from spinning from the sensations that have all but taken control of me, those cool, icy metal rings on his fingers leave frozen trails in their wake as they move. They slide down my arms, making me shiver. His hands dig into my hip, his strong, powerful arms hoisting me up from his lap.

The piano keys strum as I'm twisted and placed down onto them, a whimper escaping me as the noise slices through the air. He chuckles against my lips. I can feel them pull into a smirk as if he's amused with himself—with me.

My head falls back, gasping as those rings connect with the sensitive skin of my thighs. I'm not sure when he worked the hem of my dress up. If I'm honest, I don't care. My body aches for more, for him to venture higher, to soothe a fire that threatens to burn me from the inside out.

His teeth nip into my throat, his tongue flicking over my rapid, racing pulse, full of unspoken promises and desires. Telling me his mimic my own.

Fuck, I've dreamed of this moment. Of feeling him so close… Nothing could ever compare to reality.

Even in his weakened state, I feel like a lamb pinned beneath a predator's gaze, knowing every second that ticks by could be my last. Not caring… Only *craving it*. My movements become hurried, the need taking over, demanding *more*. Every touch, every breath, and every beat of my heart isn't enough—not even close.

My heart pounds in my chest, echoing in my ears—in my bones—as anticipation coursing through me. Asmo stands between my legs, his body flush with mine, his lips trailing down the column of my throat. Strong fingers flex, squeeze, and bite into my thighs, like he's suppressing the urge to let them travel higher, to seek out what we both need.

A soft moan slips from my lips as he presses a kiss to the hollowed space at the base of my throat, a shiver making my back bow into him. His amber eyes flick up to meet mine, like he's seeking silent permission, and I let out a shaky exhale. My fingers dive into the blue-black waves of his hair, his hand teasing the inside of my thigh.

I press my hips forward, urging him higher, needing those glorious fingers to see how deep my need runs for him, how wet I've become at the mere thought of him exploring that forbidden part of me. The coolness of his rings contrasts with the warmth of his touch, and despite how much I ache for him to move, how much I've made it known, he doesn't.

His dark amber gaze searches mine with an intensity that leaves me breathless. "Should I stop?" he asks, his voice barely more than a whisper.

"Gods," I breathe, my hands cupping his face and dragging it toward me. "Please, *please* don't stop" His mouth crushes to mine in a fury, and my fingers delve into his hair, fisting the strands at the base of his neck, demanding him to stay here, stay close to me.

His tongue dances with mine as I open for him, and I am too lost in the sensation to think clearly. I'm too consumed by the sweet taste of him, the scent of nightshade on his skin, the sounds of our ragged breathing filling the air.

My thoughts are drowned out in a whirlwind of desire, fear, and something deeper that I can't quite name. He's an elixir that can cure everything I've needed, ever wanted, and I can't help but be swept up in its magic. The world has narrowed down to this moment, the idea of war coming, of the queen knowing my secret, long lost to the ether.

24

Asmodeus

"I've never heard an elf beg before," I say against her lips, wrapping the long dark locks of her hair around my hand and pulling her head back, putting her beautiful, delicate throat at my mercy. "Our world must've frozen over if we've seen the day that an elf *begs* a demon for pleasure."

Narrowing my eyes, I wonder if I'm being played. With my other hand, I swipe the tip of my index figure around the shell of her pointed ear, feeling her body relax into me. "Those pointy ears don't come off, do they?"

"No," she half moans when I do it again.

"Are you sure?" I arch a brow.

"Maybe you didn't have anything worth begging for," she says, shoving the words through gritted teeth. Valeria wriggles her hips against my length, as if the friction alone could undo her. And when I step just out of her reach, she groans, tiring of my antics already.

"You underestimate me, Starlight," I tease, gripping her chin and stroking my thumb over her lower lip, enjoying the way her eyelids look heavy, her emerald eyes so dark they almost blend in with her pupils. "I've tortured people for a living, and they've had plenty of things to beg for."

Releasing her hair, I tease the hem of her dress up her thighs as she says, "It feels like I'm being tortured now."

"Does it?" I arch my eyebrows up toward my hairline as I find the seam of the thin lacy fabric between her thighs. Stroking my fingers over them, I chuckle under my breath. "These don't feel nearly wet enough to consider this torture, darling. If I were torturing you, I'd be able to wring them out long before I ever let you come."

Her chest shudders with an exhale, drawing my gaze to the round curves of her breasts, peeking so temptingly out from the neckline of her dress. Cocking my head, I let my eyes roam, taking in the way the moonlight highlights her all too perfect skin, has those lively green eyes glistening.

"Well, let's hear it." I flare my eyes for just a split second as I say, "Beg me."

She stares at me quietly. All I can do is watch as the point of her pretty pink tongue wets her full bottom lip. Her throat bobs as she swallows back her pride. "Please."

My hand strokes over the lacy fabric between her legs again, applying more pressure this time, and her back arches. I give her a wicked smile. "I'm going to need you to try harder than that."

"I said," she pushes the words through her teeth. "Please, oh glorious Prince of Death…" She trails off, rolling her eyes as she leans forward to cup the front of my pants in her palm, dragging a throaty groan from my lips. Her mouth is by my ear now, her teeth nipping into my ear lobe before she whispers, "Take me. Use me in every way you see fit."

My breaths are ragged as I wrap my hand gently around her throat, dragging her lips back to mine. "As you wish," I say between kisses, gripping her thighs. As I lift her from the piano, her legs wrap and lock around my torso.

Magic scents through the air, sweet like wine as my foot lifts and I step forward, folding time and space. Shadows and light wrap around us and we're in my room before my boot connects to the ground. Her back meets the wall, arching away from the cool stone into the heat of my body. Her chest swells, her hands looped around my neck.

I could devour her mind, body, and soul.

Fuck, I want to.

I want every inch of her alabaster skin painted in my teeth marks, covered in my kisses. I want every piece of her and have craved it since I laid eyes on her in those woods, falling out of that goddamn tree. For the first time in my life, I'd been jealous of leaves because they got to touch every inch of her body.

I can't explain it. I shouldn't want to.

She deserves better, and Jade deserves my suffering, yet I can't stop, even if I wanted to. I need to feel this woman beneath me, wrapped around me, to hear her moan my name, to know the sounds she makes when she shatters. I crave it more than I crave air.

Bracing her against the wall with my weight, I wiggle my fingers, and delicately pull the strings of the corset top. It's like unwrapping a present. With subtle precision, I tear the string through the eyelets, and when I'm done, the boning falls to the floor. She's left in nothing but a loose dress.

"How much do you care about this?" I ask, tugging on the neckline a bit, willing a single talon to form at the end of my fingertip.

"I can make another."

That's all I need to hear. My talon slices through the fabric, tearing it away from her with ease. Wrapping my arm around the small of her back, I guide it off her arms, bending to catch the swell of one of her breasts in my mouth. I close my eyes in a weak attempt to calm my racing heart.

Pinning her body with my hips, I grind my rigid length against her center. She moans, dropping her head back against the wall. It takes everything I have to force my demon half down, to breathe, to stay calm and be gentle. But despite the fight I put up, I can feel my eyes flicker back and forth between beast and man. The threads of magic that hold together our world shine like gold every time my eyes turn dark. Every inch of Valeria, bared to me in such a primal, intimate way, seems to glow with magic, too. It gives her a halo of light and it's fucking breathtaking.

So much so, I let go. I forget about my eyes, that I should keep them down and out of her view. The last thing either of us wants is her to become terrified of me—to see the monster the world fears.

My gaze carries up her body, taking in every glowing curve, her perfect soft skin, her hard nipples that my teeth ache to wrap around. "Gods, you're so fucking beautiful," I say, eyes lingering on the bite mark I left of her breast, then traveling higher to glimpse the flush on her cheeks as those emerald eyes widen on me.

A dainty, delicate hand settles on the side of my face, her thumb tracing my scar as she stares into my demonic eyes. "I could say the same about you."

My heart skips a beat, awe-struck by the fact she isn't beating against my chest, determined to get as far away from me as she can. Instead, she leans closer, brushing her lips against mine, and a part of me melts into putty in her skilled artistic hands, ready to be molded to her will.

I wrap my arms around her, pushing off the wall to lay her onto my bed, her body sinking into the fluffy covers as the light from the domed glass ceiling spills onto her nearly naked form. If heaven were a person, an image, it would be her in this moment.

Her hands slip down my bare torso, gliding effortlessly over every raised edge of the scars that riddle it. The gentle bite of her nails makes me suck in my stomach, flexing the muscles there. And something snaps inside me.

Bending forward, my tongue traces over the skin just above the waistband of lace, admiring the way her pupils blow. I latch onto the fabric with my teeth, dragging it down to the middle of her thighs before ripping it the rest of the way off with my hands.

Valeria lifts her knees, her legs spreading wide for me as she palms a breast in one hand and weaves the other into my hair, guiding me to where she wants me. My eyes don't leave hers as I lower my head, the heat of my mouth brushing over the most intimate part of her. My tongue lashes through the wetness that's pooled there and a groan falls from my lips.

I can hear my pulse echoing in my ears, thrashing wildly through my veins. Then everything disappears but the sounds she makes the moment my tongue slides over her again, swirling and flicking until her thighs tremble against my ears.

With both hands, I pin her legs to the bed, determined to devour her whole, to fill her with such pleasure that I become what she dreams about, that I'm who she thinks of when her fingers wander. I want her to remember the way I ravished her when she sees me, to drip with need at the sheer thought of me being here again.

My cock pushes and strains against the fabric of my pants, my hips rocking gently against the side of the bed, desperate for relief. It takes everything I have left within me not to moan as lust coils into a ball inside me, so pent up that it threatens to explode.

"Asmo," she whispers, her legs tightening around my face. My name falling off her lips nearly undoes me.

I suck hard on that little bud, where all her nerves meet, and she arches off the bed, a silent scream parting her lips. "Oh, sweet Starlight. The sounds you make for me…"

My voice isn't my own. It's not normal. It's demonic, deep, and rattled. It's grave and dangerous and dripping with lust. Valeria's body flushes from head to toe at the sound of it, as if magic somehow coiled around her, stealing her air.

Her nipples are hardened, so pink, so taught. It makes my mouth water as I dip a finger inside her. Then another, going deeper than before. Her body clenches around me greedily, her hips rising. *She's so godsdamn tight…*

"Have you ever done this before?" I brave the question with a strong feeling that I already know the answer.

"Yes," she breathes to my surprise, but when I meet her forest green eyes, I spot her wiggling her fingers. "But yours feel far better."

I should stop. I should step away, let her dress, and pretend this never happened because every plea that leaves her mouth only makes it harder to refrain from driving my aching cock into her until she doesn't simply moan my name, but screams it. Gods, I want to. My body vibrates from the need to slam inside her and chase the pleasure I crave. But she deserves better. Especially if my suspicion is right.

"I meant, has a man ever been here before?"

She stills. *Fuck… She's going to fucking end me.* It answers my question without words and I drag a hand down my face, wishing for just a moment that I wouldn't be her first. Valeria should be sharing this moment with someone she loves. Not me.

But she begged me. She wants me to do this. And if I do, then she deserves to come enough times that she sees stars, that the world tilts, and her body goes numb as her mind turns to mush. She deserves to be savored, cherished, fucking treasured. The last thing her sweet, virgin pussy needs is to be wrecked by a man who couldn't control himself to see to her body being properly prepared.

Get your shit together, Asmo.

I swallow hard, bracing a hand beside her head as I lean in to kiss her, claiming her lips as I fuck her with my fingers, stretching her for me, feeling her clench around them as she gets closer and closer to shattering.

Every cell of my being wants to see her come, wants to feel it when it happens. Gods, I'd let her stab me again if it meant a chance at this, virgin or no.

That thought is bloody terrifying.

And they say elves don't have magic of their own. Fucking liars. This is magic. It has to be, but I don't care. Not in the slightest.

Valeria pulls away from my lips, guiding my face to her throat as she breathes, "Gods, don't stop."

A growl sounds from low in my chest as I curl my fingers, thrusting them in and out of her until she's dripping with the need to be filled. Her fingers dig into my biceps, my shoulders, my chest, leaving reddened marks that only spur me on. I kiss her throat, my tongue flicking over her wild, chaotic pulse before whispering, "I can't wait to hear the sound you make for me." I drag the tip of my nose over the length of her neck, pressing a kiss to her collarbone. "It's all I've dreamed about since you came down those stairs, the scent of your desire fucking maddening. I'd wanted to bend you over those books, to make you come on my fingers," I say, driving them deeper. I nip her skin. "To taste you on my tongue and feel you around my cock." I kiss her lips, free hand wrapping gently around her throat, forcing her to meet my gaze.

"Come for me, Starlight." Power wraps around my words as I speak the command into her mind. Her muscles tense, body coiling as pleasure shoots through her. I smile down at her, enamored by the way her lips part, in awe over the raspy gasps she makes as she breaks into pieces.

Fuck, I want to ruin this girl… I want to smother her light with my shadows until she purrs in the dark.

"I knew you could do it," I whisper against her lips, kissing her deep as if I could taste those noises.

They're mine.

When she's recovered, I sit back, undoing the sword still belted around my waist, but pausing when I get to my pants. "Are you sure? We can stop if you'd like. The realms weren't built in a day."

She smiles up at me, wicked and sated, and so blissfully sexy. I'll never get the image out of my mind. "I'm—"

The door of my room bursts open. Griffin stands in the doorway, bending over to rest his hands on his knees as he tries to catch his breath. Before he can right himself, I wave a hand and one of my shirts materializes over Valeria's naked body, but she's already sitting up, startled by the noise, gripping the covers of my bed over her chest.

"What the hell is wrong with you?" I snap, glaring at Griffin and debating on whether he'd survive the fall if I use my magic to force him over the railing of the stairwell.

"Don't—*Fuck*, don't do it," he attempts, saying the words between wheezing breaths.

"Do what?" I demand, not bothering to hide the crackling power swarming my fingers, talons having already pushed through the skin there.

"Don't *fuck each other*. Gods! Give me a damn minute. I just sprinted into nearly every room of this keep looking for the two of you." Griffin tosses a hand at me, then bends back over. "I'm out of shape and drunk. Give me a break."

I wait, arms crossed, positioned between him and Valeria like some sort of living barrier, as if it'll protect her dignity.

"We've been drugged." Griffin stands, holding up a bundle of some kind of herb. "The chef thought this was lavender and added it to the punch. It's sirelouran blossoms. It's strong enough to make even the most loyal, celibate monk horny. So, whatever the fuck you two are up to, *don't*. Put clothes on, cover your assets, and for all that's holy and sacred, go your separate ways. You'll be fine by morning."

My heart screeches to a halt, every part of me going numb. *I almost…* She wasn't in her right mind. She drank the punch. I saw it.

Fuck.

I clear my throat, turning around to help Valeria up. *Shame.* All I can feel is complete, utter shame in myself. I can't even look at her. "You should go. I'll see you in the morning."

Valeria quietly slips away from me without a word. Griffin clears out of the way as she gathers her dress, pausing in the doorway for a moment. A small part of me hopes she'll look back, something to tell me that she's okay. Instead, she shuffles past and disappears into her own room, the one next to mine.

I drag in a deep breath, pushing my fingers through my hair.

What have I done? It could've been so much worse, but it doesn't take back what I did. What *we* did. I'm not sure if

I should admit that I didn't drink the punch. I left the glass on a table.

"Did you at least not get to the final act?" Griffin asks, still leaning against the door.

"You, um… You stopped us before it got that far, luckily."

He nods. "Good. Then the muscles and bruises I'll feel tomorrow from drunkenly gallivanting around the keep will be worth it."

For the first time since he's barged in here, I really look at him. His hair is a sweaty mess. His shirt and pants are gone, leaving him clad in nothing but his boxers. "What happened to you?"

He lets out a sharp, "Hah!" and shakes his head. "Let's just say I was figuring out the hard way that something was dangerously wrong. Between you and me, when you try to bang a rock spirit, check the punch. Don't wait until after you brainstorm how to make it work. I'm pretty sure I put a permanent bend in my dick."

I resist the urge to laugh, hiding the smile that threatens to split my face with my hand. "Noted."

"Anyway, goodnight. I'm going to go try to summon an ice pack."

25

Valeria

My eyes flutter open as the hell flame crests over the horizon, casting its fiery glow through the domed ceiling of my room. I lay here for a moment, basking in the warmth of the blankets wrapped tightly around me. My muscles ache in a deliciously satisfying way, a stark reminder of last night's *events.*

We didn't even have sex… Yet, muscles ache where I didn't even know muscles existed. A gentle rap on the door shatters the silence, slicing through my thoughts like a delicate blade.

"Come in," I call out, expecting to see Eep shuffling in, her broom in hand, ready to sweep the same corner she always does around this time.

Except, it's not Eep who enters. It's Asmo who slips through the doorway, clad only in silk pants that ride low on his hips, leaving his chest bare save for a smattering of scars. In his hands is a tray filled with fruits and two cups of steaming coffee. Flashes of last night rush forward, no doubt painting my cheeks in scarlet hues.

Asmodeus steps into the room, shutting the door behind him with a soft click, then gives me a sheepish smile as his eyes flicker to the tray. "I thought you might be hungry," he says, his amber gaze meeting mine.

Heat floods my cheeks as memories of last night fly to the forefront of my mind of us stealing kisses, of his hands on me, the piano keys filtering through the air…

I clear my throat and sit up, wincing at the soreness between my legs. "A little," I say, reaching for one of the cups of coffee. The rich blend of chicory and spices warms me from within as I take a sip. "But you don't have to coddle me. I'm fine."

A growl rumbles in his chest, faint, but I hear it. "I'll coddle you if I want to, now scoot." He juts his chin at me, telling me to slide over. The mattress dips under his weight as he sets the tray down on the bed and slips under the covers next to me. I try not to notice how his thigh brushes against mine, though I find myself stealing glances every time it moves against mine, that electrifying touch sparking a symphony of sensations within me.

"Are you sore?" he asks, a hint of a smirk playing at the corners of his mouth.

I narrow my eyes and set my coffee down on the tray. "From the dancing, yes."

"Of course… The dancing," he echoes with a chuckle. He pops a grape into his mouth, his gaze dropping briefly to my lips. "Is that what we're calling it now?"

A warm blush spreads across my cheeks as I fight the urge to fidget under his knowing stare. Curse this man for being able to read me so easily, to see through my flimsy excuses. I quickly snatch a strawberry from the tray and take a bite, letting the sweet juices burst across my tongue in an effort to avoid answering. But as I savor the flavor, my body remembers something else entirely. Someone else.

The taste of the punch on his lips.

I swallow hard, meeting his darkened gaze.

"We should talk about last night," he says, his voice rough.

I cringe inwardly, bracing myself for rejection or a reminder of how foolish I was to give in to temptation. But I force myself to meet his gaze and say, "Go on then. I'm listening."

He studies me for a long moment, fingers dancing over the rings adorning his fingers.

"Are you okay?"

I mean, my body aches. I'm perpetually embarrassed about the fact I took advantage of him, and worse yet, he was drugged from the punch I gave him. Xren watched me like a hawk when the chef's wife gave me my glass. I'd known something was off. *Why would Xren not say anything?*

"I'm fine, really. I'm sorry about last night, though."

"There's no need to apologize to me. If anything, I should be the one apologizing to you. Had Griffin not barged in…" He trails off, reaching out to brush a stray lock of hair from my face.

It takes everything I have not to lean into his touch. My heart thrums with hope that maybe it could happen again. That it wasn't just the punch.

"I wanted to make sure you're all right, first and foremost. What happened between us…" He pauses, gaze dropping to the bed. "I never meant for things to go so far. I took advantage of you in a moment of weakness and for that, I apologize. I should've had more control."

Silence falls between us. I'm not sure of what to say.

But then, before I can gather my thoughts to respond, Asmo's hand moves from my cheek to my chin, tilting my face up to meet his gaze. His eyes search mine, a storm of conflicting emotions swirling within their amber depths.

"You don't have to say anything, Valeria," he whispers, his voice laced with a tenderness that catches me off guard.

My heart drums a wild rhythm, threatening to escape the confines of my ribs, awestruck by the vulnerability shining through the usually composed mask he wears. His thumb traces a featherlight touch along my jawline, sending shivers down my spine.

"I don't regret it," I admit softly, unable to tear my gaze away from his intense stare.

He opens and closes his mouth, like he's unsure of what to say. "You don't?"

I shake my head, leaning into his touch.

Both of us sit here, frozen in place, as my mind wages war with my heart. Reason battles against my instincts, urging me to retract my words. If he felt the same way, he would've said so. His hand falls, but his expression gives away nothing.

Gods, what is he thinking? Did I ruin this?

With a sigh of resignation, I cave, dropping my eyes to the space between us. "I… I…" The words tumble out of me. Somehow, I've managed to make this worse.

Then his hand wraps around the back of my neck, pulling me toward him. The tray rattles from the sudden movement and he crushes his lips to mine. The shock registers in my mind a moment too late, my arms wrapping around his neck on instinct.

His lips are soft and warm, sweet like the grapes he's eaten. The scent of nightshade clinging to his skin draws me in deeper.

My thoughts dissolve like mist as our bodies press closer together. This is what I wanted. This is what I've been craving since I left his room.

When he pulls away, I chase his lips. "I'm sorry, as much as I want to, we need to get ready to go. The king and queen are expecting us within the hour," Asmo breathes against my lips, his voice laced with regret and longing.

"The meeting," I say, nodding my understanding.

As he starts to get up from the bed, he leans in to press a gentle kiss to my forehead. "I'll come get you soon. In the meantime, eat some breakfast and pack a bag."

Asmo doesn't come to get me. He summons me and my bag to the foyer without warning, smirking at me like he's won some secret bet.

"You could've warned me." I wobble on sore legs, attempting to regain my balance. "What if I'd still been in the bath?" I arch a brow, crossing my arms in challenge.

He kicks off the wall he's leaned on, prowling toward me. "It's nothing I haven't seen before."

"Well," I breathe, "Aren't you full of smiles." He's grinning from ear to ear as he closes the distance between us.

"He's been showing his teeth all morning. I'm starting to get concerned." Griffin says, pointing toward Asmo with the neck of his wine bottle. "It's unsettling if you ask me. I'm so used to seeing him grumpy and cynical. I'm not sure if this is better or worse."

Asmo rolls his eyes. "Are you going to be okay here?"

Griffin shrugs. "Don't have much of a choice in the matter, but yes. Me and the ghosts will play charades until you return. Good luck." Without another word, he slinks into the throne room.

I stare at that doorway for a long moment, hating that Griffin can't come with us. If anyone knows what it's like to be forced to live alone, trapped behind stone walls, it's me.

Gentle fingers slide down my bare arm, drawing my attention. "Are you ready?" That deep timbre has my stomach swirling with butterflies. With a nod, I take his hand, lacing my fingers with his, and the darkness and light fold in around us. Magic stings my nose, sweet like the fruit I'd tasted on his lips earlier, but stronger. The dark tresses of my hair whip around my face, swirling through the air until it disperses, leaving us on the step of Hell Hold's castle.

Massive windows stretch up stories high, arching into intricate points. The obsidian stone gleams in the hell flame light, and dozens of stairs stretch up from where we stand to the enormous oak doors, carved into depictions of angels and demons and creatures of every kind. It's beautiful and haunting all at the same time.

I turn in place, spying a bridge that connects the base of the castle to what looks like a village. The scent of fresh-baked bread storms my senses, making my mouth water. Though, it's the shape of the shops that seem to catch my eye. Whereas elvish buildings are angular and pointed, modern and sleek, these look like little cottages. Flower boxes are in full bloom in the windows, most of the walls made of stone, wood, and some sort of clay-like material. The trims of the shops are painted in a variety of colors, with round windows and doors. Trees even grow through some of the buildings, their architecture wrapping around the vast trunks. And in the streets, creatures of every kind move about.

It's nothing like I would've expected.

"Were you anticipating flames and public executions?" Asmo chuckles, his arm looping around my waist as he moves behind me, his fingers brushing my hair over one of my shoulders so he can kiss my pulse.

"Something like that, yes," I admit, sucking in a breath the moment his lips press against my skin.

"Hmmm," he says, the sound vibrating against me. "Perhaps we'll have to go exploring later."

I glance over my shoulder and he tugs me along, beckoning for us to head up the vast layers of stairs. By the time we reach the top, I'm breathless, but I stick close to his side. A whirlwind of anticipation dances in the pit of my stomach as he hauls open the large doors. And if I thought the outside was beautiful, what's waiting for us inside is nothing like I could have ever imagined.

Gold chandeliers hang in the foyer, stone gargoyles made to look like lioness creatures have been carved into pillars. Candle tapers flicker in various candelabras, and as my gaze travels over the colossal fireplace, I find a painting that's so realistic, I could swear the king and queen and their children are standing there themselves, in the flesh.

My mouth falls agape, words lost on the tip of my tongue as my eyes follow the wall, up, and up, and up, stories high. "This is incredible."

"This is my family home." Asmo follows my gaze. "Though Alice has made her share of tweaks, most of it looks just as it did when I was little. As if this place has been preserved in time."

"Sort of like you," I say. The obsidian stone's cool surface bites into me, gleaming beneath my fingertips as I trail them along the wall, feeling its polished smoothness. It's so shiny, the stone could be a mirror, and I stare at my reflection in it, making sure my hair is in place.

He chuckles low. "Yeah, I suppose. Maybe the castle is immortal, too." Taking my hand, he leads me up a tight staircase. "We'll drop our things off, then head to the meeting."

"We're sleeping here? We won't just teleport back to the keep?" I ask, huffing and puffing. My legs groan, my muscles aching from dancing and shaking and orgasms. Had I known we'd be ascending this far up, I might've opted to crawl.

"No. All lords and ladies are required to stay for dinner and seeing as war is now on the table, this meeting has likely been called to negotiate a treaty to avoid it." He speeds up the stairs, carrying our bags like they're nothing. Meanwhile, it's taking everything I have to lug my own bodyweight up flight after flight. Though his voice still echoes off the walls of the dim stairwell. "It'll take a day or two, at least, and until all negotiations and business are finalized, no one is allowed to leave Hell Hold. It's an odd rule for creatures like us who can be here at a second's notice, but for the other lords and ladies, it expedites things. Having to wait days for them to come back isn't practical."

I've completely lost sight of Asmo, his voice growing too faint to understand. Minutes of silence pass before I round the curved pillar to find him sitting on a step, a shadowy grin playing on his lips as he watches me approach.

He waited for me to catch up.

"Struggling, are we?" He presses his lips together, letting them pop. "I forgot about you being sore."

"Just peachy," I wheeze, my lungs screaming louder than my pride. They're on fire. *What does this man do? Sprint marathons across realms for fun?*

He stands and snaps his fingers. Our bags that had been sitting precariously on the ledge of a step a second ago have vanished into thin air as he descends a few levels to meet me. His hand finds mine, intertwining our fingers as he gazes down, his height more pronounced on the staircase.

Before now, I'd noticed how tall he is. Still standing two stairs up, I barely reach his hips. My eyes betray me, locking onto the pronounced bulge in the front of his pants. Heat creeps up my neck as I snap my gaze back to his face, only to find his smirk has deepened, his eyes glinting with the thrill of catching me.

Well, if there's one thing I learned today, it's that the man is highly blessed in that department.

He drags his teeth over his lip and there's no doubt in my mind… He knows exactly what I saw—what I noticed—and he's proud of it. I clear my throat, pretending my cheeks are flame, and try to look anywhere but at him.

"Somehow, you're even more awkward now that I've kissed you. I'd thought it would be the opposite, that you'd be more comfortable around me." He steps down one stair, the air turning hot as if it's vibrating with the tension between us.

"I am not—It's just my face," I say, pressing my lips together.

"Is that so?" He closes another step, his arm reaching over my shoulder, forcing me to turn my back against the stone pillar that pierces the middle of the spiral staircase.

"Yes," I breathe, catching myself looking at his lips, licking my own as the anticipation of what comes next races through me like wildfire.

"So, if I were to kiss you again, you're not going to swoon into oblivion?" His voice is a caress, his presence an intoxicating spell. Asmo's dark eyebrows lift playfully, the devilish smirk on his lips stirring something in my core that has my thighs clenching together. "You look ready to hyperventilate."

Wrong. I look ready to come. Right here. Right now. And gods, that's embarrassing. All he has to do is touch me, stroke his fingers between my legs and I'd shatter into a million pieces before him.

What is wrong with me?

I've never been this way. Not once.

I never lost my virginity because the one man I'd had the slightest interest in had kissed me and I'd felt nothing. I'd thought it was bad timing or an off day. I'd let the man strip me bare, touch me, and I might as well have been numb.

With Asmo? The man could look at me wrong and I'd turn into liquid lust on the floor.

This isn't right. It's not normal.

How the hell am I supposed to keep my wits about me now? It was bad enough when he was grumpy. But him looking at me like I'm the entire world, the center of his universe? It's like he gets off on the chase—cat and mouse—and it's become his secret mission to see how close to the edge he could drive me without lifting a finger.

And unfortunately, I suck at this game.

Asmo tilts his head down, resting his forehead on mine. My breath catches, eyes ensnared by the memories of that mouth, of the things it can do. "I suppose now might be the best time to tell you that we're sharing a room."

"Huh?" My breaths are shallow. Maybe he was right, I might hyperventilate, and gods, *pray for me*, because that's a long way to tumble down the stairs.

He slips a finger along the shell of my ear, making my knees threaten to buckle.

"Fuck…" I breathe, trying to bite back the moan.

A dark chuckle fills my ears, making every part of me tingle at the sound. "Because of these, I don't trust leaving you alone. Not with all that's happening between my people and yours. So, we can sleep in separate beds, or you can take me up on my offer to snuggle, but you're staying where I can see you. People do stupid things when they're scared, and I won't risk them hurting you because they see your ears and nothing more."

"I can't be the only elf here." Giving in, I let my hands glide off the soft fabric of his shirt. It's long sleeved, flaring around his wrists. The laces around his cover have been left undone, revealing the hard planes of muscle underneath.

"You're not, but it's not them I care about."

My heart swells as I drag in a breath, deep enough to fill my lungs to full capacity. "You care about me?"

"Of course I do. You're the Lady of Grim's Keep. It's my job to protect you. Not to mention, your life is still linked to mine."

The air deflates from me so fast, it's as if it never existed. I'm a job.

He doesn't *care* about me in the way I want him to. He *lusts* for me, the same way I do him. A pang in my gut makes me wonder, if our deal were to break, our lives untethered, would he be standing in this stairwell, pressing me against the wall? Would he have shared that moment with me last night?

I'm not even sure I can be mad.

I haven't shared with him the truth of who and what I am. Even if he did care, that might change the moment he discovers I'm a Nightborn.

"We should probably get going," I whisper, doing my best to steel my resolve, schooling my face into an emotionless wall. "They'll be waiting for us."

Asmo steps back, studying me a moment before extending his hand. "You're probably right. We've been up here longer than I intended."

When I take his hand, darkness and light explode into ribbons around us, and instead of our room, he brings us straight to the meeting hall.

26

Valeria

ASMO REACHES FOR THE door to the meeting hall, pausing before turning the handle.

"I should warn you, I might seem colder. It's not you. I promise, but it's my job to ensure they respect Alice and my brother." I hear his voice in my head, my eyes flicking to meet his.

Is he worried someone would overhear? Is that why he spoke to me this way? With a hesitant nod from me, Asmo pushes open the double doors. And as promised, his gaze turns to solid ice.

Inside the meeting hall is a vast wooden table stretching from wall to wall, surrounded by a dozen or so men and women. It could easily seat twenty if needed. As the conversations in the room die, the room falls into hushed silence, every gaze shifting toward us.

A flush rises in my cheeks, my skin prickling with the collective pressure of those curious stares. To my delight, neither of us is introduced. Though I suppose they already know him. Instead, Asmo guides me inside with a warm hand pressed to the small of my back and I keep my eyes glued to that table, admiring the way the light catches the carved details of the map on its surface. It depicts the realms and islands I could recognize in a heartbeat, and right now, those carved lines are keeping me from having to make eye contact with the other lords and ladies.

"It's nice of you to join us." I recognize the queen's voice, bowing slightly and flaring the skirt of my dress. Asmo doesn't follow suit, and instead, rushes forward to pull out an empty seat for me. Only once I've settled into it and he's pushed me forward do I lift my gaze.

He takes the chair next to mine as he answers the queen. "We'd… Gotten lost." Asmo's words hang in the air, his tone frosty and devoid of warmth.

The Queen is standing behind the king at the head of the table, eyes narrowing on Asmo as if she doesn't quite believe him. I don't blame her. It's a terrible excuse. He grew up here. There's not a chance in hell that he got lost. Even I know that.

Alice relaxes as her gaze turns to me. Her eyes crinkle with affectionate warmth as her lips curve into a nurturing smile. "Valeria," she says, her tongue rolling over my name like it's royal, "so nice to see you again."

Her blue eyes all but sparkle in the mage lights, looking every bit the queen she is with her vibrant red curls that cascade around her golden crown. She's in similar fighting leathers, like the ones I'd seen her wear yesterday, but these are made of some sort of dark golden scales. In the center of her chest is the kingdom's symbol, a deep crimson color that reminds me of blood. It's a depiction of serpents and a single blooming rose.

Last night, I was around her. She's the most powerful woman in the Seven Realms, yet her magic didn't spin through me or burrow into my bones. It was contained, leaving only the faintest of whispers floating along my skin. Just like it is when I'm around Asmo.

However, as I turn my attention around the table, taking in the other creatures, no one here should be able to radiate the power I feel. There's only one man I've known to make my skin prickle like this, like tiny thorn vines have wrapped around every inch of me.

The King of the Seven Realms.

Asmo must sense my unease. I feel something just on the edge of my awareness, like invisible hands sliding over my thigh, squeezing it, letting me know he's here. My heart settles, just a bit, still battering away at my ribs as I take in the other creatures.

One couple, I recognize immediately, seeing the subtle similarities in their faces. A man with dirty blonde hair, combed perfectly, along with a short beard. He has the same warming, and welcoming eyes as Griffin, though they're a different color. Same flirty, contagious grin, too. His gaze slips over me, then shifts to Asmo.

I can feel Asmo watching me, his attention boring into the side of my face as if he's gauging whether I'll run for the hills or not. Shifting in my seat, I lengthen my spine, making myself taller, and lift my chin, pretending the nerves aren't eating me alive.

Beside the man I've singled out as Griffin's father, a white-haired woman who embodies the very definition of goddess-like beauty twists her lips. She's where Griffin got the color of his eyes. They're so vibrant and ethereal, they're impossible to miss. She's also where he got his unmatched grace. Even the gentle twist of her lip is godly. Divine.

"You should stop staring. Trust me, the last person you want to piss off is Eva. Her beast couldn't care less about who and what you are, or who you're attached to. To it, you're dinner," Asmo warns, and I jerk my gaze away.

"Well, now that we're all here, we can commence. As all of you are aware, the Lord Elcrys of the Elven Islands has declared war." The queen places her hands on the table, standing next to her husband.

His power is relentless, filling the room until the molecules in the air vibrate. It even taunts my crystal pendant, making it hum in soft musical notes, even from afar. Bringing my hand to it, I attempt to smother its cherry glow, but it only seems to become brighter by the second. Brighter than I've ever seen it before.

This is exactly how it had been in Vanderlyth when he visited my father. Except, I'd been floors away from him then. Now, being in the same room… His raw, unchecked power is enough to make any creature tremble in its presence. It's enough to take my breath away.

"Breathe, Valeria." Asmo caresses the edges of my mind, coaxing me to calm as I turn my attention toward the head of the table, in the chair next to where Alice is standing is the king, looking as if he'd rather be anywhere but here.

The moment I lay my eyes on him, the king looks up from his laced hands, staring at Asmo and I for a long moment. His amber eyes are so much like his brothers. I nearly gasp. If it weren't for the scar on Asmo's face, and his slightly wider nose, they could be identical if Asmo were to cut his hair.

Where Asmo's is half tied back, his blue-black waves ending at his shoulders, the king's is shorter on the sides, the messy waves on top falling in wayward strands over his eyebrows, swirling around the golden crown on his head. Even those hauntingly familiar eyes are filled to the brim with latent power, causing goosebumps to rise over my arms.

The queen's hands are splayed across the wood grain, her eyes traveling around the table as she speaks. "Lord Elcrys has hinted at such idiocracy for a long time now, but he's made his intentions clear in the recent days. His official declaration accompanied an unprovoked strike against one of our shipping ports."

"Yes, what about Ogre's Landing? Any survivors?" A man with curved horns, seated across from me, speaks up, his elbow perched on the tabletop as he twists his wrist in the air. "Thornben?"

"That's Lord Zule. He controls Mythar, the only port inland, and ensures the River Styx isn't overrun with ships and boats so that the souls traversing back to the Well are uninterrupted. He's asking if the Lord of Ogre's Landing survived."

"No," the queen's voice is quiet, her head bowed. "The elves used some sort of magical bomb. It incinerated everyone within the village, the ships, the docks… There are still fish and creatures from the ocean washing up on the shore," Alice trails off, dragging a hand over her mouth as if she's struggling to continue, but she meets Lord Zule's eyes anyway. "No one made it out."

"Lord Elcrys deserves to rot for what he's done," another man says. His skin holds a bluish hue, his eyes larger than most. He squints as if the light irritates him, not in an angry way, and from between those slits, I can barely make out the vibrant neon color of his irises. It's as if he dwells underground or in the deepest areas of the forests, where the light doesn't touch. A nymph of some sort?

"And that would be Egress, Lord of the caverns. For the most part, he's quiet and more comes to these things out of duty. For him to say someone should die…" Asmo trails off, but I can see him tip his head out of the corner of my eye. *"It's gotten under his skin."*

"Elcrys is responsible for wrecking Grim's Keep, too. After I'd already been pushed through the boundary, he'd interrogated my people. When they couldn't give him what he was after, he killed the men and locked the women and children inside the keep before setting it on fire." Asmo doesn't look up from where he picks at his nails. They're surprisingly clean, but he seems to feel otherwise, as if there's invisible blood or dirt caked there that I can't see. "If he wants war, let there be war. I call dibs on ending his life."

There's a hidden promise in that last comment, one that splits me open to the bone, flaying my heart in two.

"Of course you'd say that," a humanoid looking man says. He crosses his arms and leans back in his seat. The chair groans under his weight but holds true. "The only thing you care about is yourself. Hell, if his war suited you, I doubt you'd be sitting at this table. You'd be at his side, waving your sword around."

"And that would be Rillion, Lord of Purgatory. In short, he punishes the bad souls by making them relive their worst moments in the hope that they learn from their mistakes. He's never really liked me. Not since I started an underground fight club in his district."

My brows arch as I turn to Asmo. *A fight club?* He rolls his eyes, then flicks his gaze back at me as if saying he'll elaborate later.

Asmo glares daggers at Rillion, his voice dripping with venom as he says, "If there was war, I'd sacrifice you and your *dogs* to ensure my family was safe. So, be lucky the elf lord isn't interested in the hellhounds."

"And that's precisely why you'll never be king." Rillion snubs his nose into the air. It's crooked, like it's been broken one too many times, and I can't imagine why anyone would ever want to do such a thing.

"I'll never be king because I'll ensure my brother has a long, happy life. Long enough that his son is of age and ready to take the throne in his passing. Everyone at this table knows I've never had a desire to rule, and that's as true now as it was before I'd ever gone through that boundary." Asmo doesn't look away from Rillion. I'm not even sure he blinks as he stares the hellhound shifter down.

Rillion scoffs, but says no more, turning his attention back to the king and queen.

The king shakes his head, the light bouncing off the golden serpents that have been embroidered around the edges of his billowing sleeves. He's dressed in the royal colors of black and gold, but like Asmo, he's left the neckline open. If it weren't for the sheer finery of the fabric, the crown on his head, and the power he radiates, I might not have pegged him as a king on looks alone.

A warrior, maybe, but not a king.

"War doesn't solve anything." The king sinks back in his chair, his dark eyes scanning the room, meeting those of every individual around this table. "The only thing war leads to is the death of innocent lives on both sides."

A lump forms in my throat, a mix of grief and anger swirling within me at the raw truth. The king is right. War only has devastating consequences.

"Yeah, well tell that to the Elf Lord. He doesn't seem to have gotten the memo." An Orc, easily five times the size of any creature around this table, says. He's not sitting at the table, but rather standing against the far wall. Even from that distance, he dwarfs everyone here.

"We must remember that our grievances aren't with the elves as a species, just the leaders commanding their armies to attack our villages. If there's an option to make peace, without us tossing magic back and forth on a battlefield and killing more innocents who are simply following orders, then we need to try. Now, his declaration came with a—"

Alice squeezes his shoulder, making the king stop mid sentence. Her lips tugging into a soft reassuring smile as the king peers up at her. "As much as I'd like to try to negotiate our way out of this, I don't see one. What he's demanded isn't possible." The queen meanders around the side of the table, pacing its length. "The elf lord has hated our kind for centuries. He frowns upon his own people for not being pure bloods. How do you reason with a man who sees himself superior to every other living thing?" She pauses a moment, as if waiting for someone to answer her. "You can't, because he doesn't value life outside of his own and the original elven families. To him, every creature other than the elves are ants. Ants he'd feel no remorse for if he crushed them beneath his boot."

Asmo gently nods beside me, elbows propped on the table and fingers laced, silently agreeing with her. As I stare at him, tracing the outline of his beautiful face, I'm not sure how to feel…

When my mother was alive, my father's views weren't so farfetched. He had empathy. He smiled… The day she gave her life to save mine changed something in him. Suddenly, the loving man I'd grown up with became cruel, *hardened*. I'm not sure if he was angry that his mate gave her life to save her child and left him behind, or that she did it to bring back his daughter and not his son.

She could only save one of us.

A life for a life.

Then I think of the gargoyles at Grim's Keep, what he did to them… I would've never expected such viciousness, such blood-thirsty vengeance from my father, even at his lowest point in life. It leads me to wonder if I ever really knew him at all.

"What was the alternative the elf lord offered?" Griffin's father asks, exhaling deeply as he lifts his gaze to the queen's.

"Not something we can give." The queen's gaze shifts to me.

Blood drains from my face, leaving my cheeks cold as ice, turning my soul hollow. She didn't need to speak it aloud. That look told me loud and clear.

Whatever his demands were, they have to do with me. Except, she can't do anything about it because I'd made her promise to keep my secret. She's honoring it, but at what expense?

My brows worry together, flattening slightly as I watch Asmo's face out of the corner of my eye. He spins the rings around his fingers, seemingly lost in thought.

What will he do if he learns the truth? That I'm the daughter of the man he hates with every cell of his being...

"We should have all the information," Griffin's mother says, her voice far more angelic than I expected it to be. It's impossible to look away as she speaks.

The king glances at his wife, then nods, settling his hands on the table. "He believes his daughter is being held captive here on the mainland. He's said if she's returned unharmed, then he'll settle for the Elven Islands to secedes from the crown of the Seven Realms, to become their own kingdom."

"She's his only heir, yes?" the hellhound man, Lord Zule, says as he pinches his chin between his fingers. "Is it possible for one of you to summon the girl?"

"Yes," the queen answers, her eyes drifting back to me. "Though summoning isn't an option. As elvish customs suggest, the Lord's heir in waiting is hidden away for their protection. No one has seen her."

She's not wrong. Until my courting, I had been hidden away. Whenever I wasn't at the royal balls, no one but a handful of servants were allowed in the wing of the castle I lived in. Whenever I was allowed to join my father at his gatherings, or allowed to promenade with the suitors, I always had to wear a golden mask that covered most of my face, save for my eyes and mouth.

"I thought you'd met the duchess," Asmo says, twisting in his chair, brows furrowed. "Didn't you accompany her when the two of you visited Vanderlyth? As long as her face hasn't changed much, the summoning should still work."

That was when the king came to Vanderlyth. Alice had demanded to meet me, and I could hear her yelling at my father, saying a lady shouldn't be imprisoned in her own home. That it was an honor to have dinner with the king and queen and that I should be present for such. Her efforts hadn't changed anything. I wasn't invited to have dinner with them, but she'd managed to come upstairs and bring dinner to me. She'd met me in my room. I'd never been more nervous in my life than I had been in that moment. So much that, my hands trembled and I nearly spilt my tea.

"Are we certain she's being held captive?" I ask, clearing my throat, urging my spine to stay strong, despite my incessant urge to cower when all eyes turn to me.

"No," the queen says, a grin spreading wide. "I don't believe she is. When I met her years ago, she looked miserable. And seeing as she was coming here to have her marriage blessed, I wouldn't be surprised if she took the chance to run."

"So, we're harboring an elvish fugitive now?" The orc steps closer, his green skin paling in the light. "Being it's worth war to save a girl from what? A marriage? That's their custom."

"Nothing is worth war, I assure you. However, if the duchess is here because she doesn't want to be found, then I have no intentions of going out of my way to find her. I sure as hell don't intend to put myself through the pain of having my husband or the prince scouring my memories to find a face that has likely changed too much to summon," she snaps, and the orc backs up, turning to where he's been leaning against the wall. Alice lets out a deep, steadying exhale and smoke coils from her nose, like it would a dragon. "Take the day to mull over our position. We'll convene again before dinner."

Chairs scrap the floor as the lords and ladies clear out, but Asmo makes no effort to stand, and therefore, neither do I.

When the room is empty, the king lifts his head, a clever smirk on his lips. "Well, not how I wished to meet the new Lady of Grim's Keep, but it's lovely to put a face to the name."

"Thank you, Your Majesty." I bow my head, pursing my lips.

"Kai. Family calls me by my real name." He stands from his seat, moving toward Alice to gather her hair at the nape of her neck, forcing her head up so she has to look at him. "You did lovely. Regardless of what the lords and ladies support, we'll figure it out."

"I hope you're right," she whispers, casting me a side glance, before leaning into the king, burying her face in the crook of his neck. "I will not force that girl to go back there. You know as well as I do that it took everything in my power to leave her in Vanderlyth that day. Elcrys is a bastard. A woman-hating asshat who gave me hell for years.

I'm glad he's not at this table any more. So help him, if I get the chance to run my sword through the man..."

The king smiles, chuckling slightly as he hugs her to him. "I'm glad to see you haven't lost your colorful language."

27

Valeria

Alice's lips curve into a warm smile and her blue eyes seem to twinkle, reflecting the glow of the mage lights. She bends down, planting a soft kiss on top of Asmo's head. The king simply squeezes his shoulder before tugging his wife toward the door. "Don't stay too long. I'm pretty sure the staff is putting out food already. The two of you should join us. Finn and Eva are."

Asmo doesn't flinch, his vacant stare glued to the wooden table. When it's clear he doesn't intend to answer, I tell them we will right before the door snicks shut. Tapping Asmo's arm with the back of my hand, he jerks his attention to me, like I've pulled him from a dream. "Are you okay? You've barely said a word."

"Yeah, I'm fine." Withdrawing a ring from his finger, he uses its smooth surface to trace eclipsed circles on the table.

"I hadn't realized the elves had ransacked Ogre's Landing," I say, hoping to break the silence that's fallen between us. I can only hope it's the weight of the upcoming war weighing down on him and not that he's figured out that I'm the one the elf lord seeks.

When he doesn't answer, the quiet becomes deafening. I muster up courage and try again. "It sounds awful. It makes my heart ache for people I didn't even know." Propping my head up with my hand, elbow on the table, I watch him blink, as if I've said nothing at all. My gut sinks lower, the vicious nerves clawing up my throat. "What do you think about the offer the elf lord made? Would the king really let him succeed if the duchess comes forward?"

He merely tips his head, studying the ring harder. "My brother is a man of his word. If he promised that for treaty terms, he'll honor it."

"What do you think he should do?" A part of me doesn't want to know his answer. The other half of me hopes his ruthless alter ego, the one I'd met in the keep that day, demanding to know who and what I was, will take precedence. That he'll crave revenge the same way I crave him.

Of course, the logical thing to do is like the king suggested, to find an agreement that doesn't result in innocent lives dying on a battlefield.

Asmo spins his copper ring like a top. "If it were up to me, I'd likely kill the elf lord. I'd take my time too. Except, it's not up to me, and that's not the moral choice." He bounces his eyebrows as if that morality is an inconvenience.

"And the king?" My stomach churns, making tendrils of anxiety wrap around me like a vise.

"My brother will want to find the girl, and Alice will do what she always does, stand up for those who can't help themselves. She'll happily go to war to keep one woman from leading a terrible life, just as she'd slaughter a battlefield on her own if it meant saving someone she loved. It's who she is." The ring clings against the wood, wobbling as it succumbs to gravity.

"Do you think the king will take the queen's position into account?" A lump forms in my throat at the idea of going back to Vanderlyth, swelling even more when I think of the consequences of me staying here.

There's no good option. One ends with me being with Asmo and Griffin at Grim's Keep but requires the sacrifice of hundreds of lives. The other involves far less bloodshed, but leaves me unhappy and miserable. The decision should be easy. One person's misfortune to spare the kingdom, but I'm finding it harder to make than I anticipated.

"A good king will always consider his queen's perspective," Asmo says, spinning the ring again. He hasn't once looked up from the table since he removed it from his finger. There's no one else in the room, yet his icy, vacant, hollow eyes are still hidden behind his impartial mask.

"What are you thinking about?" I gently place my hand on his arm, a wave of disappointment washing over me when he doesn't look my way or smirk.

Does he know?

Did he lie about his ability to search my head?

Would I know if he did?

"I'm manifesting," he says, the ring clanging once more as he traps it under his palm.

"Manifesting?" I shake my head, dropping my hand when he finally meets my eyes. "Manifesting what?"

"Your mouth closed," he says, his stone expression unreadable, but he doesn't look away.

"Excuse me?" I gape and rage boils my blood, warming me from the inside out.

"You didn't let me finish, Starlight." He reaches for my face, his calloused thumb stroking over my lower lip. "I'm manifesting the way it would feel to have your mouth closed around me."

The anger flees. The warmth that sparked through my veins melts into liquid lust, pooling between my thighs in the matter of a heartbeat. “I…”

Asmo shushes me with a tsking noise of his tongue, “You think so little of me.”

That couldn't be further from the truth.

His dark hair sways with the shake of his head. “I’m pretty sure daydreaming about how your mouth would feel is the only reason Lord Zule lived through this meeting. My mind was too absorbed with the fantasy of my cock twitching in your hands to care what he thought of me.” His eyes darken, the amber drowned out by his blown pupils. “I regret not telling you last night, but you’re fucking delicious, by the way. It's all I've been able to think about since I woke up.”

My eyes track the tip of his tongue as it slides between his lips. “I see,” I say, sounding far less breathless than I feel.

His lips quirk into a sinful grin, as he wraps a chunk of my dark hair around his finger. “A very dark part of me wants to lay you down on this table. To do unspeakable things… and know that when the lords meet here again tonight, that I’ve taken you on every inch of it.”

Despite the arousing nature of his words, he speaks so gently, so lovingly, that my head swims from the concoction it creates. "Oh…” I inadvertently lean toward him, and his smirk grows until his perfectly white teeth gleam, pleased by the effect his words have on me.

“Oh?” he mimics, brows raising. “No, *do as you please* or *take me as you will*, my lord?” He eliminates the space dividing us, his fingers threading into my hair, cradling my face. “Or was that just the punch talking?” His thumb strokes over my cheek, and I can’t help but lean into him.

“I thought you *weren't* a lord.”

He bites his lip. "I'm not. I'm a prince, but it sounded awfully good coming out of your mouth."

Everything about him is consuming in the most glorious of ways. I've found myself living for the moments he looks at me, for these touches, and I can feel my heart breaking at the thought of losing them.

He's so guarded… And in the little time I've known him, it's been easy to derive that he doesn't let many people in often, at least not outside his family. I've never lied to him, but withholding my lineage, knowing what my father has done to his people, is just as bad.

He'll never trust me again. He might never trust anyone.

My eyes well up, my lip trembling.

He needs to know. I just don't know how to say it. How to break his heart… but he needs this information now more than ever, before he falls for me, and I fall any harder for him.

Asmo's eyes widen, his spine stiffening as he cups my face in his hands. "Hey…" Brushing my hair away, he presses a chaste kiss to my forehead. "I didn't mean to upset you."

You didn't upset me… I did this to myself.

The dam breaks, the tears gushing from my eyes, streaming down my face so fast, not even praying to the long lost gods could stop them. Twisting out of his hands, I cover my face with my own, and a sob tears through me.

I didn't ask for this… but it's my fault. I've made choices I'm not proud of and now I'm reaping the consequences.

I decided to let my people believe I'm dead. How could I have known my father would find out I'm not? The last thing I expected was for him to be wrapped up with blood witches, that he could have them search for me and give him proof of life.

The only thing I cared about when I washed up on that shore, was not having to marry an asshole I don't love. But it was my choice not to go back. Now, people could die because of it.

I wanted Asmo to kiss me last night. I needed him to. I'd never met a demon. How the fuck was I supposed to know they could be so godawfully kind, and gentle, and loving…

He was my first demon! I wasn't prepared.

I never set out to hurt you. No matter how much I will my lips to move, to speak through the ragged sobs that barrel through me, that shred me to pieces, I can't force the words out.

Asmo pulls my hands away, his amber gaze searching my face for answers he likely won't find. "If this is too fast… If I'm pressuring you in any way, it's okay to tell me. I won't be upset." He wipes the tears from cheeks with his sleeve. Slowly, he sets his forehead against mine, closing his eyes. "Just tell me how to make it better… How do I make you smile again?"

My lips tremble as I drag in a shaky breath. "I'm so sorry…"

He sits back, brows knitted together. *Gods, those eyes…* The sheer innocence in them, the desire to comfort me, it's like a dagger driving through my heart. "What do you possibly have to be sorry about?"

"I never told you how I ended up at Grim's Keep," I say, pressing my lips together, desperately trying to push the tears down.

"What do you mean? You were stranded. Banished." He shakes his head, his eyes dropping as if he's searching his memories, trying to put the pieces together.

"You said that, not me."

"No..." His jaw feathers as he shakes his head. I don't think he wants to believe it, but he seems to have guessed where this is going.

"You have to believe me when I say that I didn't know what he did to your people." I wipe at my cheeks, sniffling as I steel myself. "Our ship was attacked by a sea monster and my betrothed rowed off in the only lifeboat. He left me for dead. I'd nearly drowned and I saw a way out of having to marry him by letting my father and my people think I had."

Asmo's knee bounces as if it's taking everything he has to remain in his seat and not pace around the room. I attempt to grip his hand but he jerks it away, lifting his gaze to mine. His amber eyes are cold, emotionless as he stares at me, like he can see straight through to my soul. "Say it."

Swallowing hard, I let myself look away. "I'm Valeria Nightborn, the Duchess of Vanderlyth."

Asmo recoils as if I've struck him. His eyes blaze, flickering between man and demon as he pushes up from his seat, pacing a moment before turning his back to me.

"Asmo, please..." I reach for him but stop just shy of touching his arm. "Please let me explain."

He whirls on me, fangs bared. "Explain? If you want to explain something then why is your hair dark? All of the original elven families, especially someone as highborn as the elf lord's daughter, have silver hair and silver eyes. Yours are green."

I flinch at the venom in his tone, wrapping my arms around myself. "That's because I died," I say, the words a whisper as they leave my lips.

Every part of him stills, like he's been petrified into a statue. "Died? Died how?"

“Our people, since the Realm of Monsters has collapsed, have been getting sick. We used to banish those who showed signs of it to the prison realm, and it kept the rest of our islands safe. We lose our color first, our skin becomes a dark gray, and as the sickness advances, our hair turns black. For some, that’s as far as it goes. The survivors were called dark elves, and they lose the ability to channel stones. Instead, they get their magic by stealing it from other creatures. However, most of those affected continue to wither away. It’s like our hearts shrivel up and die and our bodies begin to reflect the decay.”

“I don’t understand,” he says, brows flattening as he attempts to wrap his head around it. “I've seen you channel your pendant.”

“My brother and I caught the illness. Our mother had taken us to the market and the next day, my older brother turned gray, and was riddled with fever. I wasn’t long after him.” Rising from my seat, I pivot smoothly, coaxing the straps of my dress down over my shoulders to unveil the phoenix on my back to him. “When I took my last breath, my mother made a bargain with the Grim Reaper. She traded her life for him to make me immortal, to bring me back. I woke up floating in the pool beneath our sacred caverns, my skin was back to normal, but my hair was dark, and when I saw my face and phoenix branded on my flesh, I knew my father would hate me because I looked like a half-breed.”

“How old were you?” He says, helping me bring the straps to my dress back over my shoulders.

“Five.” I turn to face him, bowing my head in defeat. “My father lost his heir and he’s never let me forget that my mother sacrificed herself for the wrong child.”

“Alice knows, doesn’t she?” he asks, stepping away from me.

I can't tear my gaze away as he threads an agitated hand into his blue-black waves. The motion pulls fly away from the bun the top-half of it has been tied into. The heavy rings adorning his fingers catch the glow of the mage lights, shining through his dark strands. He's muttering under his breath, too low for me to hear, but the furrowing of his brow speaks of the deep turmoil within him.

“She has to know,” he says, shaking his head. “That phoenix is what she put on the Grim’s Keep banners. That’s how she knew your name… She knew exactly who you were the moment she laid eyes on you. It’s why she lied to the court, because she’s seen your face and would have to admit that you’re here, in the damn room.”

“Yes…” I nod, but I don’t bring my head up. “She confronted me about it at the keep yesterday. I guess, in her scrying, she’d never seen my face.” As I reach for his hand once more, he snatches it away. His eyes are filled with a mixture of rage and sorrow.

"Don't touch me," he growls, starting for the door.

“I’m so sorry…” The tears sting my eyes, rolling down my cheeks once more.

But this time, he’s not here to wipe them away.

Asmo crosses the room with lethal grace, pausing as he reaches the door to cast a glance over his shoulder. “Take a left when you leave, the hallway will lead you to the dining room.”

Just like that, he’s gone. He vanishes out the door, and I'm alone, clutching a heavy heart and fragments of hope that only his sweet kisses have the power to reassemble.

28

Asmodeus

HOW COULD I HAVE *been so foolish*... I should've known. I should've questioned more.

As the shadows and light fade, I storm through the third floor of the castle, making way for the abandoned office on this level. It's the perfect place for someone who's just realized he's been played for a fool. The office is forgotten, much like my common sense, and the maids stopped worrying about cleaning it long ago.

It's not the office itself that I'm after, rather the whiskey I hid in it two centuries ago. I'd stashed it there the day the war was over, saving it for a future time when I'd need it most. And *fuck*, is today the day to break it open.

Statues of armored figurines line the walls, watching me with silent, judgmental stares. And between them are various art pieces hanging on display. Some are of places in the Seven Realms, others of famous people of our history. Though, they mostly become a blur of colors and shapes, none of which catch my attention as I stalk through the empty hall.

The echo of my footsteps carries through the air, announcing my arrival long before I ever make it to the office door. Hand on the doorknob, I glance both ways before entering, sleeking inside and quickly shutting it behind me.

As the silence ensues, I feel a current of magic slip over every inch of my exposed skin, and with a sigh, I turn, already knowing what—or rather, who—I'll find. Even without his power on display, the feeling of being watched was enough to tell me I'm not alone.

Sprawled with careless grace atop the desk, my brother stares at me with wide eyes, his expression a picture of feigned innocence. And behind him, is his best friend, lounging in a leather chair like he's the king of the castle, legs thrown over the arms. Finn's usual up to no good grin is in place, just staring at me upside down as he leans over the arm of the chair.

"Fancy meeting you here," Finn says, his voice dripping with a mirth that grates on my last nerve.

"I could say the same," I snap back, rolling my eyes. Without another word, I stalk to the cabinets, my search for the whiskey growing frantic as I bang cabinet door after cabinet door.

"What are you hunting for?" my brother asks, a chuckle in his voice that suggests he finds my agitation more entertaining than concerning.

"My fucks to give, apparently. But whiskey will do," I mutter, rummaging through the shelves. The bottle is here. I can feel it—like a beacon calling to a sailor lost at sea. "Anything that raises my blood-alcohol content will do, actually."

"I mean, we could go downstairs, drink over some sandwiches, like *real men.*" Finn waggles his eyebrows, then sits up, shaking his head like he's dispelling the blood that's rushed there.

"Hmmm. Interesting. I didn't realize you're in the business of pretending to be something you're not." The words are out before I can stop them, each one laced with a sarcasm sharp enough to cut like a knife.

Slamming the cupboards, a snarl tears through my chest, rattling in my throat as talons push through my fingers. "Where the hell is the damn bottle?"

My brother stands, his boots clicking on the marble as he comes up behind me. "You have magic, asshole. Summon some." He flicks his wrist and a whiskey bottle appears in his hand, three cups with ice in his other.

Setting the glasses down on the shelves, he pours the whiskey with precision. The liquid swirls like gold under the room's dim light. Then, leaning against the wall with the casual arrogance of a king, he hands me a glass and holds another out to Finn.

"Your face is giving…" Finn trails off, kicking his feet off the chair arm so he can retrieve his drink. "I'm not sure." He cocks his head, tucking his free arm under the other as he points his glass at me. "What do you think it's giving, Kai? I'm leaning toward '*unexpected item in anus'* vibes."

My brother snorts mid-sip, licking his lips to catch the drops of whiskey he spilled. "That's exactly what it's giving." He knocks a fist against his chest, clearing his throat like he swallowed wrong.

Good, prick. Choke.

"Come on. Out with it," Finn says, waving at me like a child.

The whiskey burns a welcome fire down my throat, a fleeting distraction from my asshole brothers who likely won't let me leave this room without some sort of an explanation.

I scoff. "I'm not in the mood for an unsolicited therapy session. One of you putting your nose in my business is enough. The two of you together makes me want to go outside, dig a hole, crawl in it, and pay someone to bury me."

Finn snickers as if I didn't just insult him. "You're taking care of my son, the least I can do is make sure you're okay."

The least you could do is mind your damn business.

"I could just read your mind," Kai says, examining his whiskey. "At least your thoughts don't come with the attitude."

Yeah, you don't want to do that.

I shoot him a sarcastic, narrow-eyed smile. "You likely already know what's wrong, seeing as Alice is a part of this mess."

He arches a thick brow, and for being the youngest out of the three of us, he's certainly nailed the *Daddy isn't happy* face.

I'm the oldest.

That is my job.

My face.

Not his.

"Oh gods, just say it before I grow old and wither away. You two might be immortal and have eternity ahead of you, but my time is limited. I'd rather not spend it watching you two gawk at eachother like chickens."

Rolling my neck, and my eyes, and just about anything rollable to get the point across that Finn's getting on my last nerve, I turn to him. "I wasn't aware that chickens stare. Do their eyes even look in the same direction?"

Finn cocks his head, pondering that moment. "You know, I'm not sure." Hands waving, he almost spills his drink. "That's not the point. You can either say your peace now or Kai is going to pick your brain and spill your deepest, darkest secrets to me in private."

I steal a glance at the door from over my shoulder, wondering if I could make it there before they can stop me, or at least move away from the two of them, just enough to vanish. Doing so this close would likely drag them with me, or Kai could rip me back out of the shadows.

Deciding escape isn't a viable option, I huff out a long exhale, closing my eyes and praying to whoever is listening to give me strength. "Valeria is the elf lord's daughter. She just told me."

When I dare to open my eyes again, Kai's expression is unchanged. Finn, on the other hand, looks like an owl, ready to hoody hoo his shock.

"Can you fucking blink, please?" I snap at him, and Finn gets the hint, collecting himself. "Apparently, Kai doesn't tell you all my secrets." Crossing my arms, I glare daggers at the king. "When did you know?"

"Alice didn't tell me either if it makes you feel better. I found out in the meeting today."

I double take, brows flattening. If he found out today, then he… "You searched her fucking head?" I seethe through gritted teeth, poison dripping from every syllable. "Give me one good reason not to—"

He doesn't let me finish the threat. "Relax. She's an elf. We're at war *with elves*. It's my job to know who is on my court, and I was curious how the woman who stabbed you came to the meeting today on your arm."

My brows raise, but I don't say a word.

"Yeah. Alice mentioned that. I told you those poisoned daggers were a bad idea." Kai slams his cup down on the table.

Such a dramatic little king he is…

Making quick work to remove the top of the whiskey bottle, Kai pours himself a couple more fingers.

"So, let me get this straight..." Finn pinches his chin. "The girl the elf lord wants returned has been at your keep, and neither you nor my son thought to question it? I mean, it was broadcasted that the duchess was lost at sea. The very sea literally shoring your land."

Well, when you put it like that...

It wasn't broadcasted to *me.* At least I think it wasn't...

I tend to ignore the other lords most of the time. Nothing good tends to come from their mouths. If they're not reminding me of my past, they're picking apart Kai and Alice's rule. Both topics of which rub me raw.

Kai and Finn were the ones who told me to sheath my sword and only rely on force as a last resort. Well, ignoring the bastards on the court is how I'm doing that. If things were my way, I'd make an example of the first buffoon to let their mouth loose. The others would learn rather quickly to keep their wayward opinions to themselves.

They need to decide which version of me they want. The version who knows everything going on in the kingdom, that might kill a fool from time to time. Or the one that chooses to stay out of the way and ignore the blatant disrespect in the court.

They can't have both.

Well, maybe that's not true. They had both today. I managed to stay calm and poised, despite the others at the table being dicks. And I did that because my mind was kept busy with thoughts of Valeria.

It was a rare exception. One that likely won't happen again.

"Valeria doesn't look like a Nightborn. Would you have pegged her as the elf Lord's daughter at first sight? And she never said anything about it. I believed she'd been banished or something and when I'd asked, she got defensive. It made sense to me." I finish off my glass of whiskey in one burning gulp.

"Do you love her?" Kai spits the question out, nearly knocking me off balance.

My face plunges into a deep scowl. "What kind of question is that? She's been in my life a week, *maybe*, and half of that time I was in a fucking coma."

The king's eyes double in size and immediately wish I could take my admission back. "What happened?"

"Nothing *happened*. I was fine—*am fine*. I was just resting." I glance away, daring to sneak a peek at his face to ensure I saw his expression correctly the first time.

Yup, same face.

Fuck. He didn't know. I thought for sure he'd have seen that in Valeria's mind. Gods, this would've been so much easier if he didn't know about the gargoyles.

"What did you do, Asmodeus?" His voice takes on that stern, unyielding king persona and I cave.

"I used blood magic to bring back the people the elf lord killed. I'd made gargoyle bodies for them and nearly depleted my shadow trying to put their spirits into them. Those I brought back are tethered to the boundary around Grim's keep."

Finn's face turns a dark crimson-purple as if he's holding his breath. "That's why you helped Griffin? *You wanted his blood?* Gods-fucking-damnit, Asmo. That's a new low. Even for you."

I blink at him, pretending I didn't hear that last part. "Let me put your overactive mind to rest, *brother...*" Finn flinches when I seethe that endearment.

Taking a step forward, my demon form presses against my skin, screaming to be let out. It takes every ounce of strength I have to keep it at bay.

"I didn't know about the ghosts until *after* Griffin came to my keep. You're welcome, by the way. It would've been a fucking shame for the witches to bleed him dry." Shaking my head, I tsk my tongue, staring right into his big, round eyes.

Was it a low blow? Probably.

No, *it was.*

Finn was orphaned and doesn't know his true last name. And after the war, after years of him protecting Kai, my blood brother, while I was in the prison world, we'd dubbed him a Morningstar.

He deserved to be, but due to him being a druid, and not immortal like us, he doesn't feel like he lives up to the name. In reality, he couldn't be more wrong.

But right now, I want him to experience that same pang, the whittling hollow. The one that sinks into my bones and whispers that I'm not good enough, that they'll never love me, that they can't, because I'll always be different.

I'll always be the Prince who blew up the castle of Hell Hold. Who killed those inside of it… A monster.

Maybe, if Finn feels that, he'll stop inadvertently giving that pang to me.

When Finn doesn't respond, I cross my arms, glancing between the two of them, before giving Griffin's father a smug once over. "Well, go on then." I lean forward an inch. "*Apologize.*"

Finn lets out a huff of air, combing his dirty blond locks back. "Fine. I'm sorry. I jumped to conclusions."

Damn right you did.

Bouncing a brow, I pause a moment before taking the whiskey from Kai. "Now, if you two asshats are done holding me hostage, I have a queen to find."

Vanishing, my shadows swirl and light laces through them until I'm standing in front of the king and queen's quarters.

29

Asmodeus

A part of me wonders if Valeria found the dining room… but I can't think about that right now. She's a smart girl. She'll figure it out. And if not, she'll be waiting around the meeting hall when I'm done.

What I can do, though, is get some answers. And after today, I might not be the only one ready to break things.

I've known Alice for years. She's my… best friend. I know her tells. I know her faces. I don't need to read her thoughts to pick up on the fact she was ready to have a panic attack in that meeting.

I'm proud of her for keeping it together, but I'm not even sure Kai is aware of just how hard she was trying.

As angry as I am that she kept this from me, I shove it aside, take a deep breath and knock.

"Come in," she calls from inside, and I don't hesitate.

She's seated at the vanity on the far wall, her side profile to me. Her slender fingers put pin after pin in her hair, attempting to tame her wild curls. With the last one in her hand secure, she turns to me and smiles wide.

It's impossible to not smile back. "I hate you. I'm trying to brood."

"Well, you do a damn good job of that every other moment of the day. I promise one smile isn't going to damage your reputation."

Maevie, her daughter, bolts up from the couch in the living room, no doubt hearing my voice. Her red curls are just as wild as her mother's, and her amber eyes zero in on me. She squeals and sprints across the room, and my lips stretch into a grin so wide I fear every tooth is visible.

She slams into my legs, wrapping her little arms around me as tight as she possibly can. I have to stagger to stay upright. Without a second thought, my fingers thread into her hair, hugging her to me, and when she finally releases my legs, she grins up at me with big, beautiful eyes full of stars.

"I missed you!" Her head barely reaches my hip, and with her staring at me this way, every worry melts into the ether.

My heart glows, and for a short moment, I'm her entire world. "I missed you too, little mouse." Hooking my hands under her arms, I lift her up, and she clings to my torso, nestling her head into my shoulder. Carrying Maevie, I cross the room toward Alice, meeting her gaze in the mirror when I come up behind her. "Where's Lucian?"

Usually, wherever one of their children is, the other is nearby. As they would put it, it's a twin thing. Yet, as I turn in a tight circle, scanning the room, Alice's son is nowhere to be found.

"He's with Eva in the dining hall." Alice adjusts the same hairpin for the tenth time.

"Ah, precisely where you should be." I tease, taking a seat next to her on the tufted bench.

The moment I connect with the seat, Maevie pulls away, gathering a brush and two hair ties off the vanity. Tools in hand, she spins on my lap so that her back is to me, and without a word, commands me to do her bidding. I let her wave them a moment, waiting until she peeks over her shoulder in question to take them, knowing exactly what she's wanting me to do.

It's become our thing. One I sort of look forward to.

She doesn't know it, but Maevie has filled a void—as much as one can, anyway—created by losing someone just like her. And for that, I'll happily do anything she asks me to.

"I'm good for more than braiding your hair, you know," I say, parting her messy red curls down the middle.

She eyes me in the mirror reflection, too adorable for her own good. "You act like I'm not aware of your talents."

I chuckle as I twist strands of crimson hair into a perfect braid. It took me years to master it, but I've had plenty of practice. "What exactly *are* my talents, then?"

"You're a good cuddler." She ticks her little fingers off one by one. "You make the *best* ice cream sundaes. You read to me, *and* you braid my hair without me having to ask." Her eyes meet mine in the mirror and I get an eye roll full of attitude. "Well, *most of the time*. Still, that's just my top four." Maevie wiggles her fingers for me to see.

"I suppose you're right." Out of the corner of my eye, I catch Alice adjusting the same pins in her hair. *Again.* I swat at her hand and she shoots me a death glare that would make most shrivel. "You're going to primp yourself bald."

Alice's scowl deepens as she purses her lips, but ultimately she decides to listen. "Why exactly are you here and not downstairs? Please tell me you did not abandon the girl in my castle."

"Fine. I won't tell you, then."

She gapes at me, exaggerating a blink as she shakes her head. "You're joking, right? Please tell me you're joking. She's an *elf.*"

"I'm incredibly aware of her pointy ears, thank you." *I stroked them last night.*

"You can't just leave her alone, Asmo. She's an elf and we're technically at war with her people. You brought her here. *You protect her*. End of story. Oh, and let's not forget that your life is still tethered to hers. The last thing I need is you keeling over because some asshat didn't look past her ears."

"You and I both know my death would be temporary."

Alice takes the brush out of Maevie's hand—she's been holding it for me as I've twisted her hair—and before I can react, the back of the brush cracks over my bicep.

"Um, *ow.*" I rub at the spot, meeting Alice's blazing eyes. "What happened to *violence isn't the answer, Asmo?* Hmm?"

"That's not the point. What is going on with you? You're acting like your Hogwarts letter got lost in the mail." Shaking her head, then bends over the vanity, fixing her makeup.

"If that happened, I'd be crying. Do you see tears?" I get back to work on the last half of Maevie's head, while her little fingers toy with the tail of the first braid.

"You can either tell me, or the next time I go home, I won't bring you back books." Her red eyebrows arch in checkmate.

"You would hold such a thing over me?" My hands freeze. She doesn't look away. Doesn't speak.

Fuck, she's serious…

My entire life I've been fascinated with stars, but in the Seven Realms, we don't have any. Our skies are filled with twinkling lights, sure, but they're reflections of the crystals that line the ceiling of our world and the bottom of the three floating masses we refer to as our moons. Every three days, they block out the hell flame, a bright glowing fire that never goes out, embedded into the middle of the ceiling of our world, and we have a day of night.

The closest thing we have to stars is seeing those crystals catch on what little light there is. Only Earth, the world Alice comes from, has such a thing. My mother used to collect books from other worlds and the moment I read about those lights, I fell in love.

Then, Alice came into my life, and she could tell me about them. She'd *seen* them. And when she visits the mortal realm to check on her family, she makes an effort to bring back books for me so that I might experience what it's like to see the stars through words and stories.

She'd hang that over my head?

Alice is still frozen, waiting for me to pour my heart out. "Well? What will it be? Books or secrets?"

"You're one to talk. You knew exactly who Valeria was and didn't say anything," I snap quietly, not wanting to scare Maevie. As I finish the last braid, I tap my niece's shoulder. "Why don't you go downstairs with Lucian and Eva. Your mother and I will join you in a moment, all right?"

Maevie stares at me for a long moment in the reflection of the mirror, but she doesn't argue. Instead, she gets to her feet and kisses my cheek. "Thank you for the braids. Don't take too long."

"We won't," I assure her, waiting for her to skip from the room.

Alice watches the door too, and the moment her daughter is through it and it clicks closed, she scowls right back at me. "What would you have had me do? You'd just found out her father massacred your people. If I'd told you when I saw her face yesterday, you might have sent her in pieces back to her father. It wouldn't have been safe for her."

My shoulders settle, the glare falling from my face like it's been slapped off of it. "You think I'd do that to her? She's not her father. If anyone in the Seven Realms understands that children are not responsible for their parent's actions, it's me."

Alice drops the mascara in her hand onto the vanity, her chest concaving as her eyes flood with worry, with regret. Her manicured hand rests on my cheek, and it's not until her thumb swipes a tear away that I realize one has fallen. "I'm sorry. That's not what I meant."

Her thumb hovers over the scar on my cheek, knowing damn well that my father was the one who put it there. He was blinded by his need for war and revenge. So much that he'd have carved the spellbinding my mother placed on me out if it were possible. All because his son couldn't use his magic.

After years of being tortured by the man, determined to break the magic strings my mother tied around my soul, he finally got what he wanted. The darkened shadows of people burned into various walls of this castle are proof of that. I am not my father. I would never harm my child—or any child, for that matter.

"You were furious," Alice says, dropping her hand. "When people are that upset about something, they don't think rationally. They're not themselves. I couldn't be sure that you wouldn't break your deal, or that you wouldn't kill her and suffer the consequences of coming back from the dead."

"I'd hope you'd have more faith in me than that." Trapping my lip between my teeth, I force myself to meet her eyes. "So, what do I do now?"

"I saw the way you look at her. It might not be love, but you're definitely feeling something." Watching her in the mirror, she reaches for her jewelry box and pulls out earrings and threads them on.

"She deserves better." I fidget with the buttons of my shirt, popping one through the hole only to take it out again.

"She *wants* you." A necklace clings against the vanity wood in front of me. It only takes me a moment to recognize it.

It's one I'd given to Jade the day I learned we were mates—that she was the other half of my soul. The stone in the pendant has been enchanted, infused with a piece of my spirit, making it glow when it recognizes itself. It's how I'd told her. And as if it was yesterday, I can remember the way it glowed around her neck that moment the pendant touched her skin. I'd never seen her so happy before, and to this day, my heart has never been that full since.

"You should hang on to that," she says, her heels clicking on the marble as she moves about behind me, scouring for something within the room. I'm not sure when she got up.

"I gave it to you to keep safe." With trembling fingers, I pick it up, watching that clear stone bloom into a bright white light.

"That's because you were trying to be a nomad and travel the realms. You didn't want to lose it. But you have a permanent home now and you're putting down roots. It should go home with you."

All I can do is give a curt nod. With a numbness I'm not sure how to describe, I unclasp it, bring it around my neck, and tuck the small pendant under my shirt. It's only once I finish that I discover Alice watching me, a smile on her face, arms folded.

"Are you going to find Valeria?" Her question hangs in the air between us.

"Yeah. You're right. She shouldn't be unprotected, so for the remainder of our time here, I'll ensure she's not alone."

"Did she mention if she wanted to go back or stay?"

I shake my head, hating the way my insides clench and tighten to the point of pain at the thought of her leaving Grim's Keep for good.

"Well, then let's keep her last name to ourselves, yes? The lords don't need to know." With that, Alice waves me over. "Now come on. Maevie will send a search party if we don't join her for lunch soon."

A smile pulls at my mouth, knowing it's the truth. I've seen her send the entire castle guard after her father before, because she wanted to know if she could buy a dress. She'd told them it was life or death, and certainly got the response she wanted. The king had been tracked down and rushed to the village market within minutes.

As we enter the dining room, I quickly scan the table. Kai and Finn have both come downstairs, and are now seated near the head of the table. To their right is Eva, with Lucian on her lap. One hand holds a large chicken leg and the other fidgets with the boy's shaggy hair. He's a spitting image of the king, just with red hair and smattering of freckles.

Across from them is Aeress. She's the mad king's youngest daughter, but was little when the war ended. Eva and Finn chose to raise her as their own, and therefore she became Griffin's older sibling more than an aunt. Her long white hair has been braided into a crown around her head and instead of the frilly dresses I'm used to seeing her in, she's in fighting leathers, like she just came from training.

Next to her is Finn and Eva's youngest, and most ruthless, daughter, Callista. Mage through and through, she's mastered most magics and she's only ten. A prodigy in the making. Her golden blonde hair is cut into a long bob, the tips of the strands dyed crimson. If Finn were a woman, Callista is exactly how I would imagine him. She didn't even take her sword off to come to the table.

I bet if I was to look under the table, I'd find that Finn didn't either.

Valeria is next to her, and the two are in the midst of a conversation when we enter. Except, the moment she sees Alice and I, whatever Valeria had intended to say, dies on her tongue. Her emerald eyes meet with mine, and I'm immediately aware that the only two available chairs are between her and the king.

Alice takes her seat next to Kai, and I bite my lip.

Am I hungry? I could probably wait for dinner...

"Asmo," Alice singsongs, twirling her fork in the air. "We're waiting on you."

With a deep breath, I take a seat. Valeria watches my every moment, every twitch of my muscles, reading into it. "Can we talk after?"

With a curt nod, I glance at her out of the corner of my eye. My gut twists at the sight of the red rimming her eyes, the lids a bit swollen from her crying. It cracks something inside me, and I have the sudden urge to kiss her, to assure her everything will be okay, but I can't.

I don't know if it will and telling her so would only mislead her. Until we know what's going to happen, we shouldn't get any closer. If we do and she goes back to the Elven Islands, it'll only make things harder.

This is still new. The feelings are fresh. To walk away now might hurt, but it wouldn't shatter us like it would if we were to fall in love. If that happens, the choice is gone. I'd sooner go to war than let her leave me.

It's for the best.

Piling my plate with various meats and fruits and vegetables, the two of us eat in silence as the others carry on about anything and everything. They're pretending war isn't on our front doorstep and hundreds of lives depend on a decision that no one is willing to make.

In my mind, I know the right thing to do is look after our kingdom's well-being. To sacrifice a second chance at love for the greater good of our people. And Valeria returning to the islands means no one else has to die.

Aside from my burning desire to kill the elf lord, to make him suffer the same fate he bestowed on the gargoyles, doing so would mean war. And I'm not willing to let countless others die for my revenge. Especially when our kingdom isn't prepared for it. Our people have grown soft. Not many of the newer generations know how to fight because we've been at peace for two hundred years.

Still, none of us would force Valeria to go back. It has to be her decision.

Though, the ache that echoes through my chest knows what Valeria will do. Someone with generativity will choose the greater good over themselves. She's already proven herself to do so by digging graves for dead strangers and risking her life going beyond the wall to lay them to rest.

She's going to go back. We'll end up breaking our deal, and ultimately, I'll be left at Grim's Keep, surrounded by the darkness and void of her light. My only company will be gargoyles who can't communicate. And Griffin.

At some point, my desires changed from wanting to be left alone, to wanting to be left alone with her.

30

Valeria

Once we've eaten, Asmo takes me to the room we'll be staying in for the night. The tendrils of darkness and light fade away to reveal a room easily two stories tall. A large, canopied bed sits in the deepest alcove, dressed in rich, luxurious fabrics of onyx and molten gold, and embroidered in royal swirls.

It's exactly what I'd imagine his room would look like. A room that resembles his personality, dark and secretive, but alluring.

A fireplace that's at least three times my height flicks to life in the living area, sending waves of heat that surge through the room, swallowing up the chill that was present moments ago. It pricks my skin, the contrast making me shiver. The flames dance with a voracity akin to greed, enveloping the logs in shades of green.

In front of it is a fur rug and two large leather couches that frame the space. They could easily seat a dozen or so people, but they look too untouched to have been used by anyone but Asmo.

The feet step over the dark marble and admire the golden striations that wisp through the grain. Even the walls are dark, made from slabs of obsidian, and mage lights embedded into them lick over the rough natural surface of the stone.

There aren't many windows. Just one on either side of the fireplace, and both arch into points at the top, casting beams of light into the living room. I can faintly see the particles of dust floating there, even though the room appears spotless.

"Is this where you lived? Before Grim's?" I ask.

A silent pause settles upon us, and my curiosity gets the best of me. I turn in a tight circle, waiting for him to answer, only to find a vast wall of bookshelves that stretch from floor to ceiling on the wall behind me.

He nods once, driving a veined hand through his silken hair, then looks at me as if he's not here to talk about the room. "It was, yes."

I swallow thickly. "Do you know why I didn't say anything?"

"You didn't want me to take you back there, where you'd have to marry someone." He holds his hands up a moment before letting them fall back to his sides. "Is there another reason?"

"I didn't know who you were, and I knew my father had made enemies on the mainland. I wasn't sure if you'd force me to go home or if you'd take it badly. In Vanderlyth, we're taught that demons are heartless creatures. I thought the king and queen might take me prisoner."

"Do you still feel that way?"

"No… I don't." I hang my head, hating that I didn't speak up sooner. "But by the time I saw the truth, you'd gone into a coma and I didn't feel like hitting you with that was the best thing to do the first day you woke up. Then, the queen came, and well, you know the rest."

There wasn't much time. With all that's happened, I'm not sure I would've found the right time to tell him in between it all, and once we kissed, I knew I needed to.

Something inside me wanted to make sure it was done right, when the timing was better.

Except, that time never came.

"You must hate me…" I shake my head. "I'm so sorry. If I could go back, I would."

"I wouldn't." Asmo steps closer, and I glance up at him in shock. "And I could never hate you, Starlight."

"You wouldn't?"

"No. Would I have rather you told me? Yeah, but I enjoyed the time we've had together. I wouldn't take that back." He takes another step, closing the distance, and brushes the hair from my face, tucking it behind my ears.

"I don't know what to do," I say, my voice barely a whisper as I bite back tears. "I want to stay and go back to Grim's Keep with you, but I also don't want war, or for others to die because of my happiness."

He folds his arms around me, the warmth of his body seeping into mine. His heart thumps, slow and steady, against my ear, the scent of nightshade tingling my nose.

If I stay here, I could have this.

But I can't.

He cradles my head to his chest, strong fingers brushing through my hair. "I know…" Tears slip free, gliding down my cheeks as he holds me through every rattling breath. "If you choose to go home, I'll break our deal. I'll respect your decision, but just know there's always a place for you at Grim's Keep. I'll even teach you how to summon me should you need to be properly kidnapped."

I snort out a laugh, through the tears. "I'll be married." I squeeze my eyes shut. "Ugh, *gods*, I'll be *married…*"

"We have a plethora of graves—"

"No. You're not killing anyone for me." I swat at his chest.

He shrugs. "You never know." His thumb absently strokes the soft skin of my cheek as if memorizing its texture. I can't help but look up at him, finding his warm, amber eyes entranced by my lips.

"Please," I plead, cupping his face. "If I have to leave, I want to enjoy what time there is left."

"It'll only make it harder…" Asmo's throat bobs, but his stare never leaves my lips.

"It might," I admit, standing up on my tip toes. "But if I go back, I'll have to spend the rest of my life married to a man I wish would've drowned in that ocean. It's this time with you, as short as it may be, that I'm going to think about when I close my eyes."

He brings his forehead to mine, his breath rumbling in his throat. Just as I believe he's going to cave, to give me what I'm asking, he grips my wrist, and my heart sinks. But instead of pushing me away, he tugs me closer. Our lips collide, a rush of electricity surging between us.

Asmo tastes of wine, sweet and bitter and currents of his power slip over my skin, stronger than I've ever felt it before. We're a tangle of arms and breaths, until the world around us ceases to exist. It's just him and me and this moment. This heartbreaking, bittersweet moment.

Starved fingers thread through my hair, his lips searing a path down my neck. I can feel the steady thump of his heart against my chest as if it's trying to synchronize with mine. Grappling to him for dear life, a part of me wonders if I hold him close enough, tight enough, maybe I can stay. Maybe I don't have to part from him. Except I know the truth deep down in my very soul, and it threatens to splinter my soul into countless shards.

Not just because he's everything I've dreamed of when I've looked to the future, of who I'd marry one day. But, leaving him means returning to a home I hate. Where my own father blames me for the deaths of my family, where the people of our culture frown upon every hair on my head, and the color of my eyes…

I don't want to give my hand to a man who sees me as a toy, who only wishes to marry me to gain my last name. My life will be belittled to sitting next to my husband, pumping out heirs. I'll become a living puppet for him to shove his cock into as he pleases, instead of spending his nights in the brothels. There are no dreams. There's no happily ever after waiting for me. I'll just exist.

In the time I've known the man I'll be forced to wed, he's only ever made me feel inadequate. He's picked apart every dress I've worn, mentioning how it would look better on a slender, traditional elven woman's body instead of mine. He even hired a witch to glamour me into having silver hair and eyes, like most purebloods. Then took it a step further by employing the most renowned nutritionist in the islands to see to me losing weight before our wedding. Apparently, a glamour wouldn't be enough for that, though I'm fairly certain not eating won't affect how wide the bones of my hips are or the size of my breasts.

Asmo, on the other hand, every time he looks at me, touches me, I feel cherished. I feel wanted, and dare I say, *desired*. They couldn't be more opposite. I reach up, tangling my hands in his hair, feeling the silky strands between my fingers.

Between us, there is no promise of 'forever', nor vows of eternal love—we both know the truth. That reality is cruel, inevitable, an impending storm that will separate us for the rest of our lives. But at this moment, that doesn't matter. There are no distractions, no rules, no future. Just the here and now. The sensations. The lust weaving through my veins, igniting me inside and out, and pooling in my core.

My pulse quickens as Asmo's lips brush against the shell of my ear, sending waves of delight coursing through me, driving heat straight between my legs. I know beyond a shadow of a doubt he can feel my heart racing, beating like hummingbird wings. And if he doesn't feel it, I know he can hear it. Between that and his ability to smell my need, my intentions are laid bare.

Asmo's hand roams up and down the length of my back, tracing gentle patterns up over my spine. A shiver rakes through me, but as my back arches, his hard length presses flush to my stomach. It fuels a cruel desperation inside me. I want to feel it, to hold it in my hands and experience him in every possible way. I want to share this with him, something no one—not even my father—can take away from us. From *me.*

Teeth graze my neck as a growl sounds from deep within his throat. It's so bold, so visceral, all I can do is cling to it. He bites the sensitive skin of my throat, a sharp pain dragging a whimper from me, but it's gone so quick, fading into a dull throb. I moan against his shoulder, all but playing dead in his arms as my thighs squeeze tightly together.

Gods… He's so in tune to my needs, that even the slightest squeeze of my thighs doesn't go unnoticed. A menacing, knowing chuckle vibrates against my skin as he releases his hold, soothing his tongue over the spot. I can feel him smiling, as if he's discovered my dirty little secret, a weakness.

"Fuck, Starlight. This is a terrible idea, but I don't think I can stop." His voice is graveled and raw, falling an octave deeper than usual. It spiders through my veins, threading warmth and longing into the currents of my blood.

He pulls away, kissing my lips. It's slow and sensual, like he's learning me, attempting to coax those sounds from my lips at every opportunity. My head swims from the sensations that just being near him brings, and then I'm matching his steps backward until my knees hit a ledge.

My eyes flare open, finding that we've moved across the room. And the ledge at my knees? It's one of the leather couches in the living area. With a graceful swoop of his foot, mine is taken out from underneath me, and I drop into a seated position on the couch with him standing tall before me.

"What exactly is it that you wish to remember?" he asks, twirling my hair around his finger, like it's his new favorite toy.

"Everything," I breathe. "I want to remember it all."

With such a delicate touch, he guides the straps of my dress off my shoulders, and the loose, burnt-orange fabric falls toward my waist. Out of instinct, I reach for it, holding it over my breasts as I return my gaze to his. Amber, molten to the core, meets me there, and slowly, I let my hand drop, earning a rewarding smirk.

He worships the sight of me, gliding his feather-light fingers over the line of my jaw, down my neck, across my collarbones. There's a tenderness in that touch, so contradictory to everything I expected a demon to be. His gaze grows hungrier the farther down his hands travel, molding my breasts, pinching my nipples until they become hardened peaks.

"You're perfect, you know that?" He tips my chin, claiming my lips as if I'm the air he needs to survive.

"I know someone that would disagree," I say, breaking away just long enough to get the words out. However, the second I try to loop my arms around his neck, to drag him down with me, the hand crooking beneath my chin slides to my throat, pressing me backward until I'm flush with the couch cushions.

"Then he's a fool," he says, his tone becoming dark—*deadly*.

It's only when I open my eyes that I find the amber rings are gone, and the obsidian voids of his beast in their place. Dark lines leach from them, like the darkness has wormed into his veins on his cheeks. Except, what I thought before were endless pits of darkness, I can just barely mark out glowing specks floating in those eyes. They look like the twinkling lights of the night sky.

"Well," he breathes, letting his hand return to tracing the contours of my body. "If this is what you'll remember when you close your eyes, then let it also be what reminds you of this." He drops down to his knees, planting a kiss on my chest as those eyes fade back into amber. "You're the most beautiful woman I've ever met, and if anyone tells you otherwise, they can answer to me."

"You don't have to woo me, Asmo." It's impossible to hide the grin that stretches my lips though, because the truth is, I am wooed by his compliment. Even if he is likely just telling me what I want or need to hear.

He shakes his head. "I'm not. It's the truth and I can prove it."

"How?" I challenge, arching a brow.

"The day I met you in the keep, you stabbed me. You managed to take my blade off my body and plunge it here," he says, sitting back and pointing to a scar near his ribs that's slightly pinker than the rest. "No one, not even the queen has managed to get one over on me that easily. Yet, you didn't have to try."

"You're saying that you were *so stunned with my beauty* that I was able to stab you?"

"No," he shakes his head. "I'm saying I was so stunned to see a woman in my ruined keep, and one so incredibly divine at that, I wasn't sure what to think. I couldn't process it. You quite literally broke my mind for a moment. I've lived for hundreds of years, and I've seen plenty of beautiful women in my lifetime, but no one has ever stunned me so thoroughly as you did that day. And now, I'll forever wear the scar."

It scares me how easily he's pieced together my insecurities. Am I that much of an open book?

Asmo bends to kiss the curve of my breast, glancing up at me for a moment, before swirling the heat of his tongue around my nipple. My body arches into him, my eyes falling shut. His other hand slips behind my back, urging me closer, fingers splayed wide over my spine.

My legs spread for him without me cognitively thinking to do it, and my hips rock forward as if desperate for friction. Without a second to spare, he lowers his mouth to the inside of my thigh, kissing me there, and drawing the tip of his nose up toward my center and down the other leg, mirroring his kiss on the other side. It's blissful torture. Torture that has every muscle in my body tightening in a wave.

"Don't toy with me." I groan in frustration as he does it again, coming closer to the place I want him this time, but never giving me what I need.

He laughs softly under his breath. "Trust me, Starlight," he says against the hollow of my hip bone. And with a devilish smirk, he drags his fingers over my panties, pressing down hard on my clit through the drenched fabric. "I have no intention of playing."

His breath is hot against my skin and I squirm, shuddering against him, willing him to move. The air is trapped in my throat. The need to be taken so thoroughly that I ache for days has consumed every viable brain cell I have.

I want this.

I want him.

"Say please." He swirls his fingers once, making my hips buckle.

"Please," I pant, and he pulls the thin fabric away, guiding it down my legs with tantalizing slowness.

The anticipation builds until it's maddening. Where I'm trembling with the need to be sated, to have him closer—so close that I can't tell where I end and he begins—he's in the mood to savor it.

Perhaps, it's because he'll think of me when he closes his eyes, too.

At least, that's what I want to tell myself. That if things were different, he'd choose me. That we'd get to know each other. That this could become something more than one day—*one memory*—to last an eternity.

I slide my leg up, propping my foot on the couch to give him better access, and he draws his thumb over my clit, creating lazy circles. Sparks of pleasure swirl in my middle, mingling with the sea of butterflies that have taken flight there. I drag in a deep breath, forcing my lungs to fill as my head thumps back against the couch. It's become too heavy for me to keep it upright.

A soft moan escapes my lips, his name carried in it. I feel him shiver, the muscles of his stomach tightening, his breath turning ragged at the mention of his name. Power floods through me—his power—igniting and heightening every sense. I wonder if that sensation is on purpose, like he knows what it does to me. Has he noticed that it sends heat flooding through my core at the sheer thought of it being wrapped around me, whittling away every shred of my innocence.

He hooks his strong arms under my thighs, jerking my body toward him in a swift motion, taking my hips off the edge of the couch. I dare to lift my head from the cushion as his hands grip the fleshy part of my thighs. The position pins me, legs spread, leaving me prey to his predatory gaze.

Those demonic eyes have returned as his tongue darts between his lips, like he's ready to devour me whole, to feast on my very soul. White halos form around his long, splayed fingers, his grip so tight that I couldn't wiggle out of his hold if I wanted to. I'm at his mercy. And he could ruin me. He could destroy me with the snap of his fingers—that easily—and I'd be helpless. Yet, instead of terror coursing through my veins, it only makes my heartbeat wilder.

Because I know he won't.

I trust him, so wholeheartedly, and I can't even begin to understand why. But I do.

His gaze meets mine, and I swallow hard as his mouth lowers between my legs with a smirk that could stop my heart and restart it in the same beat. Asmo's tongue darts out, rolling against me in languid strokes. It's like his second language.

Shockwaves of euphoria slip through me, my body becoming pliable in his grasp as I submit to him in every possible way. I thread my fingers into his hair, pulling at the roots and I grip the back of the couch, as if that alone could hold me in stasis. Two long fingers enter me without warning and my breath catches. My lips part as my head thumps backward.

A moan, so raw, so unexpected rips through my throat as he fills me up and spreads his fingers. My toes curl, my pulse seizing while his tongue works circles against my clit, driving me so high, I swear I'll break.

His large hand creeps up the smooth plane of my stomach before squeezing my breast, rolling it in his palm. And suddenly I can't breathe. I'm bound too tightly, coiled so completely, that all I can do is hang on. Teeth graze over the place all my nerves meet, drawing my attention to every ounce of burning need in my body.

As if he knows how close I am, he sinks his fingers deeper, adding another. I release my hold on his hair and those dark eyes glance up at me, swirling with power that has my legs trembling.

"Scream it for me," he growls against me, his fingers curling inside me, hitting something that obliterates all coherent thought. My eyes flutter and I try to smother the moan in my throat, but it's too late. I'm sucked beneath wave after wave of dizzying pleasure, shattering apart.

The room tilts on its axis. I am weightless and anchored all at once—caught on the cusp of ecstasy. Through the haze, I register Asmo's wicked smile, his gaze drinking in every shudder and gasping breath. The world narrows down to this instant, lights bursting in my vision.

Just as it all starts to fade, his lips are on mine, consuming every sound, every breath. My lungs finally expand, releasing from the clutches of orgasm as I hear Asmo's voice in my head.

"You're not done yet, Starlight."

The sweet scent of magic storms my nose at the same second

"Come for me, Princess. Show me how pretty you are when you break."

His words echo through the cavernous halls of my mind, sending me reeling over the precipice into oblivion. My vision spirals out as rapture cascades through every fiber of my being. My scream rends the air as Asmo's teeth nip my bottom lip, driving me through wave after wave of bliss until I'm gasping for air.

"You're so fucking beautiful, Valeria. Please, don't ever forget that," he whispers huskily against my throat, pressing one last languid kiss against my pulse.

Then he stiffens, going so still, I force myself to sit up through the fog. "What's wrong?"

"They're convening again." He rolls his eyes up to mine, flexing his hands at my sides, making the veins rise.

I tilt my head, but before he can form the words to explain it clicks. "He told you in your head?"

"Yeah, but he's going to buy us a few minutes so we can clean up and…" Asmo trails off, his eyes glancing up at the top of my head as he attempts to smooth down my hair. "Maybe get you a brush."

With a flick of his wrist, one appears in his hand, but instead of giving it to me, he gently combs out the snags the couch friction created himself. Though, he lingers for a bit longer than necessary, letting the silky strands glide through his fingers. I'm too numb to move, to feel. After this meeting, the rest of them will know who I am, and our little bubble will pop.

31

Asmodeus

My brother has the worst possible timing. I argued with him for a full five minutes before he stopped responding, demanding he push the meeting back an hour. I would've offered him anything for just a little more time.

Of course, that didn't happen, though.

It's not that I don't understand. It's that I don't want to. I know one more hour would only leave me wishing for another. It's a vicious cycle that never ends until someone forces your hand.

And right now, that someone happens to be Kai.

I stride into the meeting hall, Valeria at my side, and our tardiness draws a collection of disapproving glances. Her hand trembles within mine, and I can feel the tautness of her nerves, like a bowstring pulled to its limit. The lords and ladies gathered around the elongated table shift with unease, attempting to hide their stares when they notice our joined hands.

And with reluctant grace, we take our seats.

“About damn time,” Finn whispers across the table.

"Hope you weren’t waiting long." It’s a lie. I really couldn't care less how long they were waiting, and I milked every second of the walk down here. I'd gone out of my way, choosing not to use magic, and purposely led Valeria down the wrong hallways. Hell, I even strode through the second floor, which I normally avoid like the plague.

Finn rolls his eyes then gives both of us a once over, choosing not to taunt me any further.

From the corner of my eye, I catch Valeria's head jerking left to right, her gaze darting around the room. She's so nervous… so *worried*. Though, I understand why. If what she's told me is true, that she feared my brother and Alice would take her prisoner before she met me, I doubt that fear has vanished entirely. She knows she'll have to tell the truth about who she is, here and now, in this very meeting.

In an effort to soothe her, I pry my fingers from her death grip, setting them on her thigh, and begin drawing little circles there. Maybe it'll bring back memories of what just transpired between us. Having her mind on that and away from the weight of this meeting might just keep her from hyperventilating.

Carefully, she weaves her fingers between mine, her clammy palm pressing down over the top of my hand. And whatever my touch did, wherever it took her mentally, it worked. Her shoulders ease, her chin lifts, and she's schooled her features into a wall of stone, letting nothing show through the cracks.

That's it. You got this.

"Now that we're all accounted for," Kai announces, his royal tone cutting through the whispers that have stirred. "We have to decide a course of action against the elves and their declaration of war tonight. So, I hope you all thought long and hard because we're not leaving this room until we have a plan."

Kai cuts a glance towards me, silently telling me that he's far more concerned about what Valeria and I decided to do than anyone else. Considering he decided to pop into my head while my face was between her legs, I'm going to assume he believes we didn't do much talking. And honestly, we didn't. But what we did say was productive.

Turning his attention back to table as a whole, my brother continues, "Lord Elcrys' offer expires tonight, so we can either throw everything we have into negotiations, or prepare for war."

"Tonight? What kind of time is that? When was the offer made?" Lord Zule stands up. His chair nearly tips over from the force as he tossed his hands about.

"We had three days to either accept or decline. Lord Elcrys gave the offer with the declaration at Ogre's Landing. By the time we saw it, we summoned all of you. This isn't disorganization, it's the elf lord being obnoxious, and trying to claim he gave us a chance to prevent war."

Each word he speaks weighs as heavy as stone. *This is our only option.*

If we go to war now, I'm not sure who would win. The elves have the most elite soldiers, ships that quite literally can slice through the oceans. They cast magic from stones, meaning their souls aren't drawn from, making their power endless.

The elves would be the only realm I fear to go to war against. Especially now, when we're vastly unprepared. The demons have grown soft, and now we're reaping the repercussions.

I wouldn't be surprised if that's why Alice has risked scrying herself into oblivion of the last few weeks. She's terrified and rightfully so, since she's against the only option to prevent such a war.

If we do this wrong, it could very well be the downfall of the Seven Realms.

Clearing my throat, I twirl the rings on my free hand, desperate to keep my mind busy. Valeria's eyes are on me. I can feel them burning into the side of my face. She's discovered the reality I have just now, that she must go home. And if she returns to the Elven Islands tonight, this meeting marks our final hours together.

A pang shoots through my chest, an unfamiliar ache that tightens my grip on her leg. It's not love that binds me to her—it can't be—but the thought of her leaving still carves a hollow space beneath my ribs. I stroke my thumb over her fingers, unsure of what to say, just knowing if I look at her right now, I won't be okay.

Kai's voice slices through the charged silence, his gaze sweeping over the assembled court. "Does anyone have comments? Suggestions?" He stares at us, pursing his lips. *"Anything at all?"*

Valeria's grip on my hand tightens, and I know he's spoke into her head, too.

Her grip pulses—a silent plea for strength or perhaps a farewell—and she stands. Every set of eyes in the room turn toward her. The weight of her decision clings to the air like a premonition, and for a moment, I can't breathe.

The air has become too thick, the light too bright. I can hear the thump of my heart in my ears as the sounds in the room fade away. It's like her lips move in slow motion, and for the briefest moment, I have a persistent need to yank her to me, to disappear from this room and never come back.

To run.

I snap forward, grabbing her hand again, and she whirls. Wide emerald eyes find mine, and her lips pull up just a bit at one corner, somehow telling me it's going to be okay. I don't care about anyone else in the room, that they're likely watching me, reading me, noting that she's somehow become my weakness.

For years, I've maintained this facade. I've willed myself to be impassive around everyone but Alice and the kids. Even then, I never showed affection toward them in front of others. It's how people get hurt—*used*. I never wanted them to get caught in the crosshairs of someone who despised me for my past.

Right now, I'm breaking every one of my unspoken rules.

"Blame me." I speak the words in her head. *"I won't break our deal. It can be the reason you can't go home. Let me be the reason we go to war. I'll tell them that I can't let you go. I'll live with the guilt, the hate, the shame, whatever comes of it. Just don't leave."*

Tears well in her eyes but she doesn't let them fall as she stares at me. The green of her eyes becomes so vibrant, like the salt somehow strengthens the color. Slowly, she shakes her head no, and it's like getting stabbed all over again.

Releasing her hand, I will my features into an impenetrable wall, sitting back in my seat like this is any other meeting.

"I will return to the Elven Islands." She lifts her chin, squaring her shoulders. "If my father wishes for my return and will drop the declaration of war, then I can do my part."

"No..." Alice breathes, her eyes wider than I've ever seen them. "You can't."

She's made her decision. Watching Alice out of the corner of my eye, I tilt my head. *But why are you so upset about it? You're not the one falling for her.*

Valeria seems to ask herself the same question, but instead says, "I wasn't meant to come here. I won't endanger people to stay."

A murmur ripples through the meeting hall. Alice's bright eyes are filled with concern as she looks from Valeria to me. I can see the white of her knuckles as she clenches her hands on the table.

Kai, on the other hand, doesn't fight her. He nods solemnly, commending Valeria's sacrifice, knowing it's necessary for peace. "You're doing what's right. For both our people."

"When?" My tone betrays me, cracking on the single word.

"She should return immediately," he says, his eyes briefly meeting mine with an echo of my own pain. "I'd rather her be there a few hours early than wait until the last second. The elf lord is cunning; we can't afford to give him the chance to take advantage of us. With the deadline being so soon, he could try to drag out the signing of the treaty when we arrive, then claim we waited too long, keep Valeria, and still declare war. I wouldn't put it past him."

I nod, doing the best I can to mask the roiling emotions, but the thought of her leaving, of her marrying someone else, shatters something fundamental within me.

My hands tremble. I wish she'd given me her betrothed's name. I'd like to know what I should have on his headstone. There's no way in hell I'll let him make it down the aisle. Not with what she's told me.

Any man willing to let her drown to save himself, isn't good enough.

As Valeria retakes her seat, my hand finds hers again, a silent promise of solace even as my heart splinters. The room bursts into chaos as multiple lords attempt to speak at once. Except, instead of waiting their turn, they just get louder, urging the king to hear their grievances. Most of which happen to be about me bringing the elf lord's daughter to the meeting, and not telling them her true identity.

"Enough," Alice commands, her hair bursting into vibrant flames as her power rolls through the room. It's enough to raise the hairs on my arms, and make goosebumps pepper the surface of my skin. "We have preparations to make and farewells to bid. This meeting is adjourned. *Go home."*

Most of those in the room are too shocked to move, staring at the queen like she's committed murder. It's not until she growls that they flee from their seats, taking the hint. Whispers flood between them as they file from the room, leaving my brothers, the queen, Eva, and us behind.

The silence is heavy as Kai sits down in his seat. "I'll open a portal and take Valeria there by myself, except with a couple guardsmen. However, I have to tether the treaty to something. Elcrys will want me to put someone or something up as collateral to keep us from breaking it, and the same will go for him."

"What are you going to put up?" Finn asks, scratching his beard. "Or who, I guess is the better question?"

"I don't know," Kai says, drawing his hand down his face. "He'll want a person close to me."

"Use me," I say, trying not to react to Valeria's gaping mouth as she glares daggers into the side of my face. "Treaties are usually bound by life, so if you break the treaty, I die. Just don't be a bastard and I'll be just fine."

"If we have to, you won't come back," Kai says, brows raised. "You know that right? You'll be dead for good."

"I do. But I'm fairly certain I can find a loophole in a rushed treaty." I shrug, feigning nonchalance as I play with my rings. "And it's better than you offering up someone else. I have no children, no wife. It's just me. And Elcrys knows I'm important to you. He's not going to let you put just anyone on that treaty, and neither should you. It needs to be someone close to him—just not Valeria."

"Well, Finn and I will gather the guards. We'll let the two of you have a moment to say goodbye." My brother stands. "Please, try to be as quick as you can."

Eva is the first to join him, setting her hand on my shoulder as she follows the king out the door.

"It was lovely to meet you," Finn says, nodding to Valeria with pursed lips as he takes his leave behind them.

Alice nods, but I can tell by the stiffness of her movements, that she's not pleased with how this is ending. Still, she doesn't press, just stands from her chair and looks at me. "You're okay with this?"

"I'll support whatever decision Valeria makes. If she wants to go home, then I'll see her safely home. I won't force her to stay."

"Good luck to you, then. May your sacrifice not be in vain." Alice storms from the room, muttering under her breath too low for me to make out the words. The heavy oak doors click closed behind her.

There's no time to waste. And as much as it hurts to be losing our one night together, I'll do what needs to be done.

I turn to Valeria, my voice quiet. "I need you to listen closely. Summoning is awful for a demon to experience, but I'd much rather wade through a tunnel of black sludge then you need my help and not get it in time." Using my power, I draw a sigil on the table in darkness, the edges of the lines wavering like liquid floating in the air. "If you need me, draw this. You'll need to place a candle at every point. Once the candles are lit, you're going to call me forth using my full name and title. Asmodeus Morningstar, Prince of Death."

"That's it? It seems so easy." She blinks at me.

"It is, but you don't hear about it often since the demon coming through that summoning circle is usually pissed off. The person who summoned them doesn't typically survive the encounter."

"Oh," she mutters, eyes doubling in size.

"You have nothing to worry about, though." Drawing my dagger, the blade stings as I slice open my palm, then hold the hilt out toward her. "Ready?"

"As I'll ever be." Reluctantly, she takes it, wincing out a hiss as she mimics me. For a moment, she watches the blood well in the cut, then presses it to mine.

I let my demon side take over, glimpsing the golden strands of magic. I search for the origin thread of our deal, and pluck it with a sharp talon. A pulse of power barrels through me, knocking the breath from my lungs. The blood we exchanged that night in the woods passes through my palm and into hers and vice versa, and just like that, our lives are no longer one.

"Are you sure about this?" I ask, sliding my fingers into the spaces between hers and giving them a final squeeze. "It's not too late."

"This is the way it has to be." Her smile is sweet but it doesn't reach her eyes. "Though I wish things could be different. Maybe in another life." She cups my face and I try to memorize the way her fingers feel. "You're a good man, Asmo, and you're going to make some woman very happy one day."

"I was hoping that someone would be you." Twisting my lips, I pull my head away from her touch, trying not to look back at her face. It's only going to make this harder. "Is there anything I can get you? Anything you want to take from Grim's?"

"Maybe some paper and a pen. I'd like to write a note to Griffin. Otherwise, I'd just really enjoy hugging you for a moment."

My lips tip up as I breathe out deep. "Of course you would." Daring a glance, I find her lips pressed into a line as she blinks back tears. Without a second thought, I gather her from the seat, cradling her in my lap like I would Maevie, or any other small child. Valeria loops her arms around me and buries her head into the crook of my neck.

"You smell good," she says, the words muffled against my shirt. I can't help but smile, and I hate it.

"I'm glad?" I've never had someone tell me that before. No one has ever really told me the opposite, though, either. Well, maybe Alice once. But in my defense, we were also trapped in the Enchanted Forest for two weeks. Both of us desperately needed a bath.

Tucking my chin to her head, I hum out of instinct. I'm not sure how much time passes of me smoothing her hair, brushing it from her face, but I pray to anyone that'll listen to not let this be the last time I see her.

The oak door creaks open and Finn peeks his head inside. "Hey, sorry, but it's time to go."

Valeria sits up, the warmth of her body fleeing with her, and my blood turns to ice in my veins. She quickly scribbles something on the paper and pen I summon, having forgotten about her wanting to write a note to Griffin.

"Please ensure he gets this," she says, pressing the folded parchment into my hand.

"Of course." Words clog my throat. I'm suffocating on all the things I want to say, but it's too tangled to get any of them out.

Together, we follow Finn through the castle. Apparently, Kai picked up on me lingering before the meeting, and sent Finn to ensure we didn't get *lost.* Our footsteps echo off the stone. There's not a soul in sight, creating an eerie silence. With the meetings finished, I wouldn't be surprised if the staff is assisting the court, packing and loading their carriages or horses. Whatever they brought here.

Though, without the people in this castle, the click of our shoes against the marble floors becomes that much louder. It's like a slow march toward the gallows when you know the prisoner you're transporting won't be coming back.

Reaching the foyer, I push open the door, and just at the end of the stairs, Kai and a handful of guards are gathered. Except now, he's in his golden armor, crown on his head and sword clipped at his hip. He looks every bit of his part, like a true king.

Kai was born for this job, and honestly, I'm glad it didn't pass to me. I'm not sure I could've gone through with this, even if it was to protect my kingdom. In my head I know it's right, but seeing her stand at that table, knowing what was coming, I would've taken war…

Gods, I begged, and she's still doing this.

A swirl of energy gathers at Kai's fingertips as we near, every stair making the reality hit harder, like a punch to the gut. The beginnings of a portal shimmer to life, a dot in the air that grows bigger and bigger by the second. Valeria's grip tightens on my hand and for a moment, I don't want to let go.

Would she hate me if I took her away? If I simply hid her against her will, until the deal timed out? Could she ever forgive me if I did?

"Don't take this choice from her," Kai says into my head. *"Trust me."*

I meet his eyes as we reach the cobblestone, and the air hums with magic, thick enough to taste.

"I'm—" She swallows hard, her voice barely above a whisper. "I'm not sure how to say goodbye."

"Then don't." I turn toward her, tucking her dark hair behind her pointy ears. "But I won't forget you, Starlight. Not in a thousand lifetimes."

"Until we meet again, Starlight," I say, cupping her behind her neck and bringing our foreheads together. I close my eyes a moment, then plant a kiss on her brow.

"In the next life," she breathes as I pull away. Her emerald gaze finds mine and the sheer sight of the tears threatening to fall from her eyes is like a vise around my heart.

"Turn around," I say gently. "Lift your hair."

She complies, and with shaky hands, I unclasp Jade's necklace from my neck. The metal feels like ice against my fingers, or maybe it's just the loss already setting in. Looping the chained pendant around her throat, the silver chain rests against the golden one of her red stone, the one that gives her magic.

Valeria's arms move, like she's reached up to touch it, but I can't bring myself to see how it looks on her. All I know is no one has ever captivated me the way Jade had until her. No one. And I hope that the magic in that pendant, the one that houses a piece of my soul, will keep her safe. I hope she looks down and senses my presence there. That it gives her comfort and reminds her someone believes she's beautiful.

"Don't turn around," I whisper in her ear, staring at the portal a couple of feet in front of us.

My brother's men have already poured through that swirling light, but he's still waiting for Valeria beside it, watching us. If I didn't know any better, I'd think he was on the verge of tears, too.

"Just walk," I say, my voice raw with unshed emotion. "It'll be easier, I promise."

It's a lie. There's nothing easy about this.

With one last touch, a brush of her soft skin, I step back. She nods once, so small, so brave that fractures my heart anew. Her steps carry her toward the portal where Kai waits, hand outstretched, ready to steal her away from me.

Kai reaches out, taking her hand, and guides her toward the shimmering gateway. But at the threshold, she hesitates, turning back to give me one last smile, one last look. My gaze falls to the necklace, and I catch the white glow emanating from within the crystal. The sight steals the breath from my lungs, and a quiet gasp escapes me.

My heart lurches, every beat a drum of war within my chest, but I remain motionless, watching the glowing crystal as she enters that portal. I'm too stunned to move, to speak. The crystal should only glow when it touches my soul or my mates, yet it gleams against her skin, a flare of light so bright that sears through the space between us.

She's... my mate.

Valeria grips the pendant I gave her, her form barely visible from within the portal as Kai tries to pull her through. Her hair whips through the air, and that image will forever be burned into my brain. Panic claws up my throat, but it's too late. There's no time for words, for declarations or pleas.

The portal swallows her whole, and as it fades, so does a piece of me, leaving nothing but shadows and the memory of her touch. The air dies down, leaving me rooted in place, like a statue cursed with a beating heart. Suddenly, I'm drowning, and pain radiates into every bone.

I just let my mate leave. I agreed to honor her wishes to be the sacrificial lamb and marry a man she doesn't love, for my family, for our kingdom, for the peace of both of our people.

No... No, no, no. This is all wrong.

32

Asmodeus

ALICE KNEW.

And she didn't fucking say anything?

She just let Valeria leave.

Alice is the only person with access to Jade's soul. It was kept in Hell Hold for a reason. And I know damn well my brother doesn't have an itch for creating happily ever afters.

The signs were all there. At the keep, the day I was stabbed, she'd asked me if I thought I could ever fall in love again. Why now? Why, after all of these years of knowing each other, was she interested in my love life?

Then there's the way her eyes lit up when she discovered that Valeria stabbed me with my own blade. Alice is incredibly intelligent and deductive. She'd put the pieces together and had known I hesitated because Valeria wasn't just some random woman. She was my soulmate.

It's why she left Valeria a letter. It's why she fought to keep her here. Why she kept her secret from me. She didn't want history to repeat itself. Only this time it wouldn't be my spellbinding breaking or some accident. Alice thought I'd kill her to get back at the Elf Lord.

At least with Jade, I know it wasn't entirely my fault. I still hold myself accountable, but I know some of the circumstances were out of my control. Had I killed Valeria out of spite, or revenge, there was no one else to blame but me. Her death would've weighed ten times as much on my soul.

My mind spirals as I stand in the same spot until the day draws to a close. Bringing the whiskey bottle to my lips, I find it empty and curse under my breath. It's been hours since Kai left. We're past the deadline, and it won't be long now until the rest of the servants and castle staff that live in the village and not within the servant's quarters return. I'm not sure what I'll say to them when they stroll by, happy as can be, mumbling hellos, oblivious to the hell I've unleashed upon myself.

Kai should be back by now.

I have to do something, but there's no right move. If Valeria leaves Vanderlyth, I die. The treaty will be broken, and my life will be its penance for going back on our word. Until I find a loophole, she has to stay there, but I can't even examine the wording until he returns. That's saying I can find a loophole at all.

The only thing I know for sure is there's no way in hell I can go through with this. Valeria deserves to be happy, and seeing as she's Jade reincarnated, Jade damn well deserves the world after what I did to her.

Valeria won't remember her past life. No one ever does, but I do. Fuck, I'm certain my heart recognized her… I should've noticed. I should've listened to it.

But I can't take back what's been done, so how do I fix this? How do I keep her safe?

If she can't come here, then I'll have to go to her, and the only way Elcrys will let me be in his brand-new kingdom is to not be a threat. The puzzle pieces fall into place, and I know beyond a shadow of a doubt what I have to do. Standing up from the stone step, magic swarms around me, making Hell Hold disappear and Grim's Keep come into existence.

I barely make it through the front door before Griffin is gliding down the stairs. "What happened?" He looks past me, his brows drawing together when he doesn't find what he's looking for. "Where's Valeria?"

Digging the folded parchment from my pocket, I hold it out to him. " I need you to come with me," I say, brushing past him on the stairs. I don't stop until I'm on the second floor, digging through the drawers of the desk in my office.

My fingers graze on rough stone and I pull the tablet from the drawer, placing it on the wooden surface of the desk. Grim did this for me. Now, I'll do it for him.

Yanking my dagger from the sheath on my hip, I reopen the wound on my hand and clench my fist until my blood pools on the desk.

"What are you doing?" Griffin asks, breathless as he reaches the room. "And what the hell? Why would you let her go back there?"

"It wasn't my choice." The words are cold, emotionless, but it's what I'll need to be. What I have to be to save her. "Come here." With a single finger, I draw a sigil, using my blood as ink, and write Griffin's name on the stone face.

"What is that?" he growls, leaning away from the desk like the tablet will bite him.

The blood turns into a bright yellow light, illuminating every stroke I made, then fizzles out and the stone wobbles before disappearing all together.

"It hid itself. Only you will know where it is. It should've spoken to you."

Griffin swallows hard, his face pale as he nods. "It did."

"Don't be scared of it. It sounds meaner than it is." I cross the room, gripping his hand and pulling up his sleeve. The moment my fingers meet his skin, the sigil I drew scars on his wrist. The smell of burnt flesh fills my nose as Griffin yelps and jerks his hand back, eyeing the shape that matches one of the various scars on my chest.

"Gods, Asmo. What is going on? And what was the *thing?"* He stares at me, his chest rising and falling with every jagged breath.

"It's a titan. Its bones support this keep, and its spirit is what enchants the wall. It lives below ground, existing just like the gargoyles. It's how I knew to tether them. Should something happen, you can call upon it. It'll wreck the keep again, but it might save you should someone invade, buy you time to get everyone out."

"Why are you telling me this? What happened at the meeting?" He tosses his hands, storming toward me. "Just spit it out."

"Valeria went to the Elven Islands so that a treaty could be made, but she's my soulmate, Griffin. She can't come back, and I won't live here without her. So, the keep is yours. Congratulations, *Lord* Morningstar. Please look after it."

Griffin hasn't moved—hasn't blinked.

"Did you hear me?"

He nods, slowly trying to regain his composure. "I don't want to be a lord."

"Well, you became one the moment that tablet disappeared." Stepping closer, I rest my hand on his arm, shooting him a flatline smile. "I'm not sure what's going to come next, but I trust you to look after the gargoyles. I wouldn't have left the keep to you if I didn't."

"But Valeria… How?" He shakes his head, his mouth opening and closing as if he's trying to form the words.

"Alice is how. She placed a soul in the well. Jade's soul. I don't know why she did it, but I'm going to find out." Without another word, I vanish.

With my keep protected, I can do what needs to be done. I'll become what everyone has thought of me. I'll be the traitor. The monster. I'll embrace it for her.

The stairs of Hell Hold face me, and the longer I stare at the front door, the more my blood boils.

Jade and I knew there would come a day that she'd die, that I'd outlive her. She'd told me the night we got engaged that if something ever happened, should she grow old and die, or otherwise, that she never wanted to be returned to the Soul Well. She wished to be contained, saved, until I could be reborn with her. So that we might find one another again in the next life and not risk being reborn at different times.

Her wishes were taken away from her the day she died, when I was labeled a traitor to the crown and made a fugitive. I didn't know what became of her soul while I was trapped in the prison world, but I'd found it after the war. Alice promised me she'd keep it safe. That when the time came, Jade's wishes would be honored.

But she lied.

Valeria is proof of that.

The smell of roses storms through my senses as I climb the stairs and throw open the door to the castle. Fury rages within me, for the deception, for Valeria, for Jade. I want answers and I'm not stopping until I get them.

One of the servants meandering through the keep spots me and drops into a bow. "My Lord, I'm sorry. We weren't expecting you back so soon."

I yank the man closer to me, feeling my eyes flicker between demon and man. "Where's the fucking queen?"

"In the gardens," he stammers, his frail body trembling in my grip.

I don't wait for him to get out his terms of respect before dropping the man and heading toward the back door of the castle. Finn and Eva are seated in the dining hall, but neither of them speak as they watch me stalk through the room and out the back doors.

The moment I step outside, the scents of flowers slam into me. Alice's fiery red hair comes into view and I shout over the courtyard, ensuring she can hear me over the distance. "Tell me you didn't!" My voice echoes through the twisted paths of roses.

"I'm not sure what you're talking about," she says, arching a manicured eyebrow. Her ruse won't fool me. Even from across the garden, I can see her lips twitch up into a knowing smirk.

Leave it to her to smile. I just said goodbye to the woman who's had my heart for centuries. "How fucking dare you?" My feet float down the steps as I close the distance between us. It's not until I round the last bush that I see my niece and nephew sitting by her feet. I inhale deeply, straightening my spine. "I was not aware the children were here."

Two sets of eyes stare up at me, contrasting their bright red hair as Maevie leans toward her brother and mumbles, "He said fuck…" and I can't help but smile. Though the amusement is gone in seconds.

My hand scrubs over my jaw for a moment as I pace away, only to come back. "Why?" I ask, carefully choosing my words. "Why did you do it?"

"Because even you deserve your happy ending." Alice leans in close, whispering the last bit so the kids don't hear. "Don't fucking waste it."

"Waste it? It's a bit late for that, isn't it? She's in the Elven Islands and my life is bound to the treaty that put her there." I toss my hands up, my mouth falling open, but nothing else comes out.

"I tried to stop it, but it's what you both wanted." She presses her lips together and turns her gaze to the sky for a moment. "I thought I could give you a chance at happiness. You looked so miserable. I'd scried and saw the two of you together, and gods, Asmo… If you could see it. It might look messy now, but it will get better. I can't tell you how. You know how this works. If I tell you before you're supposed to know, then it could alter things. If I steer you away from the fated path with what I know, then it could change everything, but this is how it's supposed to be."

She's right. I know exactly how this works. I learned such when I'd tried to scry a future where I didn't exist and lost my eye to ether. It was a damn miracle that Alice was able to get it back, but I still lived like that for decades, one eye seeing the present, the other seeing the past, the future, and everything in between. I've played this game, wondering if I could play god and use what I knew to alter courses that were painted by fate. It hardly ever works out well.

Alice couldn't tell me what she had done, because the path she'd set in motion was promising. Telling me might've changed that outcome.

"I fucking hate scrying. It should be outlawed," I say, quiet enough so the kids can't hear me. "Promise me you'll stop doing it now that the treaty has been made."

"I promise." She nods, blinking long and hard. "No more. Honestly, the only reason I did it wasn't to protect my people, it was to protect your future."

"You could've died. All it takes is one mistake, one stray thought, and your soul is gone. You'd risk that for my happiness? You'd let your kids grow up without a mother?"

Tears brim her eyes as she looks away for a moment. "Yes, because they won't have one without you. You're the reason I'm still here. The least I can do is ensure your existence isn't spent wallowing in your own shame because of something you couldn't control." She shoves a finger at my chest. "You loved her, I know. But I can't bring Jade back, Asmo. This is the best I can do."

My eyes drop to my feet. "I can't leave her there."

"I know." She cups my face, bringing my gaze back to her's. "I know you can't. And I want you to know that I trust you. Whatever you do from this moment forward, I know is to save her. I won't hold it against you."

"Brother!" Kai's voice sounds behind me, and I turn, letting him get an eyeful of the frown on my face. "I was told you arrived. I thought you were staying at Grim's Keep?" He grins, flashing his perfectly white teeth. "It worked. The treaty has been finalized."

Finn… Of course he'd blab to him that I came back.

"Did you know? About Valeria's soul?" I ask, scowling so deeply that death himself would cower.

He had been for Valeria leaving from the start. Was his determination to truly save his kingdom, or was it to fulfill this fantasy that Alice created?

"Knew? I went with her to give the soul to the ferryman." His eyes fall, giving me the answer to my question. "If there was any other way, any version that Alice had seen that didn't involve hundreds of people dying, you have to know I would've steered you in that direction."

They'd both kept this from me. Hell, Finn likely knows, too. I was left in the dark and now the other half of my soul has been sent away to suffer.

"Make me an ambassador. I'm already tied to the treaty. I could go and ensure Elcrys holds up his end of the deal."

"Part of the treaty I signed ensured no one from my kingdom enters his lands and vice versa. Being an ambassador isn't an option." Kai checks the inside of his lip, worrying filling his eyes.

"There has to be some way—"

Kai snaps, "There isn't. I'm sorry. In order—"

Alice slaps him in the chest. "Don't." Her eyes go dark as her voice takes on a demonic tone. "He has to choose."

Kai swallows his words, tucking his lips between his teeth. Suddenly it makes sense why he's kept me at arm's length. It's why he's kept me in the dark about this war…

They knew I'd leave.

"I'll come back. Once I can find a way to get her out."

Alice smiles, holding her arms out to me. I tug her close, wrapping my arms around her. "You're leaking."

She dabs at her cheeks with her sleeve. "It's the roses."

"Sure it is," I say, a weak smirk playing on my lips.

33

Asmodeus

Elcrys' voice carries through the hall. His guards escort me in magical shackles. Before they can push open the door, I kick out with my foot, slamming the taller elf in the ribs before bringing my hands down over his head. I tear away his crystal pendant, using the shackles to deflect the blade slinging toward my face.

Magic erupts from my assailant's fingers as the last guard channels the crystals in his gauntlets. And at the last second, I dodge before a bolt of lightning slams into the wall behind me. Right where my head had been.

I pause, looking over the scorched mark, shaking my head. Then turn back to the man. "Rude."

His eyes widen as I kick up the sword on the floor, discarded by the unconscious guard, and catch it in my chained hands. I rush on him, our blades colliding, getting close enough to snatch his crystal away. He swings low, and I barely have time to drop my hand, the thick metal cuff around it taking most of the impact instead of my leg.

Taking a page from Valeria's book, I snatch his dagger out of the sheath on his side and drive it through the man's throat before he can react. Blood sprays, soaking my chest, coating my hands as I yank it free. The man clutches his neck, desperate to stop the crimson pouring from the wound, but it's too late for him. He slips in the mess it's made on the aseptic white floors, his head thumping into the ground, and his body goes weak.

"How unfortunate…" I say aloud to myself, then dig in his pockets for the keys to the cuffs that are holding my magic hostage, preventing me from calling upon it. I hadn't intended to kill anyone today. Honestly, I've made an effort to turn over a new leaf, but… *circumstances.* I'll try again tomorrow, but with what I'm about to do, I doubt my hands will be any cleaner any time soon.

With a jingle, I yank the keys free from his pocket, making quick work to shed the cuffs. They rattle against the floor, tinkering a moment as they tumble. The gold metal circles next to the guard's dead body before falling flat, diverting his blood spreads into a puddle near my feet.

Great. This was a new shirt.

I strip it from my body, using the fabric to wipe the spatter from my hands and face. This isn't how I wanted to walk in there. Her people already think mine are savages, I'd hoped not to look the part. With a huff, I discard the stained shirt, not bothering to summon another one. I toss it on the dead guard, retrieve his sword and dagger, and push open the heavy carved doors.

They fly open with such force that they clap against the gray stone walls.

The sound echoes through the vast chapel-like room. Pews line either side of the main aisle, and three thrones are positioned at the end of it. The rows are filled with citizens. All of which are dressed in fine linens, decorative hats, and adorned in more jewels than should ever be necessary. For a brief moment, I fear I've interrupted her wedding. Except when I find Valeria, she's not wearing a white gown.

Staring like she's seen a ghost, she's on her father's left, seated on a throne made of tree limbs. The branches have been wrapped and shaped into a chair, yet remain alive, budding with new leaves. Her hair is silver, her eyes matching, and the raw, unbridled rage that rips through me has talons threatening to push through my fingers. *They glamoured her.*

Elcrys bursts up from his chair, crystals in hand, ready to cast. "What is the meaning of this? Your king signed—"

"My king? Are you sure?" I hold up a finger, pouting my lips as I slowly make my way down the aisle, channeling every ounce of predatory grace I possess. "My brother has a throne, yes. It does not make him my king. In fact, he believes I'm a monster. His people,too."

"He listed your name on the treaty. You can't lie to me, boy. I know his wife is fond of you, enough that I allowed him to place your name up as collateral." His voice is gruff, but it's changed since I saw him last, holding more of an authoritative ring.

The silver beard on his face is longer than he typically keeps it, coming down to the base of his throat. His long metallic hair has been braided tight against the sides of his head, the top left loose and swept back. But those piercing eyes, ones I'd like to carve out and save like trophies, are just as cold as I remember.

"That's exactly why he put me there. He couldn't care less if I die. In fact, I came, out of the kindness of my heart, to *warn you."* I spin around, arms wide as I make a show of my lies. "Your treaty is useless."

"I don't trust you." He eyes me skeptically, sitting back down on his tree limb throne.

Examining my nails, using the dagger I stole off the guard to fish the blood out from underneath them, I say, "I wouldn't trust me either. My reputation isn't exactly commendable, but I suppose that depends on how badly you want to win your war. You know what I can do. Wouldn't you rather that power be on your side?"

He cocks his head as I stop just past the front row of pews. "You want to join me?"

I smile wickedly, slipping the dagger between my belt and pants, like a makeshift sheath. "No, my king. I want to serve you, but I have conditions."

"Which are?" he asks, cutting straight to the point, tapping his fingers on his throne.

Good. Bite. You wouldn't ask if you weren't interested.

I hold a face of indifference, but for a moment, I let my eyes wander to Valeria. She's gripping the arms of her chair so tight that her knuckles flare white. She hasn't taken that terrified stare off me since I stalked into the room.

"You didn't think I'd let you leave that easy, did you?" I push the words into her mind.

She grips the chair tighter, trapping her lips between her teeth as if she's fighting to keep her mouth shut.

"Have you told him about Grim's Keep?"

Ever so slightly, her head shakes no.

"Then breathe, Starlight. The last thing we need is you passing out on your lovely throne."

Her face falls into discontent, and I resist the urge to roll my eyes.

"Please," I add.

Her shoulders ease, and only then do I turn back to the king. "Who is she?" I ask, pretending not to know Valeria.

I doubt my brother mentioned our time together, and Elcrys doesn't need to know. It's best if Grim's Keep remains a broken keep in his mind, and the gargoyles stay a secret. If Elcrys knows of the last few weeks, he'll ask questions and dig into how we met. Griffin and the gargoyles don't need his attention.

Shooting Valeria a flirty grin, I let my eyes wander down her throat to the faint mark on her breast, knowing it was made by my teeth. Then there's the necklace I gave her, beaming brightly next to her red crystal.

My mate… The thought alone sends a spark of pride deep into my veins.

"She's no one you should be concerned with." Elcrys waves the question off and I scoff.

"She must be important if you're willing to forgo *war* to get her back." I turn my grin on him, biting my tongue to avoid calling him a prick out loud.

"State your demands, Asmodeus. I'm growing tired of your antics, and you're dropping blood on my floor." Elcrys' mouth forms a flat line, his brow furrowing as he rests his head on his hand.

"My demand is her. I'll swear fealty. I'll even make a blood deal to serve you as my king, but only if she becomes my bride."

Gasps sound from the pews behind me. I've almost forgotten about the audience in the room. They've been utterly silent. Even now, their gasps are so poised it makes me sick.

How dare a demon marry a pureblood elf? I roll my eyes. *They can suck my—*

"She's my only heir. I won't make someone *like you* next in line to my throne."

A deadly silence falls over the room, the tension palpable. I stand my ground, meeting Elcry gaze with a defiance that shocks even myself. "I have no desire to rule. As far as I'm concerned, the succession can skip me. The throne can fall to your grandchildren."

"Mutts, you mean," he arches a brow.

Rage flares up within me, so fast, I can't stop my eyes from flickering into obsidian voids. "I meant, the most powerful elves in existence."

The king's gaze shifts to Valeria, then back to me, a silent calculation behind his cold silver eyes. He rises, the air thick with anticipation.

"If you say no, I'll ensure my brother finds a loophole in your treaty," I tease, stepping up to Valeria's throne. The guards in the room grow restless, but Elcrys makes the smart decision, demanding they stay put. I swoop a lock of her silver hair around my finger, tugging on it ever so slightly as I move behind her. "And I'll be here the day he declares war, raising the dead. Everyone your people have laid to rest will join my army. Then I'll take what I want anyway."

Letting my demon half take over, I search for the origin strand of the glamour she's wearing and snap it like a twig. It melts away, her hair turning dark, her eyes becoming that emerald green I love. Gasps ring out, but silence the moment I glare through the crowd.

Valeria plays the part, grimacing at my touch, flinching even, but I can hear her pulse racing. I can see the subtle shift of her dress skirts as she squeezes those pretty thighs of hers together, so desperate to be touched that I catch myself licking my lips.

Soon, my love. So soon. I promise.

"What will it be?" I say, dragging a bloodied knuckle over her cheek, right beneath the edge of the golden mask she wears, leaving a crimson streak in its wake. "And if I were you, I'd make your decision quickly. Every minute that passes, one of your people die."

He starts to speak, the words jumbled as he shoots up from his throne. "I... You can't..."

But I can. With a snap of my fingers, one of the men in the front row of the pews jerks, his head swivels around twice, shattering his neck, and his body slumps to the ground.

Screams shatter the silence in the crowd, some rush for the door, but my magic seals it shut. No one is getting out of here. Not a damn soul. Not until I get my way.

As I glance at Elcrys, his eyes narrow, the intrigue battling with disdain. "Stop this, this instant."

"Or what?" I let out a dark chuckle, shaking my head. "You'll kill me? Then your treaty really will be all for nothing. My brother would storm these islands so fast, you wouldn't be able to escape as the walls of this castle tumbled down around you. I'm offering you a way out."

Raising my hand, fingers poised to snap again, I feel a tug on my other hand. I turn to meet Valeria's eyes, a storm of emotions swirling in their depths. Fear, hope… and an unspoken plea.

Death is unsettling for her… I know that. She's so kind and empathetic, that seeing this has struck a chord. But it's what must be done.

Death has become a comfort to me in the oddest way. It's power, raw and unyielding. I've sworn to myself that I'd never chain myself to a wretch king again. I'd promised to never put myself at someone else's mercy, to never bargain my own freedom. Yet, here I am, agreeing to serve someone who murdered my people in cold blood, who embodies everything I hate, that I wish was rotting in the ground.

I never wanted Valeria to look at me with fear in her eyes, but I'll be the monster everyone believes me to be. I'll be the traitor, the villain. I'll do whatever is necessary to protect her and ensure her happiness.

Because she is the very thread that creates my own.

And this is the kind of monster it will take to save her from this fate.

"Don't. Please don't." Her voice is but a whisper, but if I cave, there is no saving her. This is what it takes to convince a moralless man… Her father has to see it, feel his people dying in this chapel to veer from his most time-honored tradition. I'm not an elf. Even then, he'd never marry her to someone that wasn't a pureblood, not without having no choice.

"I'm sorry," I speak the words into her mind, cupping her face. *"I won't lie to you and say you haven't been promised and bound to darkness. I'm the Prince of Death and the title fits me well. But I swear to you, Valeria, you are my brightest light. I'll be better with you at my side. I'll become the man you deserve; I just can't be him today."*

I snap my fingers and two more bodies drop. Cries and screams envelope the space around us, and she tears her face away from my touch. My jaw tightens, the muscle feathering over my cheek as I make my way to stand in front of Valeria's throne. "Tick Tock, My King."

My eyes become voids, talons pushing from my fingers as my magic swarms around me. Palms up, I push my awareness out, focusing on the bodies on the floor. They jerk and spasm. Bones and muscles flex in the empty husks of his people, and slowly, they begin to stack, one limb after another, until all three of them have been reanimated. Glassy clouded eyes scan the room.

"Eyes on me, Starlight. Don't look away." Without glancing over my shoulder, I know she's listened. I can feel that stare on my spine, like a bead of water trickling down it.

Right as I'm about to give the command to attack, Elcrys shouts. "She's yours!" His voice slices through the air and I let the magic dissipate.

The bodies drop lifelessly to the ground as I turn my head toward him. "I'm glad we have a deal."

THE END… For now.

The story continues in book two of the 'Of Death & Starlight' series, titled A Fated Crown.

Want to Stick Around the Seven Realms?

Turn the page to check out the other books in the world!

Get A Bonus Chapter...

By visiting the website below:
https://amandaaggie.com/bonus-content

Rapunzel meets Robin Hood but with DRAGONS in this standalone romantasy!

- Prisoner Princess
- Dragon Shifter Hero
- Warring Kingdoms
- Mate Bonds & Magic Rituals
- A Merry Band of Dragon Shifting Thieves
- A Floating Kingdom

Captain Hook hates witches, but little does he know, he's about to be arranged to marry one in this standalone romantasy!

- Ruthless Gauntlet Competition
- Arranged Marriage
- Warring Kingdoms
- Pirate Shenanigans
- Morally Gray Shadow Daddy
- A heroine who can control living things

Brave meets Reverse Beauty & the Beast in this standalone romantasy! The one where FINN gets his happily ever after.

- Only One Cage
- Escaping an Arranged Marriage
- Warring Kingdoms
- Funny Golden Retriever Hero
- Snarky & Grumpy Princess
- Monster Shifter Heroine

Alice in Wonderland meets Hades & Persephone in this complete romantasy trilogy!

- Deal with the Devil Gone Wrong
- Arranged Marriage
- Warring Kingdoms
- Morally Gray, Shadow Daddy Prince
- Snarky, Spellbound Witch
- Funny Monster Cat Familiar

About the Author

Best known for her #1 Amazon bestselling series, Dark Halos, Amanda Aggie writes steamy dark fantasy romance. She's a wife, a mother to two beautiful tiny humans, and has a stellar caffeine addiction. More importantly, she writes choking-hazard fantasy romance that will have you laughing out loud, swooning, and biting your nails all in one sitting. Almost all of her books take place in The Seven Realms, which she's often described as, "If Hell and Wonderland got together and had a baby." You'll find creatures of all kinds—fae, demons, dragons, witches, and more—along with morally gray villains, and steam. So, grab you some pearls to clutch and get lost in the chaos.

Check out the link below for extra goodies and places you can find Amanda! https://linktr.ee/AmandaAggie

Acknowledgements

To you, my reader... Thank you for picking up this book! Asmo has been waiting for so long to have his love story and it's been a pleasure to take him from a disgruntled ex-villain to a full-fledged murder muffin, ready to embrace his monster-side. I think we all have a little monster in us, especially when it comes to protecting the people we love. I hope you're beginning to fall in love with him! While writing him as a villain in Dark Halos, I knew this man would have a special spot in my heart, and I hope his story helped you to escape the real world for a bit! Here's to book two!

To Margie... Thank you so much for everything you do! You've become more than a PA to me, but a close friend and I absolutely cherish that friendship so much! I might not say it enough, but I'm so proud of everything you do and how you've thrived so much in the year I've known you. You're there to hype me up when I'm down and always let me know that you have my back. I love ya, girly. Thank you for putting up with me and my quirkiness. You're the best!!

To my husband, Jacob... You might not be a villain who makes up nicknames like *Mouse* or *Starlight*, but you're my cinnamon roll, golden retriever, and I love you for it! You've been there for every up and down. You've listened to me ramble about people I've made up in my head, like they're real. You're my best friend, my other half, my other pea in the pod, my burrito to my taco. P.S. Thank you for making me your badass character in your Xbox game. It made me feel loved… BUT I am still going to pick on you for naming your character Nugg Daddy, and mine, Nugg Wyfe. Your Denver Nuggets obsession has officially gone too far.

To my beta readers… Thank you so much for everything! You guys truly helped make this book better and your comments help in so many ways. They get me out of my writing slumps and soothe my nerves around release day. Knowing y'all are in my corner to hype me up is absolutely EVERYTHING. I love y'all!

To my critique and sprint partners, Carey Richardson, Michele Lenard, and L.R. Friedman… Thank you so much for all of your input and helping to make this book the best it can be. I appreciate you guys so much!!

To my ARC readers… Thank you so much for reading my stories and being so passionate about them. It fills my heart with such joy to see your posts in the group and sharing about the characters with the world! Your support is incredible, and I seriously appreciate it!

To those that helped me share the cover… Thank you! I know it was completely last minute, but I appreciate your support and efforts to help spread the word about my book so much! I absolutely ADORE the covers for this book, and my dream is to see them decorate people's shelves, like people I don't personally know lol. So, just know I see you and it doesn't go unnoticed!

To Sam and DeAnna… Thank you so much for supporting me and A Fated Vow and throwing together a tour last minute! It took so much stress off of me and it meant so much! I'm glad that I got the chance to meet you both! Y'all are such a bright light in the world, and it makes me so happy!

www.ingramcontent.com/pod-product-compliance
Lightning Source LLC
Chambersburg PA
CBHW020340310726
48979CB00015B/2444/J
* 9 7 8 1 9 6 3 1 8 4 0 0 6 *